"[An] intricate, excellent first mystery . . . the writing is so good. Private eye Wil Hardesty . . . must turn over some very old rocks when the skeletons of seven murdered children are found in the California desert. What lives under those rocks must be read about to be believed, and this skillful new author makes you believe."

—*Oregonian* (Portland, OR)

"The book's strength comes from the chances it takes . . . Add some fresh characters, a couple of clever plot twists and you have an auspicious debut."

—*Chicago Tribune*

"Impressive . . . Whether the ends justify the means is Barre's theme, and the scenes between the priest and his 'money man' take on chilling philosophical overtones. The real strength of *The Innocents* is the superbly drawn priest. His moral dilemmas are sadly believable and Barre resists sentimentalizing him or the church. It's a brave stance that pays off beautifully."

—*San Francisco Examiner*

"A private-eye novel, and a very good one . . . An absorbing, fast-paced, and violent tale."

—*Wilson Library Bulletin*

"An intriguing plot . . . plenty of promise here."

—*Knoxville News-Sentinel*

"Interesting . . . an auspicious debut."

—*Mystery News*

"One of the best mysteries of the year. Richard Barre's first novel . . . has the potential to do big things."

—*Firsts Magazine*

continued...

THE
INNOCENTS

RICHARD BARRE

BERKLEY PRIME CRIME, NEW YORK

THE INNOCENTS

A Berkley Book/published by arrangement with
Walker and Company

PRINTING HISTORY
Walker Publishing Company, Inc., hardcover edition / 1995
Berkley Prime Crime mass-market edition / December 1997

All rights reserved.
Copyright © 1995 by Richard Barre.
This book may not be reproduced in whole or in part,
by mimeograph or any other means, without permission.
For information address: The Berkley Publishing Group,
a member of Penguin Putnam Inc.,
200 Madison Avenue, New York, New York 10016

The Putnam Berkley World Wide Web site address is
http://www.berkley.com

ISBN: 0-425-16109-9

Berkley Prime Crime Books are published
by The Berkley Publishing Group,
a member of Penguin Putnam Inc.,
200 Madison Avenue, New York, New York 10016.
The name BERKLEY PRIME CRIME and the BERKLEY PRIME CRIME
design are trademarks belonging to Berkley Publishing Corporation.

PRINTED IN THE UNITED STATES OF AMERICA

10 9 8 7 6 5 4 3 2 1

For Ruth Groves Barre
Life and Inspiration

Larry and Jody Rudd
for their knowledge
of the genus Harley

ACKNOWLEDGMENTS

Much love to Susan, who always knew.

Many thanks to Cheryl Lyons and Fidel Gonzales of the Los Angeles County Sheriff's Department, Robert Dambacher and Judy Suchey for all the coroner-type questions they answered, and to Jim Rochester for his guidance. Thanks also to Shelly Lowenkopf, Leonard Tourney, and Alan Rinsler for their invaluable input; Fred Klein for his advice and counsel; Philip Spitzer, Michael Seidman, and George Gibson for their faith; Susan, Mary, Ruth, and June for their fine-tooth combing; Keith and Bill for their artistic efforts; and to the many other friends and relatives who gave their support and good cheer.

THE
INNOCENTS

Mexico, 1967

*The man's hand was hurting his—he wanted to pull away,
to run. He said he was sorry about the medal. Why couldn't
they understand?*

*Papa must know that Gilberto had put him up to it. Gil-
berto was jealous. Gilberto fooled him, and now look what
happened. First the beating from Papa and now the man
taking him away. Sad faces, his brother not looking at him,
Mama crying.*

*Yesterday had been so happy. He wanted to go back to
the bright time with the shouts and the blindfold and the
clay rooster he'd whacked with the long stick. Even getting
up at dawn had been exciting—before the church bells,
before anyone. All winter they'd coughed in the chill wind
off the mountains. But it was warmer now, and night rain
had washed the sky, leaving pinks and golds.*

*Finally he couldn't stand it, so he woke them, all but
Mama, who stayed behind. How could they have been so
slow?—hanging back to tease him, laughing as he tried to
hurry them along. In church, with Papa watching, he'd
been good the whole time. Even the old priest went to sleep,
but not him. Next year he would join his brothers at the
rail, receive the wafer, feel the shiny disk touch his throat
before it moved on. Then he would close his eyes and taste
the Bodyblood. Made him want to make a face, but he'd
be brave.*

Mass was endless, his toes jumping beans—and then it was over. Skipping home in the sunshine, ahead of Papa and the rest. The door opening suddenly. Mama there and the flowers and the piñata and the singing: Happy Birthday to him! As they sucked on little sugar cones, Papa gave it to him, the most beautiful thing he'd ever seen, silver with his name on it and everything. It was only later, when he and Gilberto were alone examining the medal, that Gilberto dared him. "Pretend it's First Communion. Go on, don't be a baby." He was no baby. He showed Gilberto.

Papa's willow switch had stung like fire through his thin pants. Never had he seen his father so angry. At least he knew Gilberto hurt just as much.

But that was yesterday. Now the man's hand was tightening on his, pulling him toward the door. Papa met his eyes and looked down, then Gilberto. Was the man going to take Gilberto away because of the medal? Mama was crying again, Papa holding her now.

He didn't like the man, didn't want to go. Would God know where to find him? Couldn't they give him another chance?

He would never do it again.

ONE

Dawn was bringing shape to the greasewood by the time they unearthed the skeleton and sifted for clues. Montoya, part of the initial wave of law, watched as first light touched Saddleback Butte and the Tehachapis. It had been a long night, wind off the Angeles Crest dogging them for most of it, rising again with the sun.

Soon they'd kill the generator-powered kliegs.

Montoya slugged down the last of the coffee, raised the fur collar of his jacket as a gust stung him. Still snow up there, obviously; months before the warm desert evenings, the kids laughing in the backyard pool.

He wondered if the kid they'd found liked to swim. All kids liked to swim, certainly his did. Jesus, what next, he thought, rubbing his eyes. In fourteen years he'd seen children die in smash-ups, a baby electrocuted, a family of five wiped out in a fire. This one was different, though, put in the ground with intent; chilling beyond the sadness of it. Montoya recalled his first glimpse of the skull, multicolored quartz chips embedded in the small eye sockets.

He scratched his scalp under the L.A. County Sheriff's cap. From the looks, this one was about his daughter's age. Hard not to think it.

The coroner and crime scene people were nearly finished, the gravesite photographed, evidence bagged. Montoya, who'd supervised until the Homicide team from downtown arrived, tossed the thermos in the 4WD, then crunched over coarse gravel defining the flash flood channel.

"Can't tell much yet from the bones." Weiss, the name tag read; Montoya remembered her from a Palmdale rape-murder she and her partner drew a couple of years ago. Her breath showed in the morning cold.

"We maybe got lucky, though." She held up a clear plastic bag, something small and round inside.

Montoya took the bag, felt the Saint Christopher medal. It was a cheap plated one, with some of the silver around the staff and the Christ child stripped away. He turned the bag over. The engraving was worn but deep enough to read:

Vaya con Dios, Benito. Papa, 1967.

Montoya puzzled a moment; something clicked. "What about a chain? One turn up?"

She exhaled. "Not so far. Kind of expect one, wouldn't you, Sergeant? Certainly it would have lasted as long as the medal."

"Detective Weiss," a voice called. "Over here."

One of the Lancaster deputies was hunched over something several feet from the area they'd combed. "More bones," he said. "Spotted 'em as it got lighter. Look there."

They looked. Barely visible outside the circle of artificial light, beside the exposed roots of a mesquite bush, white finger bones poked up from gray gravel. Like the others they were small, perfect. A child's hand.

There was a moan of wind, a crackle from one of the radios.

Weiss spoke first. "Merry Christmas," she said.

"Son of a bitch," Montoya added.

"Slow it down, Patty, how many?"

The news director was trying to open his eyes and find his glasses at the same time. From the floor where he'd knocked the alarm, the hour glowed early, too early for somebody who worked as late as he did.

"What's the source?" he mumbled. She was calling mobile; he could hear truck sounds and a car radio in the background. McGann wasn't the best field jockey on his news team, but she was young and ambitious and covered a lot of ground. Things he liked.

"Scanner, Chief, heard it coming home from a date. At first it was a single, kid's remains out near Saddleback Butte—some man and his son shooting at cans found 'em. I got curious, made coffee, and sat with it. After a while they came on again and upped it to three. Figured I'd get rolling."

The news director grunted, sat up, fumbled on bifocals; he'd crossed the line now, more awake than asleep. "Okay. How quick can you get there?"

"I'm on the Golden State near Burbank," she said. "Traffic's a bitch. An hour if I step on it."

"Step on it, then. Any idea about the three?"

"Not yet."

The news director heard a horn and a muffled curse, half-smiled, reached for his cigarettes. He'd spent twelve years in the field, knew the pressure the kid was under. Delays were slow death.

"Too early to tell, I guess," she said. "Scanner's been pretty sketchy. I just hope I got the jump."

"Stay with it, you'll be fine. You got a shooter yet?"

"Lombardi's a mile or so back." Gears shifted. "Here we go," she said. "Might scoop this one yet, Chief."

"Just get there in one piece, okay?"

"Rodge."

He was about to hang up and put the department on alert when he heard Patty McGann swear again, only this time it was full of wonder. A little prickle went up the news director's spine. He'd heard a CBS correspondent swear much the same way passing a shot-up rifle company near Hue, 1968. It had been him.

McGann came back, but her voice sounded far away.

"Scanner just updated. They've got five so far." There was a pause. "My God, they're still counting."

TWO

Pumping for speed, Hardesty dropped down the waveface, hit bottom, then angled up for a move off the lip. After reentry and a cutback, he'd close it out with five on the nose—maybe ten—show 'em how it's done. Nirvana coming up.

Then the wind. All day it had stoked the breakers, turning wavetops into needle spray that reached windshields driving past the Rincon. All day it had been his friend.

He was coming off the top when it hit, a maverick burst of gusting energy. Unbalanced and overcompensating, he staggered, then flipped headfirst into the green wall, the weight of it rolling over him like a highballing freight. He came up breathless, tasting salt. The longboard, like a dog on a leash, tugged on the cord strapped to his ankle.

Gringo flashed by him on the next swell. "Hey, Kahuna. Gotta show me that one."

Hardesty grinned. He and his board were relics to these kids and their racy tri-fin thrusters. They knew him, though, got a bang out of his wipeouts. What the hell, so did he.

Even with the wind the day was perfect: lapis sky, clouds long gone, Channel Islands clear enough to see the canyons etched like claw marks in the hills. And two miles south, the roof of his La Conchita house. Lisa'd have the Viennese brewing by now, burnt bitter stuff—words that made him wonder if it wasn't the way the marriage was heading.

Hardesty ducked under an incoming. The early-December swells were the best he'd surfed in years: ten-foot bluebirds, the pulse of far-off storms, a blast to the younger guys like Gringo. But for Wil Hardesty, the waves ebbed and flowed in his veins, part of him.

He'd started at the Wedge, bodysurfing at fourteen, and nearly drowned. The exhilaration, though, stuck around long after the water had left his lungs. In a month he was riding breakers under the Newport Beach pier—shooting the shit afterward with the foggy morning crowd, sharing lukewarm coffee and sugary Winchells with sand on the glaze. Life then was surf odyssey and outlaw-freedom mystique, San Onofre to Malibu to even-then Rincon, Mickey-this and Corky-that, slow dances to tremolo guitar bands, Coppertone on warm skin. Fun to kick around now when he bumped into other surfing graybeards.

Back then he'd even done some money gigs before walking away. Ultimately, it had come down to him and the water.

Thinking how much Devin would have loved it today, he headed in.

The '66 Bonneville eased out of Rincon Park and turned south, Wil's nudge on the pedal conjuring throaty exhaust. He still had hots for the car, virtually stolen from a widow anxious to dump it during the gas crunch. The Bonnie had style; it went like a white bat. It also carried a 9' 6" long-board in a partition he'd punched through the backseat. To improve its handling he'd replaced suspension and steering. Other than that, the car was mint.

Wil rested his arm on the open window; to his left, La Conchita appealed to some inner sense. It was so unexpected: half a mile long, scrunched against the coastal cliffs, a vest-pocket colony not even on most road maps. Northbound drivers escaping L.A. for the red-tiled splendors of Santa Barbara another fifteen minutes up the road rarely caught more than two blinks of it in the rearview.

Which suited him fine.

Like most locals, he dug the closeness of it. People co-existed—like the mobile homes, beach shacks, stucco houses, redwood decks. Roses grew next to cacti, fuchsias next to Spanish bayonet. And up the street at the north end, bananas, the fruit tree-ripening in bright blue bags. La Conchita itself hadn't grown much, though. Laid out in '24, it had waited for the movie stars and city folk to come, some getting as far as Mussel Shoals. After a while the coast highway had brought others: oil workers, smugglers, retirees, surfers, all attracted by cheap lots and two miles of sloping beach.

Wil checked his watch, knowing Lisa'd be annoyed: Given her accounting practice and his schedule, Sunday was their day. He pulled the car in under the port, between her black Legend coupe and his ancient Harley SuperGlide with the For Sale sign, and caught a glimpse of her looking down.

He waved, unloaded the longboard. Southern Cross: his cornball name for it after the blue stripe crossing red aft of center. Designed to impress other teenage surf rats, fashioned one distant summer following evening shifts at his father's place. Like himself, it had held up despite hard use.

Up the wood stairs: cinnamon air, Edward greeting him cockatoo-loud, Lisa with silence. She was in faded jeans and the long-sleeved tee with the parrot on it he'd bought her in Cabo; at her throat the gold heart held a splash of sunlight. She was curled up on the couch, concentrating hard on the travel section.

Wil poured coffee, tasted it, heard "Glad you could make it" from behind him.

"The waves were outrageous," he said, turning. "I was hoping you'd understand."

She folded her paper and laid it down. "What I don't understand is how you can surf at all. Nothing I haven't said before."

"You see the water?"

"Through the scope, yes. That's not what I meant, and you know it."

"I know what you meant. Can we talk about it later, please?"

"Later, Wil, sure." She returned to her paper.

He peeled out of the wet suit, showered, toweled off in front of the mirror, more or less pleased with his chest and shoulders, the stomach less so, his evasiveness definitely not. He ran a comb through his hair, its dampness concealing the gray.

"Everything's ready," she said from the doorway. "I'm just reheating." She handed him part of the muffin she'd started on.

"Ummm. Corn and jalapeño?"

She nodded. "They're probably dry by now."

"I'm sorry," he said. "Staying out that long was selfish."

"I know."

"Forgive me?"

"Wil . . ."

He kissed her, got some heat, tried it again; this time she spun away. As he dressed, he flashed on the photo—silver-framed longhairs in tie-dyed shirts, him tall in leather hat, her short and headbanded. Lisa Shigeno, with the smooth skin and almond-shaped eyes that still bored holes in his libido. She'd been a junior when he first met her at a 1969 UC Santa Barbara basketball game, surprised at how sport-smart she'd been. Interested, he asked her to a photo gallery opening and found out she knew more about Herbert Bayer's work than he did. Much later, she took him home.

Her father raised orchids in one of the big greenhouses south of Santa Barbara. Tojio Shigeno had planned on a black-haired samurai for his Japanese daughter and was un-impressed with a six-two blond Aryan—the point driven home with shouts, sulks, and threats. To no avail. They'd married right before Wil shipped out the first time, and it had stuck—unimaginable to most of their friends, some already on thirds. Which made him hate even more where they seemed to be heading.

His eyes settled on the smaller, newer frame: Devin Kyle Hardesty, forever ten-almost-eleven. Child of water and to water returned—standing beside the surfboard Wil would always see him on. Four years of trying to have him, two more in therapy . . . He took a deep breath, finished dressing.

Later, as they ate, he said, "About this morning—I'd like to make it up, dinner in town tonight. We can talk then if you want."

Lisa shook her head. "No. Paul phoned while you were in the shower."

"Rodriguez?" Wil looked up from coring a winter nellis.

"He's coming up, said it was important. About a friend of his. Said he hoped you were between jobs."

"Okay. You want to talk now?"

"Ruin our one day—isn't that what you really mean?"

"What's it going to solve, Leese? Beyond dredging up a lot of old—"

"Four years this February, Wil. I love you, and I hate being a bitch, but I'm running out of time."

THREE

While Lisa worked on her computer, Wil settled in front of the window, trying to remember the last time he'd seen Paul Rodriguez. Ten months, a year? The occasion was easier: wrecked in a bar down on lower State where Paul had come to pull him off the reef. Telling his friend to fuck off, leave me alone—taking a swing at him finally and falling down in a cascade of Coors bottles. Vintage Hardesty then.

His eyes drifted up and down the coast to nineteen years back.

He had them in the field glasses.

They were on a small dock; nothing much, a few boards sticking out into the river—the mother waving frantically, the baby under her arm screeching and kicking, the toddler clutching her leg. It was almost dark.

Miller ordered the Point Marlow *slowly toward shore. Full alert: They'd been briefed on the* Point Faro *ambush, VC snipers picking off a man and ripping up the bridge.*

Wil joined Rodriguez aft at the .50-caliber.

"What do you make of it?" he asked the gunner's mate.

"I'm not too thrilled about them bushes," Rodriguez said. "Congville, you ask me."

Both dripped with the heat and humidity. The smell of rotting vegetation rolled over the deck in waves. Actions clicked as the crew checked their weapons.

Rodriguez spat. "But hey, women and kids in distress? Semper Paratus, Lieutenant. Watch your ass."

Wil could hear the baby's screams as they made shore. His grip tightened on the M-16; close in now, the mother's eyes hollow with fear. Miller reversed engines, then backed off, preparing to board the trio. The Point Marlow *drifted momentarily.*

Then they lucked out. The first mortar round fell short.

Twenty yards away, the pier dissolved in a dirty wall of mud and flame. Degtyarev fire spat from the undergrowth.

"Sheeit!" Rodriguez opened up with the .50-caliber.

Five-foot geysers single-filed along the water's edge as the ship's other machine guns hammered at the thicket beyond. Miller shot the Point Marlow *ahead and starboard toward the safety of mid-river. The mortar mount was thumping now; bullets pinged and sang in the rigging.*

Turning with the ship, Wil heard himself scream as an arc of automatic rifle fire caught him, the impact spinning him over the side and into the muddy wake.

He was drowning by the time Rodriguez found him, spitting brown water while Rodriguez somehow kept them afloat and Miller swung the gray patrol craft around and the crew covered them with everything they had.

Back on deck he remembered the tracers, the explosions, yelling and blood, the numbness becoming pain. And three figures blown apart in a fountain of brackish muck. Then nothing until Rodriguez's happy wake-up call at the field hospital.

"Fuck me, it's alive."

Wil watched the Sunday traffic, heavy now with people going home. He'd been lucky as hell: three rounds, clean exits, no extensive damage; scarring and a shoulder that now and then told him when to come out of the water. Four months recuperating.

A year after that he'd returned—five months aboard his own eighty-two-footer, intercepting Delta contraband before going ashore for port security work: off-loading explosives, boarding vessels, inspecting cargo. The odd run-in with profiteers and hotshot brass.

What intrigued him most was the people stuff, the sabotage, assault, smuggling, murder. He'd been drawn to it and in time become well enough known to get requested for a number of interservice investigations. And the politics that went along.

Frustrated as he'd been by Vietnam, there were small victories: he'd helped people, been enriched by the diversity, given—and been given—friendship. Indeed, some of the friends had gone from active duty into law enforcement. In a sense, he had, too—well distanced from administrative structures and chains of command.

Rodriguez pulled in at six, climbed the stairs puffing and grinning; appraising Wil. "Lookin' mellow, bro. Glad to see it."

"You, too, *Jefe*." Wil held him at arm's length: still the bearish five-ten he remembered, but with a layer of softness now over the military muscle. He grinned back. "Always knew you were a man of substance."

"Brought you some'n, smart guy. Homemade tamales." He handed Lisa a paper sack. "Compliments of Raeann."

"Thank you, *Raeann*," she said, putting the bag in the fridge. "Can I get you something, Paul? Nachos?"

"No thanks, *chica*, ate before I left." He hugged her. "You still crunchin' them numbers?"

"Them crunching me is more like it. It's been crazy lately."

Paul laughed. "Must be pretty good, judging by that little black number in the carport. *LISA CPA*, no less."

"It keeps the corporate types impressed."

"Oh, right, can't be fun or anything." Paul rested an arm on her shoulder, faced Wil. "Must be nice, huh?"

Wil nodded. Despite himself, the Acura was an issue— nothing rational; Lisa deserved it, and they weren't hurting for money. *Her* money. "How's retirement?" he said to change the subject.

Paul went with it. "Shoulda stayed in, man. I sleep late, eat good, chase mama, and the checks come in regular as ever. *Que vida!*"

Late fifties by now, Wil figured. At his retirement bash everyone turned out, admirals to E-1s: E-9 gunnery Paul Rodriguez had played well over thirty years. The face was round and weathered and quick to let you know where you stood with it, the lines etched deep. Service-length hair, ebbed back a bit now, was remarkably free of gray, as was the mustache he'd let bush out.

Lisa popped him a Corona as Wil freshened coffees they'd been working on. For a while they admired the Channel oil rigs, Christmas-tree-festive on the horizon. Talked of old times. And new.

"Man I know needs help, Wil. I thought of you—who else, huh?"

"Not that I made it easy."

Paul dismissed the remark with a wave.

"It's appreciated," Wil said. "You know how it's been."

"Hey, *por nada*, okay? Anyway, Rae and I are friends with this guy, Ignacio Reyes. Little hard to get close to, but a good man. Couple times a week we eat in his restaurant."

Paul drained his beer. "Lately he's been real standoffish. Looks tired, drawn out—like his blood forgot to circulate. I ask him polite what's the matter. He shines me, nice, but distant. I persist—friends, right?

"So he pulls me off in this corner booth. Time he tells somebody, he says. Then he comes out with it—you ready for this?" Paul got himself another Corona, swigged some and sat back down.

"My friend tells me he's a murderer. Yeah, sure, I think. Tears come then, he tells me he killed his son. More tears. Benito, he says. Now this man ain't just anybody. He's made it, owns ten restaurants—Papa Gomez, chicken places, good ones. He works like a mother and goes to church and minds his own business. I know this man's family, know his wife's dead and mostly by himself he's raised six kids. No way the guy's a murderer.''

He paused. ''But there ain't no Benito. At least not that *I'm* aware of.''

Lisa set down her mug. A prickle started to crawl up Wil's scalp.

''It's late, so he closes the restaurant, gets out the mescal. The one with the worm? We drink awhile, the mescal works. He tells me the bodies they found in the desert, one of 'em's Benito's.''

Lisa joined Wil in the big chair.

''It's the medal, he says, the Saint Christopher medal. In the desert, he says.'' Paul massaged the back of his neck. ''Then I get what he's talking about. Sheeit.''

Wil sat forward. ''Saddleback?''

He watched Paul nod. For days there'd been little else in the news: gallons of ink, grim-faced TV reporters, sagebrush, solemn lawmen, Saddleback Butte silhouetted against the sky. The Innocents, they were calling it, child murders. Seven graves they'd found, bones, and the medal—all that had been released, anyway, that and the inscription, in the hope that someone would come forward.

No one had. Without breaks, the national news had eased up some. Local pubs, however, were still in a frenzy, aspiring politicians demanding greater efforts of the sheriff's department. Dead kids stuck in the public's craw.

Wil said, ''You think he's serious?''

Paul drew a breath, exhaled. ''I'm out of my league here, man, that's why I told him about you. But I saw his face.'' He paused. ''Hell yes, he's serious.''

''Has he been to the police about it?'' Lisa asked.

''He's afraid of the law, *chica*, doesn't know what to do. I told him I thought Wil could help. After a while, he said okay.''

Wil rubbed the scar between his eyebrows. "You tell him anything about me?"

"Sure. That you're a private dick and real closemouthed. Faster than a speeding bullet, more or less."

"Seriously."

"Lighten up, man. The guy wants to hire you."

"To do what?"

"Said he'll tell you himself," Paul said.

FOUR

Wil covered the seventy-five miles to the San Fernando Valley in just over an hour. Winter Santa Anas had blown out the usual murk, leaving a tapestry ringed by unexpected mountains, the effect one of revelation, like focusing a lens or seeing the girl next door in a party dress. Sharply defined, the Valley, like L.A., wasn't pretty—he'd never call it that—but it made you look.

For over a year now most of his jobs—those that panned out—had taken him south, away from the local rep he earned during the two-year tailspin after Devin. Anything to cut the pain, slice through the black, paralyzing bouts of depression, he'd done: pills, booze, dope, women, insane risks—hazy flashbacks that still raised a sweat. Lost in her own grief, Lisa stuck it out, but the investigations business Wil built up after Nam had nearly foundered. As it was, area law enforcement agencies and insurance companies were still gun-shy. Lawyers called occasionally, new ones who didn't know him. But unlike before, they were now the ambulance chasers, accident stagers, workman's-comp shaders. Fringe types who worked the system's cracks—and who didn't give a damn about how good you'd been and how far you'd been down and that you were finally getting it back. Long as you were flexible.

Following Paul's directions, he took Topanga to Ventura Boulevard. On both sides things sprawled: supermarkets, shops, malls, multi-movies, billboards. The empty-promise land.

Wil made a turn toward the hills and thought about the Innocents.

Seven kids they'd found, one of them fathered by the man he was going now to meet, a man whose pain was his, the wound still fresh. For the umpteenth time he pondered motives: pedophilia—serial murders—a smuggling deal gone sideways. Somewhere somebody knew something. Maybe Reyes.

He took a peppertreed drive to a looping cul-de-sac and parked, looked the place over. The house was newish, pseudo-Spanish, and white, except where storm runoff had left a brownish residue around the foundation. Curving red tile undulated on the roof, the three-car garage, and what looked to be a cabaña in back. Under a Chinese elm patchy lawn spread out, bisected by a resined pebble walk.

His bing-bong was answered by a Mexican woman who studied him for a moment, then took his card. "*Venga,*" she said. Looking back frequently, she led him through a tiled entryway, watched his feet for tracks down gold shag stairs, across a vast living room to a pair of oak doors.

As the housekeeper rapped, Wil glanced around at dated sectionals with matching chairs, arched brick fireplace, a big-screen. Nondescript landscapes claimed vertical surfaces, family pictures in various frames, the horizontal ones. The Virgin Mary smiled forgivingly from a distressed triptych. The oak doors opened.

The man was dressed in a navy jogging suit with white piping and appeared older than the mid-sixties Rodriguez had described. He was tall, pale-skinned, and blotchy, with a line of mustache under a hawkish nose and eyes that hungered for sleep. Second thoughts seemed to compete with resolve until he motioned Wil inside.

"*Pase, por favor,*" Ignacio Reyes said. "Come in, come in."

The den had a loungelike comfort. Bookcases lined three

walls; against the shuttered window was a desk, on it a coffee set and two china cups. Reyes motioned Wil toward a small couch, seated himself in a chair. He examined Wil's card, then spoke quietly, as if it were an effort.

"Private investigator. My friend Rodriguez said you were good at it. That he'd known you a long time."

"Since Vietnam," Wil answered.

Reyes poured them each a coffee from which rose the faint aroma of chocolate. "How old are you, Mr. Hardesty?"

"Forty-six."

"You have little ones?"

Wil shook his head, flashing on a brief ceremony: Dev's ashes scattered from the back of a boat. "In My Life" playing on the tape deck.

"I have six, grown now," Reyes said. "My children have been everything. They run my places, worry about me. They keep Serafina alive; I see her constantly in them." He pointed to a small ornate frame.

Wil leaned for a closer look: a hopeful-looking bride and groom, restored and hand-tinted, gazing into each other's eyes.

"Twenty years she's been gone," Reyes said. And then, "I killed her, too."

A brass clock chimed the hour. Beyond the doors a vacuum cleaner prowled; over the hum, something being sung in Spanish. Reyes struggled with his thoughts.

"We lived in the Sierra Madre, northern Mexico, in one of the mountain villages." He looked around the den. "There was no heat, no running water, no electricity. In the summer we baked, in winter we froze. All the time we were sick. We had barely enough food—a little cornmeal, greens we grew. Every so often, if we were fortunate, a squirrel or chicken." He put a hand to his temple.

"We had nowhere to go, our families were as poor as we were. Our only hope was in coming here." He reached for his cup. "But that was no hope at all because we had no money."

Wil shifted on the couch and wondered where this was going.

"Then we heard about this man, a border runner. We expressed interest. After a few days he came, in the night. It didn't take him long to see we had nothing—and how badly we wanted to go. He made"—Reyes sipped, set down the cup unsteadily—"a proposal. First he told us we were lucky to have such a fine family. People he knew in Los Angeles were not as fortunate, people who wanted children, wanted to give them a good home. They would have every advantage. Be loved, have clothes, go to school. Be something. I remember the way he looked at us and at the house.

"He told us he would take us where we wanted to go." Reyes pulled an earlobe. "If—"

Wil waited.

"If we would let him have Benito." A hoarseness crept in. "He kept saying Benito was perfect for the people he knew."

There was a knock. The housekeeper entered with cold turkey and a blood pressure pill for her employer, *rellenos* and a disapproving stare for Hardesty. As they ate, Reyes went on.

"At first Serafina and I were adamant: Unthinkable, we said, absolutely not. But he was persuasive. He kept asking us how we could deny Benito such a life. Didn't we want to save the family? And hadn't we already been blessed with six fine babies, and Serafina pregnant again? Over and over. Finally we had no more answers. Finally we agreed."

He shut his eyes, fought for control.

"Try to understand, Mr. Hardesty. We adored him. But we were also desperate. Giving him up seemed the only way." He got up stiffly, moved to the desk, where he reached into a drawer, emerging with a yellowed envelope.

As Reyes eased back into the chair, Wil pulled out a small photo.

"He was the youngest," Reyes said. "Our baby."

Wil looked into the face of Mexico: dark eyes, large and full of promise under thin brows; black hair parted over a high forehead; a guarded smile. The boy stood there trying to fill out a coarsely woven shirt. Around his neck was a homemade drum, the sticks poised to play.

"What could I give him?" Reyes said. "I could see the life he had, the life he *could* have." His voice broke. Slowly at first, then harder, he began to weep.

"*God forgive me. He was six.*"

Drying his hands, Wil took in the gold fixtures, hand-painted tile, expensive mirrors, and thought about the boy with the big eyes. Of guilt like a millstone around a father's neck; wounds denied their healing: things he understood too well. Reyes's decision had gotten him here, brought him what he wanted. Then, like an Aztec priest, it had ripped his heart out.

Reyes was picking at his lunch when Wil returned. "The *rellenos* were quite good," Wil said.

The older man raised his head. "My doctor says they're bad for me, too much fat. All my life I've eaten *chile rellenos*. Pleasures become fewer and fewer, Mr. Hardesty. My due, perhaps."

"The man who took your son, who was he?"

Reyes put down his fork, regarded his hands. "His name was Zavala—a bad man, it turned out. We crossed over a month after he took Benito. Seventeen of us he put in a small delivery van, twelve hours, no food or water. We could barely breathe. I heard later one of his trucks broke down crossing the desert, that everyone inside perished." He swallowed his pills with a gulp. "Bolo Zavala."

"You know what happened to him?"

"No, but he would be a hard one to kill. I know that."

Wil got out a notebook and pen. "Can you describe him?"

"I wish to God I remembered more. Short, young then, and very muscular. Broken nose, I think—" He shrugged, refreshed their coffees.

"What happened after you got to California?"

"Relatives of Serafina's let us stay with them. I got a job in a restaurant, then another. A few years later, we opened a place selling chicken the way Serafina's father cooked it in Mexico. Papa Gomez. We lived over the kitchen. We did well."

Wil recalled Reyes's comment. "And your wife?"

A deep sigh. "My wife did not do well. Losing Benito was very hard—even the new baby failed to cheer her. She stopped eating, then talking, then living. I was at work so much, I hardly noticed. By the time I did, it was too late." His eyes went flat, then closed.

Wil stirred milk into his cup; the spoon made a thin brittle sound. "Señor Reyes, what is it you want me to do?"

The eyes opened slowly. "Can you kill Bolo Zavala for me?"

"No," Wil said. "I can try to find him, if he's still alive. But it sounds pretty uncertain." He laid the spoon on his saucer. "You're sure the bones are your son's?"

Reyes nodded as if it hurt. "I chopped wood three months to pay for the medal. We had it engraved for his birthday. I knew the writing."

"He was six, you said? What date?"

"April ninth, nineteen-sixty-seven. A Sunday." He rubbed his hands. "He looked like an angel, Mr. Hardesty, but my Benito loved mischief. He swallowed it on a dare from Gilberto, his brother. I was furious with him. The next day he was gone.

"You see," he continued, "Benito wasn't wearing the medal, it was inside him." Reyes's voice sounded distant, and he looked old.

"The bones are my son's."

• • •

Before he left, Wil briefed Reyes on his fees. The man who was once poor was now rich, three bills a day plus expenses dismissed with a shrug. Reyes tore a thousand-dollar advance from his checkbook. "Find him. I don't care what it costs," he said.

"What about the cops?" Wil asked.

Reyes gave him a weary look. "Police don't like fathers who sell their children to murderers so they can cross the border in the night."

"What you've accomplished since then would certainly be taken into account."

"I still have my family to think of, Mr. Hardesty. The hurt they've already endured."

Wil wondered how much of that was Ignacio Reyes's pride, but he let it drop. He caught sight of a group photo in the bookcase. "Do your other children know?"

"So far they've said nothing." He paused. "Gilberto would remember the inscription, but I doubt the others would. They were older and wouldn't have stayed long at a birthday party with six year olds."

"Benito swallowed the medal at the party?"

Reyes shook his head. "Afterward, when he and Gilberto were alone. I had been resting, but when I woke up I knew something was wrong—they both looked so guilty." His eyes drifted to a point beyond Wil.

"I'll want to speak with Gilberto."

The eyes came back slowly. "Gilberto runs the Papa on Ventura Boulevard. Please, only if you think it will help—"

"One thing more," Wil said. "Have you any idea why your son might have been killed? What motivated Zavala— or the people he turned Benito over to?"

"No. And I think of nothing else, imagining how it was for him. That is a terrible thing, Mr. Hardesty. Lying there in the dark assuming the worst. Hearing him cry out to me."

Wind rasped a tree branch against the house.

"I have to know what happened," he said. "If it means my life, I have to know."

The phone rang just as he was raising himself off the big woman with the spiderweb tattoo. Sweaty, panting, he picked up the receiver, caution having taught him never to speak first. As he waited he admired himself in the mirrored ceiling: *muy hombre*, even at fifty.

"I see they found your little family." The voice was steely. Familiar.

His mood vanished like smoke in a breeze; immediately he hustled the woman from the room: "*Vete, vete, vete, vete, vete. Tengo negocios.*"

"An act of God," he said, uncovering the receiver. "Who would predict a flood in the desert?"

"God acts in ways mysterious. Not so men. What about the medal?"

"*No se preocupe.* An oversight, nothing." He fingered the pinkish line that ran from his chin to his right ear. "What do they know from it that could hurt us? None of those sheep would dare speak to the police. They know what would happen. They have everything to lose."

There was silence, then, "*Recuerda, compadre.* So do we."

FIVE

Using the car phone, Wil left a message for Lisa not to expect him, then called Mo Epstein and set up an after-work at Musso's. He drove to Paul's house, parked beside the sycamore in front, told him of the meeting, what he faced going in.

"I don't know. Reyes wasn't sure he was even alive."

Rodriguez thought a moment. "I know a Border Patrol guy—and another in Immigration. Big a bastard as this one, somebody must know something. Lemme help, huh?"

Wil was shaking his head when he had second thoughts: If Paul could get any kind of a sniff, he could pick up the trail from there. Meanwhile he could use the time to see what the law had learned. "Two conditions," he said. "One, you're on the payroll. Two, you take no chances." He saw the grin, sharpened his tone. "Hear me on this, *Jefe*. It's too nice a deal you got here to let me screw it up for you. Okay?"

"Your call, bro."

Wil hesitated. "I was a horse's ass, Paul, the things I said in that bar. Hope you understand what was doing the talking."

"More'n you think," Paul said. "Now go on, get outta here."

• • •

Cruising Hollywood Boulevard, Wil took in the dazzle. The City of Dreams lived in the bright billboards, the few remaining deco facades, the glowing marquees. Real Hollywood, though, lived at street level—in the human pinballs who bounced around mumbling, in the hungry angry ones snarling for spare change, in the timid vacant ones who avoided eye contact. Bits of flotsam, they streamed and eddied past leather shops, greasy spoons, curio dives, low-fi outlets, T-shirt emporiums—the new inheritors.

Musso and Frank was an island in the polluted stream. Wil reserved a table, savored red leather booths and old wood, the long bar, the juniper smell of crisp, cold gin. At lunch the restaurant was crowded with dealmakers and doers, revved by the race. Dinner, early dinner particularly, brought out the old-timers and a nice sense of calm.

He scanned the bar for Mo Epstein, saw him in a rumpled suit rolling for rounds with the barstoolers on either side. As Wil approached, he looked up, grinning, from a spread of dice.

"Hey, Wilson, we were just celebrating the occasion. These gentlemen are buying our cocktails."

"I see you brought your own dice again." He shook Epstein's hand; to the losers he said, "This man isn't usually allowed out by himself. It's good you kept him occupied." He ordered a club soda, watched it being poured while Epstein collected his beer. They followed the maître d' to a corner booth.

Settling in, Wil regarded the man he'd first met defying authority in Saigon: compact stature, homely face, intelligent eyes over a generous nose. A pain in the ass, Wil had thought initially. Never keen on the military way, Epstein resigned his commission after Nam, kicked around, and to Wil's amusement joined the L.A. County Sheriff's. "Can't live with it, can't live without it," he'd kidded. Still, Moshe Epstein had done well. Their paths had crossed a couple of times since, unofficially. Once over a teenage runaway when Mo had been in Missing Persons, the second on a wife-killer who'd disappeared into the San Rafaels.

They touched glasses. "My friend, the independent one," Mo said, raising an eyebrow. "Club soda?"

"Penance," Wil said. "Six months now."

"At least I haven't had any morbid drunken calls from biker bars lately. Figured it must mean something."

"You miss those, do you?"

"About like nighttime incoming. You working again?"

"Here and there, nothing I'm too proud of."

"Lisa?"

"Just fine, quite the business executive. She outearned me again last year—thank God." He sipped his drink; the waiter came and they ordered dinner. Epstein tore a piece off a slab of sourdough.

"And how's copping?" Wil asked.

Epstein stopped. "Business is terrific, thanks, very uplifting. Just had a little girl beaten to death and burned up by her junkie mother, somebody's been slicing Lynwood hookers, and Jesus, the gangbangers. Last week a grandmother minding her own business, this week two grammarschool kids and a three year old. Proving themselves, or they're bored, or you're wearing red, or something. And the weapons: riot guns, assault pieces. Like Ma used to say, it's no place out there for a nice Jewish boy." He waved at the waiter for more butter, steadied on Wil's eyes.

"How you farin'—really?"

"All right."

"I mean about Devin."

"I know." Wil stirred ice around and sucked in a breath. "What-could-have-been still gets to me, usually at odd times. I see him in crowds occasionally. But the worst seems over. Except now Lisa hears clocks ticking—she wants another child. We keep going round and round about it."

"Changed her mind, huh? You think you might?"

"Not in this lifetime. Your shop handling the Innocents, Mo?"

"All right, I can take a hint. We are, yeah. There's another piece of work—the kid murders."

"Think of the bright side," Wil said. "Everybody watching, no more laboring in obscurity."

Epstein grimaced. "Gimme obscurity. Anybody with an ax to grind is out there grinding it. As we speak."

Wil motioned the waiter for a repeat on the club soda. "Anything new turned up?" he said as it arrived.

Morris's attention had drifted to a woman across the room; at the question, he swung back. "What, on the Innocents? Can't tell you much."

"Policy, or don't have much?"

"Fulla questions, aren't you?" He spun his beer glass slowly, watched it settle, eyed Wil. "I know you, Hardesty, the way you sneak up. You wouldn't have something going—"

Typical, Wil thought; well, here it was. "Actually I have, Mo." He watched his friend's eyes widen. "I'm representing someone I can't disclose, someone with an interest. I'm prepared to share what I can."

"Jesus," Mo said. "Lucky I asked."

Wil met his eyes. "It was coming if you hadn't. I invited you, remember?"

"Yeah, I suppose you did at that." Epstein paused to let the waiter set down their orders, then started on his. "How'd you fall into this honeypot?"

"C'mon, Mo."

Epstein gave him a long look, then shrugged. "What the hell. What we got is a lot of media hype and circling politicians. Carl Vella's the task force coordinator—good man, grist for the mill, though, the way it stands, everybody out for blood." He removed a bone from his fish. "That's it mostly. Thing's a bitch."

"I'm sure it is," Wil said.

"So what's up?"

"I hear you say *mostly*?"

Epstein flushed. "Games—seven dead kids and a good

cop with his tail in the wringer and it's fucking games.''
He took a deep breath. ''Sorry. I know you'll do what you
can to help. Okay, to date: they were found about seven
feet apart, regularly spaced, like in a graveyard. Except for
the medal we got no physical evidence. Not even a fiber.
Nobody's come forward, no Missing Unidentified Person
matches. All the databases have come up zero. Sound good
so far?'' He used the napkin, then dropped it beside his
plate. ''Whoever did this was real tight, they'd never have
turned up at all without some freaky storm and a boy shooting at cans. Maybe God plain had enough.''

Wil smiled faintly at the logic. ''Kids—how old?''

Mo looked at him. ''We're expecting the report on that
tomorrow. First blush, though, fairly young.''

''What about the medal?''

''Maybe you should be telling me about it.''

''It's been all over the news, Mo, *Vaya con Dios, Benito.
Papa, 1967.*'' He put down his fork. ''The paper said something about sex murders. That the feeling at Homicide?''

Mo swallowed the last of his beer. ''Among some.
We've got a search going for similarities and offender pro-
files. NCIC, VICAP, our internal system; we're even cruising through the Unsolveds. So far nothing.''

When the waiter returned Wil ordered pie, Epstein coffee. In a few minutes, the waiter was back with both. Mo
resumed after he left.

''You mentioned a client with an interest.''

Wil drew a breath and leaned forward. ''What if I had a
name, Mo? Not my client's—that's out—but a name that
could open things up?''

''That'd be up to Vella and Captain Freiman. I don't
know, they might be in a mood to listen. Suppose it depends on what you're asking for.''

''What I'm asking for is in. Access.'' Wil chased pie
with ice water. ''I need to know what you guys know.
Everything. Until it's over.''

''That's all?'' Epstein looked incredulous. ''Look, *ev-*

erybody wants this thing cleared. If you know something, Freiman's going to want it in the worst way—he'll dance on your head if he has to. Christ, you know about withholding evidence.''

Wil bristled. "So far it's not evidence, Mo, just dinner conversation." He gestured for the check. They sat awhile, looking around, not seeing much.

Epstein broke the silence. "Look, all I can do is ask. Maybe you'll get lucky. But if that's what goes down, I'd watch the independent act if I were you. Freiman's by-the-book and not without ambition. Vella's a good enough guy, but he'll toe company rope. Now, what is it you have to offer?''

"Sorry, Mo, you're a good cop. What would you do if I told you, and Freiman wouldn't deal?" Wil pulled out a credit card and laid it on the table.

SIX

Paul was up and glad for the company; as he listened to Wil's plan to meet Freiman and Vella, he blew on decaf, then offered his opinion. "Sheeit. Probably just my Hispanic instincts about cops, but I'd be careful, I was you."

Wil said he would.

Paul looked skeptical, then brightened. "Hey, I got through to my sources. Two're researching, but my Border guy knew Zavala. Some bad mother—got into a scrape with some of my guy's people near Calexico. Early seventies, it was, after they got a tip he was coming. Four in the morning they spring an ambush. Zavala opens up on 'em, using his illegals as a shield. They hit him, but somehow he gets away." Paul inhaled coffee. "After he guns three of them and a couple of his own."

"Just a gentle misunderstood soul," Wil said.

"Yeah. Mexican authorities told my guy he was pretty good with a knife, too. Not long after the shoot-out, their snitch, fella named Pacheco, winds up in the Colorado with his throat cut. So happens the Mexicans have been after Zavala for years. Nothing recent though. Prob'ly dead, they thought."

Wil leaned back on chrome legs and stretched. "Your guy's connection say where in Mexico he operated?"

"Hermosillo," Paul said. "Drugs and guns but mostly flesh-peddling, although he thought there were some six-

ties-vintage murders. No convictions—Zavala had a lot of
friends in the local police. Every time the *federales* got
close, he'd disappear.''

Wil said, ''Shame Reyes didn't know some of this
stuff.'' He complimented Paul's detecting.

Paul smiled, hesitated. ''It's kind of off-the-wall, but my
cousin Gabe goes to church in the north Valley, St. Some-
thing-or-Other . . . Boniface. They're big into Mexican outreach, always after us for donations. I remember him
mentioning once the distribution end's based in Hermosillo.'' He slid his empty mug on the tabletop.

Wil narrowed his eyes. ''And you were thinking they
might know somebody down there to talk to.''

Paul's smile went to grin. ''More'n I would. I'll check
it out tomorrow, give me something to do. The extra bed's
yours if you want it.''

Wil nodded. ''Be great. I'm beat.''

''Um—I know how rough it's been, man. But I was telling Raeann about how much better you guys seem, you in
particular. You still seeing that therapist?''

''I'm fine, Paul, really. Lisa too. Everything's fine.
Thanks for not pushing it.''

Wil got Raeann's sewing room with the hide-a-bed, a little
milk-glass reading lamp on behind him. Hands under his
head on the too-soft pillow, he lay awake, gut fluttering at
the risk he was taking.

Two ways to go, the dice already rolled: If the cops were
as flat as Mo Epstein indicated, they might agree to let him
into the loop. If not, they could make it tight—threaten his
license, haul him in, generally harass him trying to get what
he had.

But finding Zavala was going to be a bitch, especially
with as cold a trail as this one. He needed what cops could
put their hands on readily—files, documents, reports. For a
while he tried putting himself inside Freiman's head, jug-
gling possible scenarios, weight given to how much heat

the department was taking. After a while he gave it up, clicking instead on a little boy in a desert grave and a father who, now that he had the money, couldn't get his son back at any price.

Six, Benito Reyes had been. Four years younger than Devin.

Feelings flooded in: hearing Dev pronounced dead, blaming himself, taking whatever Lisa'd said all wrong, the same with her. Trying then to be strong, the agony of it, finally just numbness and not knowing how the hell to act—even in bed.

Lisa found the therapist; they'd gone together for a while, then each alone. It hadn't helped. For months it seemed they were on different cycles: one up, one down; him angry, her depressed. Vice versa. Then there were the harpoons of pain from unexpected sources, tears when he least expected. For two years he'd wiped out in waves of his own making, each wave bigger than the last, each battering them both hard. One day he broke the surface like a drowning man clutching a spar and began to function again. Enough to swear with Lisa that as long as they stayed together they would never again risk the loss of a child.

They'd almost rebuilt when Lisa decided otherwise.

With effort Wil spun his mind away from it to the who and why of the Innocents, getting nowhere before his thoughts turned abstract. A species that preyed on its own: Every day there was some new horror; picking up the paper was like waiting for the other shoe to drop. There seemed to be no bottom anymore.

Gradually the room brought him out of it, Raeann's passion for creating everywhere. In one corner, a group of footstools shared a needlepoint pattern; from an upper shelf, watercolor owls stared at crocheted homilies. He spotted a photograph propped up in a brass frame: the family, scrubbed and smiling.

Counterpoint.

He snapped off the lamp.

• • •

What once had been full was now empty, raucous now stilled. Cigarette smoke drifted in harsh light over green baize. There was the soft click of pool balls as two men took their turns. Now and then a sip of beer.

Far away, audible now in the bar's late quiet, a ringing. Feet padding closer and a pointed finger. "*Teléfono*."

The man with the long scar, the shorter of the two, moved toward the alcove, the waiting call. Anyone noticing might have been struck by the man's orange hair, light skin, freckles—especially knowing he was Mexican. No one was there, however, as he lifted the receiver.

As always, he listened first.

"It's happening," said the voice. "What you said would not happen is happening."

He allowed a respectful silence to pass, then, "*Cuénteme*, talk to me. What concerns you?"

"Not what, who," the voice said. "There have been inquiries—a man named Rodriguez has been very curious about you. Calls have been made. My sources told him you were dead, but the man persisted. Words to the wise, *cuate*. A small effort now would be time well spent."

The listener waited; when nothing more came, he sighed deeply. "*Comprendo, patrón*. Tomorrow—after some personal business."

"This Rodriguez lives in Van Nuys." There was a soft rustle of paper. "The first name is Paul. I leave it to you."

The connection went dead in the man's hand.

The voices woke him, quiet as they were trying to be. He found them in the kitchen: Paul sitting with the paper, Raeann scurrying.

"Wil, honey." She smiled, stopped for a hug. "You look good, not so thin. We worried, you know—even if Rodriguez never told you."

"Thanks, Raeann. You're looking good, too." Raeann Rodriguez was *gringa negra*, the cocoa-skinned daughter of a black shopkeeper Paul's family knew in Santa Barbara—how often had he heard the story? They'd noticed each other about the time Paul enlisted, spent the next thirty years riding out the calms and storms: one son, Tommy, a lot of service-mandated separation, flak from families deeply rooted in different ways.

Not to mention cultures.

Wil had long figured the reason he and Paul originally grew close stemmed not from common interests or professional respect but from the women they'd chosen—the unspoken bond between them. He also knew that whatever prejudices he'd felt directed at him and Lisa could be magnified a hundred times for Paul and Raeann.

They were good people, enduring.

Raeann Rodriguez eyed him. "You still could gain some."

"Time to have your eyes checked, babe." He sniffed. "Whatever it is, I'm sold."

"Eggs and chorizo's all." She pointed to Paul. "Watch him, or he'll be swiping yours." She winked.

Wil grinned; Paul rolled his eyes.

"I'd love to hear what you're up to," she said. "But I'm off after bulrushes." She jammed some things into an already stuffed bag, nodded at Paul. "I keep trying to interest the Chief in basketmaking, but he won't do it. Tell him it's fun, will you?"

"I don't know, he might bite me," Wil said, watching her. She was still relatively trim, with deep hazel eyes and a burnished look to her skin. High cheekbones, a comfortable sort of pretty. She hoisted the bag and backed out. In a minute they heard the car starting, a good-bye toot.

"Bullrushes my ass," said Paul, pouring more coffee. As Wil ate, Paul told him they'd missed Ignacio Reyes last night. "He's always at the restaurant. You think he's okay?"

"Yesterday was tough on him," Wil said. "You know Gilberto?"

"Sure, he runs the place. Nice enough kid—worked there long as we've been going, ten years about. Doesn't seem very close to his pop, though." Paul forked in illicit chorizo. "You gonna see him?"

"Tonight, yes. You think he knows about this?"

"Hard to say. Gilberto doesn't let on much."

"Guess we'll find out," Wil said.

Paul left for St. Boniface as Wil phoned Mo Epstein; they'd meet at eleven. At ten-fifteen he hit the Ventura freeway, then the Hollywood toward downtown. Gas fumes caressed the slow-moving traffic; ahead, high-rises lurked behind a gray curtain despite sun and blue sky overhead.

By ten forty-eight he'd eased off the Broadway exit and parked at a meter across from the Hall of Justice. Waiting for the light, he ran his eyes up the Prohibition-era wedding cake. Stone leaves circled it; Doric columns pretended to support the top floors; air conditioners poked out. A dreadlocked man slept curled up near the doors Wil entered at five-till.

Mo Epstein was there in the lobby under an intricately waffled ceiling and large overhead fixtures with most of the bulbs lit. TV crews were waiting their turn while bright lights inside the Information Bureau signified interviews in progress.

"Feeding time," Mo said, watching two reporters argue. "What there is. Every day just makes everybody that much more peckish."

"Apply to the gentlemen we're about to meet?" Wil asked.

Mo nodded as they entered the elevator. "Them in particular. Watch your step here, pal. I've told them you're okay, but they're in no mood to futz around."

Homicide was seventh floor, down a lifeless marbled hall. Wil followed Mo Epstein into a conference room. Two men sat at one end of a long table; without rising, the larger man motioned them to hard-looking chairs, then spoke.

"Mr. Hardesty, August Freiman, Captain to you. Lieutenant Epstein says you have something about the Saddleback killings that might interest Lieutenant Vella and myself. He also tells me you're something of an investigator, actually make a living at it. Kind of an independent son-of-a-bitch as well. That anywhere close?"

Wil tried a smile. "Lieutenant Epstein is too kind, I'm not that independent." He waited for a reaction, got none. Freiman was big and Germanic, blond gone bushy gray; florid face on a thick neck above a civic-lunch gut. He was dressed in the bottom half of a dark glen plaid, a starched yellow shirt, red tie. As though interrupted from something important, he looked out over half-glasses. On his right Vella was tall and dark-suited; vulnerable-looking by comparison. Fatigue showed in both faces: indoor pallor, dark bags under eye-drop eyes. And something else Wil knew well: the taut look of men too long on alert for a shadow adversary.

He flashed on Mo's warning look and started again: "What you said is correct, Captain. I'd like to help."

"Then do it."

"And be helped in return."

Freiman's jaw twitched slightly. "Mr. Hardesty, I've met remoras like you before, and I'll tell you to your face I don't like private cops. You know something about the Innocents, I want it. Yesterday. And not just because of the well-meaners and wackos breathing down my neck."

Administrative menace: Wil had seen the act before, and he knew Mo had. Vella regarded the backs of his hands.

Freiman went on. "Seven dead kids, Mr. Hardesty. You are familiar with the rules governing evidence, I assume. Particularly the part about withholding it?"

"Yes."

"Well, then?"

"Enough to know I'm not obligated by law to tell you anything."

Freiman looked at Mo Epstein, then back to Wil. "Perfect—just perfect. Our reward for laws like that, I suppose. Mr. Hardesty, you even have kids?''

''Captain—'' Epstein began.

''No,'' Wil said.

''No, I didn't think so. This your great white hope, Epstein?''

''Look,'' Wil said. ''What you think is your business. My situation is that I represent a client who is peripherally involved. Not as a suspect, but with a possible link to one of the victims. My client remains anonymous—that isn't negotiable. However, in addition to the link, which could shed light on the possible reason for the killings, I'm prepared to offer you the name of a potential suspect. Now, that's my situation. With all due respect, yours is best explained by that scene in the lobby. To be blunt, you seem to have a creekful of shit and no paddle.''

The blood left Freiman's face for a few seconds, then came pumping back. Epstein looked at the ceiling as Vella jumped in.

''Not a real productive attitude, Mr. Hardesty.''

''Real sorry about that.''

''More like a luxury you can't afford. Maybe you need time to reflect on that among types who'd be less interested in your attitude and more with your involvement. Men with a steel-door code about child murder. You think I'm kidding?''

''No, Lieutenant, I don't,'' Wil said. ''You'll come up with a reason to lock me up and who'd care? But remember who requested this meeting. I want to help. I just need something in return, access to information—now and down the line. You get what I know and find out, I get what you know and find out. Everybody wins.''

Freiman and Vella exchanged looks; Wil could see the hunger in them, the specter of time. Fingers drummed the table. Finally Freiman spoke.

''Mr. Hardesty, you'll excuse us a minute.''

• • • •

"Talk to me," Freiman said. "This guy for real?"

Epstein met his eyes. "Captain, he and I served together in Nam, toward the end of the war. One time a shipment—food that we'd seized—turned up missing and embarrassed some brass. Hardesty found out a South Vietnamese who worked with us took it to feed his family—things were tough then for locals who'd helped us. Anyway, the brass was convinced Hardesty knew what was up, so they tossed him in the brig when he wouldn't come across." Epstein paused. "After forty-five days they gave up. Point is, Captain, we can sweat him, but it'll cost us time. He didn't have to come here. My gut feeling is he has something we can use."

Vella lit a cigarette, frowned. "I keep trying to think why the name's familiar."

"His son died in a surfing accident," Epstein said.

Vella frowned, shook his head.

"Hardesty went after a deputy who fronted him for letting the boy surf where he did. Things got out of hand—the deputy's arm wound up busted. A photographer happened to be there, and it got splashed around."

The frown cleared. "Right, several years ago."

Epstein nodded; Freiman shifted in his chair. "This a red flag here, Epstein?"

"No, sir. Both men apologized. I wouldn't have let it go this far if I'd thought so. For what it's worth, he's helped me out a couple of times."

Freiman pondered the input, then turned to Vella, got a what-have-we-got-to-lose shrug. He exhaled loudly and motioned to Epstein, who was gone and back in seconds.

After Wil sat down, Freiman fixed him with a look.

"If we agree, this conversation stays here or you won't believe the trouble you bought yourself." He picked up Wil's card, snapped it for emphasis.

"All right," he said. "Let's do it."

SEVEN

The Camaro, an IROC model with the big engine and a midnight-blue custom paint job, turned left off La Cienega and onto Slauson. After a number of blocks it hung a right at Central, drove south across Firestone and into the 'hoods. The driver brushed back orange hair, levered down a smoked-glass window, and spat.

Fucking coloreds, he thought, eyeing a group of men drinking outside a market with gates on the windows. Turn anything into a goddamn slum, live in shit, then whine that everybody disrespected them. He pulled a small shape out of his jacket and spun the top, hit the inhaler twice, sighed as the coke hit back. Graffiti and run-down storefronts gave way to shabby streets and hurt-looking houses.

Close now, there it was.

He circled the block, left the IROC in an alley, eased up from the rear. The place was small, squeezed in behind another and down a cracked driveway, invisible from the street. The Junkyard Dogs insignia was right where Ronnie'd said it would be.

Bolo Zavala watched the house from cover, saw no signs of life behind windows boarded-up and barred. He racked a nine-millimeter round into the chamber of his double-action Llama, slid the gun into his coat pocket, then approached and knocked. The door opened a crack, a black face in shades asking, "The fuck you want?"

"Want to see Collins. Ronnie sent me."

"Ron knows better'n sending somebody here. Do a ghost, Taco."

Zavala put two silenced rounds into the man, pushed through the door, and scanned the room: nobody else there, noises coming from a room down the hall, the sticky smell of ether. He checked the body on the floor, dragged it behind a counter stacked with boxes. Then he started for the sounds.

There were two of them: a heavyset black man with a goatee and a fried-looking girl whose features said black and Mexican. The girl wore only underpants; scabs lined the inside of her arms. She looked up from wrapping crystallized cocaine, regarded him with hollow eyes, but said nothing. The black man was tinkering with the coils of an electric range.

"Jerome let you in here?" he said.

Zavala took in the girl's brown nipples, her watching him vacantly. "Uh-huh. Got something for Wendell Collins. You him?"

The man glanced at a pump shotgun in the corner, then back at the visitor, who was pulling a kilo-size package from his coat. He relaxed, went back to tapping the coils. "Already got suppliers, Essey. On your way out, tell Jerome I want to see him."

Zavala tossed him the package. "Not *selling* garbage, *pendejo*. Returning it." He brought the gun up as Collins regarded the package. "You think I'm some cherry who don't know coke from baby lax? Aguilera never cut his shit. Makes you think I take that from some fuckin' gangbangers just because they move in on the turf?"

Collins's eyes got large. "Hey, man, be cool with that thing. We ain't cuttin' no shit. Straight up. You unhappy, hey, lemme see what I can do while you take the bitch in the other room. You know, she's real—" As he reached for the phone, it was blown out from under his hand.

With the gun, Zavala motioned the girl over closer to

Collins. In Spanish he asked her, "They tell you to cut the white with menita?"

She nodded, her expression unchanged.

"What you tellin' him?" Collins bleated. "The bitch don't know shit, man. *Jerome, get in here!*"

Zavala turned to him. "You think the dope's so good, you try it."

"Hey, fuck you. *Jerome!*"

Zavala took a folding knife from his pocket, threw it down next to the kilo. "Jerome's dead. So's Ronnie. Now open that thing up and start eating."

Collins undid the blade, looked at Zavala and the gun, then slowly made an incision in the package.

"Wider," Zavala said.

"You Aztecs? Malvados? Whatever, you better get your brown ass home while you still got it."

Bolo Zavala smiled.

"Suicide what you be doin' here, man. Junkyard Dogs don't take no dis from nobody."

"Wider."

Collins thumbed open the slit, brought the package up to his face. When he lowered it, his mouth was white. "There. You happy now, muthafucker?"

"More," Zavala said.

Wendell Collins had the package at his mouth, adulterated cocaine spilling down his front, when Zavala fired. There was an explosion of white. Collins hit the wall behind him, leaving red before bouncing off.

Zavala turned to the girl.

"Dandelion," she said dreamily.

"What?"

"One'a them things you blow on and it goes poof. What his head looked like." She scratched the needle tracks on her arm. "You got any heroin? I could sure use some heroin."

"No," he said, picking up a sealed plastic bag from Collins's table. "This stuff pure?"

"Yes. Am I yours now?"

Bolo Zavala stuffed the bag into his coat and retrieved the knife. He shook his head. "*Lo siento, hermana.* Wrong place, wrong time."

"My story." She began to shiver; her pupils were pinpoints. As he raised the gun she turned away from him. "Just don't hurt me, okay? Other than that, I don't much give a shit."

Father Martin Desantis was worried; his meeting with the Gentes de Ciudad operations committee had not gone well. They were having renewed problems with the landlord, an unsympathetic man of Middle East extraction, and the van scheduled to pick up donations this week had been crunched in a head-on with a drunk. He was sure something could be worked out with the landlord, but the van was another matter.

Leaving the administration building for the rectory and yet another meeting—this time with the Amigos de Hermosillo ways-and-means people—Father Martin was deep into it. Hermosillo was big, no Band-Aid solutions this time, and yet it seemed only yesterday they'd opened the doors.

So much work.

He reached into his pocket, peeled a mint, popped it in his mouth. In his haste, he nearly ran down the shorter, plumper man.

"Father Martin? Excuse me," the man said. "Paul Rodriguez, Gabriel Ortega's cousin. If you could spare a moment, it would comfort a friend of mine who needs help."

Separated from his thoughts, Father Martin stopped, noting the earnest expression. "Of course," he said. Ortega? He finally gave up—there were so many now. He offered the man a candy.

"Thank you, Father," Paul said, chewing. "We've donated clothing and food several times before. Do I remember correctly hearing they were meant for Hermosillo?"

"Los Amigos de Hermosillo, yes. But those things you give us go out to all of Mexico." Father Martin smiled. "My thanks, Mr. Rodriguez—as you can imagine, we never have enough contributions." He began walking them toward the rectory. "You have a family?"

"Just the wife and myself at home now, Father. I'm retired military."

"And what has your friend to do with Hermosillo? Is he a part of our work down there?"

Paul shook his head. "Father, you remind me of someone—who is it—Ricardo, um . . . Montalban. Anybody ever said that?"

Father Martin smiled, wishing he had a dollar for every time. "Poor Montalban," he said, smiling, his standard reply. "But thank you. You were saying about your friend?"

"Yes. My friend is trying to locate someone. He was told this person had interests in Hermosillo at one time."

"I see."

"I was hoping you might be able to suggest some people down there I could ask. If he was still around, where he might have gone, what he's doin' now, things like that. My friend thinks he might've been there off and on going back about twenty years."

Father Martin paused in front of a natural stone grotto. On a ledge was a statue of the Virgin appearing to a smaller figure kneeling below; a waterfall spilled over the rocks at the Virgin's feet, past the saint, and out into a quiet garden. He fixed his gaze on the rushing water, then turned to Paul. "Names we have, Mr. Rodriguez. Perhaps this man even helped us at one time."

Paul smiled politely. "I'd be surprised."

Father Martin resumed their walk, Paul following in step. They passed a row of deodar cedars and headed toward a brick residence with stained glass in the door. They were almost there when Father Martin said, "You know, I visit the city rarely now, but I wonder if I might know this person."

"My friend remembers him as something of a character. Short, with reddish hair. Had a reputation, he said." Stopping as they reached the door: "The name is Zavala. Bolo Zavala."

Father Martin pursed his lips. "No," he said after a pause. "But our Amigos chairman lived there at one time, he may remember. If you wish I will speak to him."

"If it's no trouble, Father."

"Another mint?"

Paul took the candy.

Father Martin had his hand on the latch when the thought struck him. "Even better—speak to Leonardo Guerra yourself, Mr. Rodriguez. He's here every Sunday at eleven." He checked his watch: late again, never enough time. "As for the other, see Mrs. Diaz in the administration building, tell her you talked to me. She'll give you a list of some people to call. And now, *Vaya con Dios*."

He waved a blessing, then hurried inside.

Later, in his office, he checked his afternoon, then buzzed Mrs. Diaz. "Isabel, please convey apologies to my four o'clock. I will be unable to attend the meeting after all." He tapped the desk.

"And Isabel, dial Leonardo Guerra for me."

Freiman's face was a storm front.

"Here's how it plays, Mr. Hardesty. Lieutenant Vella will show you everything we've gathered, plus the coroner's report we got this morning. You then will give us your information. All parties agree in advance to share future findings as they occur. Which means that should you act independently, as Lieutenant Epstein indicates you have a penchant for, it will be grounds for serious can time to celebrate your independence from peeking through keyholes. Am I quite clear on this?"

Wil met his eyes. "Clear."

"Consider yourself warned." Freiman stood, announced he had another meeting, and left the room.

As Epstein got them foam-cup coffees, Vella brought a thick file up from the chair next to him. He spread a large-scale map showing the crime site and its relative location to Saddleback Butte. Then photographs.

Wil concentrated on the close-ups. Small skulls, ribs, spines brushed free of earth; rulers to lend scale; the Saint Christopher medal once in open palm and then tighter in to show the inscription.

Vella brought it out and opened the plastic bag. "Handle it if you like."

Wil did. It felt small and rough and insignificant, not much to show for a kid's life. He recalled Benito's face, then focused on what Vella was saying:

"—definitely kids, all seven. Fairly young, we think, impossible to tell exact age after that amount of time in the ground, which we don't know for sure either. Only thing we do know is since sixty-seven on the one kid, and that's assuming the medal belonged to the victim. Condition of the other bones was more or less the same, clean. No clothing, no threads, no soft tissue, no traces of blood, nothing in the surrounding soil—killed someplace else, we figure, buried about four feet down. The flood that uncovered them must have been fairly recent, though. Coroner's anthropologist found almost no external weathering."

He pointed to some extreme close-ups. "This nick on the front of the neck vertebrae, each skeleton had one. The coroner says knife, possibly curved from the unevenness here and here." Vella glanced again at the report.

"The angle would indicate an upward cut from behind, like so, all of them. Whoever did it had to have been strong—much deeper and they would have been decapitated. As for motive, the sex-killing stuff is media generated so far. It's certainly possible, but from the bones we don't know if we've got boys or girls or both." He sucked in coffee, tapped a photo. "This one's our medal kid. Like the others, no hacking or saw marks. One nick to a customer."

Not a customer, goddammit.

"He was a nice-looking boy," Wil put in quietly. "I saw a picture of him. I met his father." He watched their expressions change. It was still enough to hear Epstein's cheap watch.

"Jeezus," Mo said finally. He took off his suit coat, slung it over a chair.

Wil went on. "Benito was payment to get his family across the border the same year as the medal, sixty-seven. They were dirt poor. The man who brought them over promised the boy would be adopted by a wealthy family. The parents believed they were doing what they had to do and the right thing for him. Obviously something went wrong."

"Illegals would explain why we weren't able to make dental records," Vella said to Epstein. "What about the others, Hardesty?"

"I don't know, but the pattern would seem to hold if nothing's turned up. There'd be no shortage of interested buyers, judging from the stuff you read in the papers."

"Who's the man the parents gave the boy to?" Epstein asked.

"The name the father remembers is Zavala, first name Bolo." Wil waited for both cops to write it down. "You'll want to check it, but twenty years ago, he shot up three border patrolmen at Calexico, got some of his cargo killed using them as shields." He paused again. "The kids must have been a side venture for him. Just so happened my client had no money. It was Benito or nothing."

They drank coffee in silence.

"I'll save you more time," Wil continued. "Zavala worked with a man named Pacheco. Apparently they fell out, because after the shoot-out Pacheco wound up in the Colorado River with his throat cut."

Epstein sat up in his chair. "You get all this from your client?"

"No," Wil said. "This man would never have given his

flesh and blood to a jackal like Zavala if he'd known what he was like. I've done some checking.'' No sense involving Rodriguez, he reasoned.

Vella scratched his head, smoothed thinning hair. ''This Zavala alive, dead, what?''

''That's why I'm here, Lieutenant. So far nobody I've talked to seems to know. Or is saying.''

''Your client, why won't he come out?''

''Selling your child in exchange for illegal entry? Funny thing is, up until last week he'd imagined Benito a successful doctor or lawyer somewhere. I'm sure you can guess how he feels now.''

Epstein bit the rim of his cup. ''That would explain why nobody else has come forward. With no ID on the other bones, how would you know it was your kid out there?''

''Assuming the parents are even around,'' Wil said.

Vella checked his notes again. ''What about the medal? We found no chain, so the kid wasn't wearing it. If he was killed somewhere else, he couldn't have had it in his hand, it would have fallen out. If the killer dropped it, which I doubt, the medal could have belonged to some other kid.'' He pulled out a cigarette and lit it, waved away smoke. ''The killer himself could be named Benito.''

''You're right except for one thing,'' Wil said. ''The day before Benito left with Zavala, they had a birthday party for him, his sixth. The medal was a present. Later, another kid dared him to swallow it, which he did—the father remembers spanking him for it. That's why you found the medal where you did. It was inside him.''

Epstein flipped his cup in the trash. ''Which means he was killed right afterward or it would have passed through his system. It also fixes nineteen-sixty-seven as our year.''

''April ninth,'' Wil said.

''What?''

''The day he swallowed it. His birthday.''

Vella shook his head. ''Makes no sense. If the kid—''

''Benito.''

"I know his name, Hardesty."

"Then use it."

"Fuck off. You're here by dispensation, remember?"

"Right. Like you had so much going."

"Come on, people," Epstein said. "We're on the same side here. Carl?"

Vella glowered, then spoke. "What I don't get is, why kill Benito and the others? Delivered alive the kid means big bucks to Zavala from somebody."

"A double-cross, maybe," Wil said. "Money up front that Zavala splits with. Not much recourse when you're adopting illegally."

Epstein said, "Unless the kids were worth it to Zavala for sex. Wouldn't be the first time." He rubbed his forehead. "Your client remember what Zavala looked like?"

Checking his notes, Wil described Zavala for them, and they concluded with that. Vella went to brief Freiman and to turn the task force loose on the lead, telling Wil he'd let him know when something turned up. Mo Epstein accompanied Wil down the elevator into the lobby, walked him to the door.

"Really stepped in it big-time, didn't you?" he said. "I'll give you this, you did better than most with Freiman. Don't take him for granted, though, he's not nice when he's mad."

Wil was glad the sweat-soaked shirt under his jacket didn't show. Or the craving for cold beer and warm shots. "Far be it from me to upset the captain," he said over his shoulder. With the shouts of the reporters, he wasn't sure if Mo heard him or not.

EIGHT

Leonardo Guerra put the phone back in the onyx cradle. Sunlight slanting through the French doors illuminated the smoke from his cigar, an exceptionally fine Havana. For a moment he watched it waft upward toward polished wood beams, then he rose from the desk.

Father Martin was right. They were going to have to raise the stakes for Hermosillo; the work there was too important, the old facilities inadequate. The run-down hotel they'd converted was beyond repair, the orphanage similarly decrepit. They needed another drive, another huge effort. Money, and a great deal of it.

He flicked a long ash into the fire Julio had laid, then panned his eyes over the photographs on the mantel. The charitable missions of St. Boniface: Gentes de Ciudad, caring for L.A.'s downtrodden; Casa de Bienvenidos, assisting immigrant families; Dirección, the urban resources network; Work Etc., jobs for the indigent; Justicia para Todos, legal help for L.A.'s Hispanic poor; Friendship House, spearheading human rights; Comfort Zone, helping poverty-level disease victims; Amigos de Hermosillo, their first project together. Framed ribbon-cuttings, freshly painted signs, earnest volunteers wearing change-the-world smiles. He and Martin; Martin's look. Martin growing increasingly distinguished over time.

Guerra took in cigar smoke, let it out slowly. When

viewed dispassionately—a talent of his—St. Boniface was simply another diversified market-driven corporation. With attendant responsibilities, of course. Planning for the Amigos fund-raising would begin tomorrow.

He moved away from the hearth, pressed the button for Julio, and a slim youth appeared. Guerra's eyes appraised him: fourteen now, not a youthful or awkward fourteen either; no, far older. His brown skin glowed in the light from the fire, the black eyes deep and expressionless as empty vaults.

"Julio, start my bath," Guerra said, brushing a fleck of ash from his smoking jacket. "And before that, I would like a massage." He watched Julio nod and withdraw.

Then he dialed a familiar number.

Wil had to sprint from the corner, barely saving the Bonneville from a city-sanctioned tow truck. Driving away, he reflected on the meeting. No turning back now: Dead or alive, Zavala had to be in somebody's computer. And if they found him, what then—engineer a deal for Reyes to testify? Maybe; worry about that later.

He stopped for a quick lunch, called Lisa and got the machine, left a message he'd be back late. Outside the murk had intensified, thickened by lumpy clouds into a steel-wool sky. With the traffic already stacked up at Vermont, it was an hour to Reyes's place. By that time rain was making soft sounds on the leaves.

Wil walked toward the house, the low gloom making it seem larger than he remembered. Shrubs glistened on either side of the walk; somewhere a metal wind chime stirred. The housekeeper directed him partway to the study, then returned to her vacuuming. Built-in job security, he thought; finish one acre, another one needed it.

As before, Reyes was in the study. Wil briefed him on the border patrol incident, the killings, Zavala's trouble with drugs and guns. "As you said, a bad man."

Reyes shook his head.

"I am going to see Gilberto," Wil continued. "Tonight if I can."

There was no mistaking the expression, the twisting of blue-veined hands. "I know," Reyes said quietly. "It makes sense to speak with Gilberto." He sighed. "What doesn't make sense is how his own father could sell his brother to a man like Zavala." He looked around the room as though seeing it for the first time. "And for what—for *this*? *Jesumária!*" He got up awkwardly, fists clenched; picking up an urn-shaped lamp, he raised it over his head and smashed it on the floor.

Pieces flew, and the room dimmed. In seconds there was banging on the door. "*Señor Reyes, está usted bien?*"

As quickly as it happened, Reyes's composure returned. "*Si, Marta, gracias. Solamente un accidente. Estoy bien.*" Turning to Wil, he said, "I will speak to my son this afternoon. For now I am tired. Please excuse me, Mr. Hardesty."

Ignacio Reyes's feet crunched across lamp shards. Opening the doors, he walked past sliding glass, beaded now with rain.

Bolo Zavala checked his watch: eight-fifteen. From his position up the street, he watched the three leave the house and take two cars, the white coupe following the station wagon.

The fat one had to be Rodriguez, he guessed, the black woman his wife, since they left together. No telling about the tall one—blond he looked in the greenish night glasses.

After the taillights vanished, Zavala took a double hit off the inhaler, then timed off twenty minutes. Satisfied they weren't coming back for something forgotten, he left the IROC, put up his collar, and made for the house.

A snap: He was inside in less than a minute, pausing in the darkness, getting a feel for the place, then twisting on the flash. He looked around: four doors down the hall, the kitchen to his left. Start with the front room: stuff everywhere—knickknacks, knitted shit, family photos. He examined the photos.

It was him all right. Paul Rodriguez in uniform, with the woman, with babies. He swung the light down the hall. Bathroom on the left, sewing room, then master bedroom.

Zavala stepped inside, saw a canopied bed, throw rugs, plants: a woman's room, a woman's house. What kind of man lived in a place like this? He almost spat. If they were here, sleeping, it would be easy to take them both, pigs in a slaughterhouse. He fingered the knife: her first to keep her from screaming, then Rodriguez—

Some other time, maybe.

Back in the hallway, pushing open another door with the flash. Papers strewn on the gray metal desk, trophies; on the wall, more photographs: Rodriguez at some ceremony, posing in uniform, shirtless, cleaning a machine gun. Rodriguez with— He stopped. It was the tall man Rodriguez had left with, younger but recognizable, standing on a gray ship by a mounted deck gun. He lifted it off the wall, turned it over, saw writing: *With Wil, Cam Ranh Bay, 1969.* He flipped it back, wondering about this Wil. And Rodriguez.

Why had he been asking about him? For a friend, the voice had said. On a whim, he slipped the snapshot, frame and all, into his coat pocket.

Next he shuffled through desk papers: junk mail, gun magazines, insurance come-ons, a take-home restaurant menu. He picked up the menu, paged it, turned it over: on the back was a yellow Post-it with a name and phone number, under that a story about the restaurant and the family who owned it. The name meant nothing, and he went on.

There were envelopes addressed to Paul Rodriguez, United States Coast Guard, Retired; next to the phone a business card. Directing the light, he read, *Wil Hardesty, Private Investigator.* The tall guy, the Wil in the Vietnam photo. La Conchita, wherever the fuck that was. He pocketed the card, useful perhaps if the tall man came too close.

An investigator—maybe he'd find him first, see what he was made of.

Finished in the den, he searched the kitchen, found nothing of interest there. For a moment Bolo Zavala stood very still in the darkness, his hand on the frame in his pocket. Then he slipped outside, retracked the glass door, and headed up the street toward the IROC.

Papa Gomez was bigger than Wil expected: Mexican tile in abundance, stone fountain in the lobby. Blenders whirred, mixing in with clatter and hum from the dining areas. In a mural behind Raeann, jaguars crept among jungle vines.

Paul drank amber beer and talked about St. Boniface, showing Wil the list of Hermosillo people Isabel Diaz had given him. "Then there's this Leonardo Guerra," he said, working salsa onto a chip.

"Guy's head of the outreach program in Hermosillo. He lived there once, he'll be at mass this Sunday. What do you say we chat him up?" He saw the look on Wil's face. "I won't let the door fall on you, and you'll like Father Martin. See what he gives good boys and girls." Paul reached into his pocket and flashed the mints.

"I can't believe you actually took those," Raeann said. "With that stomach? I *mean*."

Paul winked. "Just being polite, hon."

Wil sipped his pineapple soda, flashed on himself as an altar boy, responding in Latin, pouring wine, shaking the bells—sometimes at appropriate moments, sometimes not. He tried to recall how many years since he'd been back, drifting instead to why, to the too many questions, those even before Devin. Paul's eager look brought him out of it. The truth was, he questioned this direction Paul was taking now, this whole thing with St. Boniface. Coincidences like that rarely paid off. Still, he could be supportive. "All right," he said. "Anything but the six o'clock."

Paul grinned and left for the men's room; Wil touched

his glass to Raeann's. "So, how's life among the bull-rushes?"

"If I'd done the boat, Moses never would've made it." She giggled, the sound high and youthful. "Seriously, it's a kick. We never had the time before." Hesitation. "Which reminds me, what are you guys up to, anyway? I haven't seen Paul this excited in years."

Wil poked the straw around in his drink.

"Actually, Paul's told me a little." She sobered. "Not dangerous, I hope. He's the only Rodriguez I've got."

"What he's been doing for me hasn't been, but it could be with the man we're looking for. We have an agreement."

Her face said it.

"No danger, Raeann, that's a promise. All right?"

She nodded. Paul sat down and dinner came; halfway through it a slightly built man approached. Unlike the colorfully clad waiters, he wore a conservative suit and tie. Wispy hair, thick glasses—thirties, Wil guessed.

"Mr. and Mrs. Rodriguez," he said, "twice in two days. The chicken pleases you I take it?"

Paul told him if it was any better they'd sprout feathers, then introduced Wil. Wil felt a cool, moist palm.

"My father mentioned you, Mr. Hardesty. If you can wait, I'll be free around ten." Gilberto Reyes left for other tables.

"Good enough kid, from what we know," Paul said, returning to his plate. "Polite, quiet. Bit intimidated, maybe."

"I can understand that," Raeann said, "knowing the father."

Wil was about to say something when mariachis appeared, making conversation impossible and speeding up the rest of dinner. Paul and Raeann left then; after a while Gilberto Reyes returned and led him to a cramped office. Wil complimented him on the restaurant as their talk drifted to why he was there.

"I knew, Mr. Hardesty," Gilberto said. "From the medal. From my father calling." He lowered his eyes to the desk, picked up a pencil, began tracing nothings on the calendar blotter. "I'd not heard my father cry before. Odd how little things stick in your memory. I was seven, Benito six. We never had or did much for birthdays, but that day we had a small party for him. It was supposed to be a surprise."

On a shelf above the desk Wil saw a small print, blurry but recognizable: Serafina Reyes holding a baby and smiling.

"I think he knew. He couldn't wait to get home." Gilberto laughed without humor. "Then the party was over and it was just him and me and we were looking at how shiny it was. I started daring him—you know how it is when you're kids. I never thought he'd swallow a Saint Christopher medal, for God's sake." The laugh became a sigh. "I was jealous—he had a treasure and I didn't. Afterward, Papa beat us both so hard we couldn't sit down." He lifted his glasses, rubbed his eyes.

"All those years I thought it was my fault Benito had to leave. That the man took him away because of me." His voice trailed off; outside the office, kitchen sounds got louder. Gilberto started again.

"After that everything changed. We came here, I got to go to school, there was plenty of food. But it was never the same. Papa would hit us for nothing. He never smiled. It was as if he couldn't stand to be with us anymore."

A hostess poked her head in the office, saw Wil, and quickly excused herself. Gilberto nodded to her, resumed when she'd left.

"Now I know why," he said. "He was paying for what he'd done. Mr. Hardesty, have you any idea what it's like to compete with a ghost? We weren't blind—it was obvious how he felt about Benito. For a while I actually was glad he was gone. Now, at last, my father would pay attention to me."

He made a short sharp sound.

"Instead he worked. Brooded. Told us not to talk about Benito. But my brother was there—all those years. In a way, when Benito left, we all left." He leaned forward, elbows on the desk, chin on his hands.

"The man who took your brother, what was he like?"

"Since my father called, I've been trying to remember. He was strong looking, with a mustache. He gave us candy. But he had mean eyes."

"Anything else?"

"Freckles—like a kid's. And reddish hair, frizzy. I remember he hardly took his eyes off Benito the whole time. It was like none of the rest of us existed."

"What about your brothers and sisters? Would they recall anything?"

"I doubt it. As for the medal, I'm not sure they even knew about the writing. I've heard nothing from Connie or Humberto or Felix. Esperanza lives in Albuquerque. Rafael hadn't been born yet." He hesitated. "Then again, we're not a family that talks. Anymore."

The man was visibly out of steam; Wil finished making some notes, gave him his card, rose to leave.

Gilberto Reyes stared at the card; his voice, like an echo, was detached. "What is it like out there where they found him, Mr. Hardesty?" he said. "I would like to see it sometime."

The rain was coming hard, intermittent drumrolls on the car's roof, by the time he left Papa Gomez. Traffic added freeway splash to the pattern of fat drops.

Wil set the wipers on high, tuned in a jazz station.

An alto sax riff, sweet and sad, drew his thoughts to the seven graves. Raining there, too, likely—or maybe not, the storm blocked by the mountains, the desert an apt metaphor for Benito's family. Not knowing where he was, unable even to speak of him, their love for each other had dried up and blown away like so many tumbleweeds.

Wil remembered the sword stroke, his parents dying in a car crash. It hurt like hell, but it was clean and had healed, despite the reason for it. There had been no healing for the family Reyes.

North of Conejo Grade the storm slackened; by the time he turned off 101 it had played out altogether. La Conchita, after L.A., looked small and safe. Few lights shone in the lateness—Christmas strings, pinpoint stars through broken clouds. The damp air felt like freshly washed laundry hung out to dry.

He let himself in as quietly as he could; from the bird-cage, cockatoo murmurings started.

"Just me, Edward, don't get up."

"Wil—?"

He came to the bedroom door, crossed the room, kissed her back to bed. "Right in," he whispered.

Lisa rolled over and began breathing deeply. He watched a moment, thinking the composition would make a stunning silver-print, her black hair splayed on the pillow. He shut the door softly and made for the fridge, cracked a mineral water, walked to the window.

Across the freeway, surf rolled up on the beach; this late not much else moved, a few big rigs pulling all-nighters. He wondered where Bolo Zavala was tonight if he was alive: a quick upward stroke, all seven, all the way to the bone.

Christ.

Gradually Wil wound down with the remaining Calistoga. He stuck the empty in the recycling bag, let Edward nibble his finger affectionately, and slid into bed, grateful for the normal things in his life.

The phone was picked up on the second ring.

"There may be someone else," Bolo Zavala said. "A man named Hardesty, a private investigator." He spelled it off the card. "I saw photographs. He was with Rodriguez on a boat."

Silence on the line, a signal for more.

"Your Rodriguez is retired Coast Guard," he continued. "Nothing on what they want."

"All right," the voice said. "For now we will watch closely and consider what comes next. If this man is an investigator, the friend Rodriguez mentioned is likely Hardesty's client. Private investigators work for money. We will find out who is paying him and put a stop to it. *Comprende?*"

The line clicked, the voice replaced by dial tone.

NINE

Lisa's hair smelled of jasmine; their lovemaking had been like old times: unforced, silly-serious, hot enough to start Edward squawking. An E-ticket ride that afterward, as Wil lay there while she slept, had him wondering at this kind of uneasy peace between them. He got up finally and put the covers back. Taking care not to wake her, he set the timer on the automatic drip, spoke softly to the big white bird, then let himself out.

The wind was calming, but the clouds had re-formed low on the horizon. The ocean was a vast gray plane dotted with whitecaps. Gringo was already there, juking in the breaks—paddling in when he caught sight of Wil.

"Saw the Bonnie, dude, figured I'd see you today."

"Been in L.A.," Wil said, struggling into the wet suit. "I need this." He walked into the surf and floated the Southern Cross toward Gringo, and they headed out toward the swells. "How's it holding up?"

"Looks better'n it is," Gringo said, "like most things." He was as tall as Wil but more wiry, with surfing-ad features and sunstreaked hair he wore long. "Backup waves. Every now and again they're in sync."

Wil nodded. For an hour they fooled around, then made for shore and hiked up the trail to the parking lot. Gringo put his tri-fin in the carpeted bed of a weathered Ford Ranchero. Slapped on over a rusted spot was a bumper sticker trimmed to read, Practice Random Senseless Acts.

"Don't you get tired of packing that old piece of whatever?" he said. "How you turn that thing anyway?"

Wil set down the longboard. "Turn? I thought the idea was to ride."

"One of these'd change your mind." Gringo tapped his board. "Thrusters rule, dude. Evolution and all that."

"So that's where the rest of that little thing went," Wil said. "My sympathies."

Gringo snorted.

Wil said, "By the way, you keeping up your quota?"

"Told you about that, huh? Pam's big idea."

"Seems fair to me—she just wants you working as many hours as she does."

"You punch a time clock at home?" Gringo said. "Damn, I get enough of that at the sites."

Wil opened the Bonneville's trunk. "I thought you had an arrangement. Surf, work, live cheap, save up. Like that."

"We do. Pam likes the trailer fine, just not forever. I can understand that. Her way just seems kind of programmed. Probably not used to it is all."

"You're working, then."

"Drywall mostly—single units. Next week a convalescent hospital." Gringo yanked on the Ranchero's door handle without success. "What the hell. It buys groceries, doesn't add to the worry lines." He looked closely at Wil. "Speaking of which."

Hardesty laughed; Gringo never had two cents to rub together and zip for possessions, but Gringo hadn't many wrinkles either. He shed his suit, dried off, loaded the longboard while Gringo coaxed a metallic screech out of the Ranchero's sprung door.

"Hang loose," Wil said. He cranked the engine over and on the way home contemplated a gray figure in a white house and the cost of things.

Her note was on the dining table: *Got an IRS meeting,*

then the McTeer Research audit. Home late. Encore? L.

"Goddammit, Ed." Wil let the bird out to walk around. "Next time say something." Fucking schedules; there went their day together. Bakery scones she'd left soothed him somewhat. He carried one to the window, watched for a while, then turned his attention to the smallish two-story they'd added onto. Enlarged kitchen, a deck, bathrooms redone. To make a small space look bigger, white paint with indirect lighting, spots to illuminate their collection of photographs: Ansel Adams, a Muench White House Ruin, early Annie Liebovitz, some promising local work.

Decor they'd kept simple: trestle table and matching Windsors, nubby sectional, the oversize Danish chair. Their bedroom, being upstairs, faced the bluffs; the second bedroom was all-purpose: futon, computer and desk, file cabinets. The third bedroom was Devin's. A thousand or so square feet, the house's size was sometimes an issue—as was distance from certain amenities. But every time moving came up, they looked out the window.

Wil put on a CD: Jennifer Warnes smoothing "Bird on a Wire." The bamboo palm slow-danced to an onshore breeze. Gilberto Reyes called about one.

"I remembered something," he said. "Zavala had a tattoo, a squarish thing on the inside of his forearm. I know now what it was: a razor blade, dripping blood. There was writing, too. Benito and I were doing our alphabets then. We spelled it out after the man left."

Gilberto paused to call instructions to someone.

"Mr. Hardesty, the writing said, *'Ahi viene la muerte.'* You know the meaning?"

"Yeah," Wil said. "Here comes death."

Wil waited for the Lapsang Souchong, its aroma reminding him as always of the tarry hold of a lumber schooner once toured in San Francisco; a privy on a hot day, according to Lisa. The tea store had been only too happy to sell him the last of it. Romance is dead, he thought, pouring some as the phone rang again.

"My ear's about to fall off," Paul said. "Ma Bell's gonna send me Christmas cards."

Wil assured him it was covered.

"Came up with a lotta nothing this time," Paul said. "One man down there'd heard the name is all. What the hell—hard to see Zavala having anything to do with Amigos de Hermosillo and vice versa." His tone was discouraged. "Nothing from my other contacts either. I dunno, maybe the whole thing's a dry well. Sheeit, I thought we'd have the sucker by now."

The opportunity was there, and Wil took it. "Take it easy, the guy's likely dead in some unmarked grave. If I haven't told you, this is the work. Some days are like that."

Paul was silent.

"Listen," Wil said. "You've been great so far, a regular Dick Tracy. But it's time to let the heavies and their computer nets have a crack at Zavala. Give that girl of yours a break."

Paul's voice hardened. "Ain't dumping me, are you, hotshot? I been that route already."

Suddenly it dawned: Paul hadn't retired voluntarily. Money was always a big deal for the Coast Guard, Wil knew, and Raeann had certainly wanted it. But Paul hadn't, and nobody had noticed.

"Look," Wil said, "we'll see this thing through on Sunday, then talk. I'm just concerned that you're getting too involved. We agreed it was my call, remember?"

He could hear the voice deflate.

"You're right, I got baskets to weave. Be here Sunday at ten if you're going to St. Boniface." Then Paul hung up.

TEN

Wil aimed the .45 and fired; a plume of reddish dirt rose and fell with a clatter of stones. Aiming again, he squeezed off another round: Fifty feet away, the soup can jerked in the air and clinked against the hillside.

He replaced the clip.

Reaching into his duffel, he pulled out the beer cans, lined them up slightly apart on the fallen cottonwood. Twelve paces he stepped off, closer this time. Assuming a two-handed stance, he let loose all seven rounds at the six targets. Four spun off as the sound rolled away down the canyon.

Most of the time he hadn't much occasion for the .45. But today he'd dug it out, bought ammo, headed out on the Harley for some fresh air and hand-eye stuff, Zavala-inspired. Most everybody who packed a sidearm now was into the teen-shot nine millimeters. Wil liked the .45 for its stopping power, despite the limited capacity: eight rounds he carried cocked and locked, the extra bullet in the chamber, compensating for the seven-round clips by carrying several.

Hand and arm throbbing, he policed the area and left, gentling the motorcycle through Wheeler Gorge. Fragrant air rife with the smell of California laurel, the sycamores turning shades of gold; even the SuperGlide was behaving.

He gunned it a little and was home in an hour, making coffee when Mo Epstein rang.

"Vella asked me to call," Mo said. "We turned up some things on your boy Zavala. Pacheco, too."

Wil got out a notepad. "Was I right about you guys or what? Before you start, though, add a tattoo to what I gave you." He described it, then said, "Okay, ready."

"First, we confirmed Hermosillo," Mo said. "Zavala worked in a slaughterhouse there and did some boxing. Man has a record going back to the late fifties: drugs, assaults, typical shit. Plus he's still wanted in connection with stealing armory weapons, early sixties."

"How about the people stuff?"

"That came later, apparently. The authorities knew about it but were never able to catch him. Got a half-dozen old killings—witnesses and the like—they think are his. No Bolo, though. Incidentally, our sources said he was known for the kind of knife he used, ergo the nickname. Real name is Antonio."

"Antonio," said Wil, writing. "Probably had a mother even."

Epstein went on. "September 1971, he pushed his luck like you said. The Border Patrol got a tip he was coming across predawn near Calexico and caught him in a roadblock with a vanful of customers, including women and kids. The guy was armed to the teeth, killed three patrolmen. He got it, too—they found blood—but somehow he escaped. Incident stirred up hell with the feds."

Wil heard him take a pull on something wet.

"There's speculation he's dead," Mo continued. "But no hard evidence, either here or in Mexico."

"Any local contacts?"

"Sketchy. He had a girl in East L.A., but she died the same year from drugs. FBI staked out her place for about six months after the shoot-out and came up snake-eyes. They spotted him a couple of times in the late seventies, nothing since then. Figured he got his comeuppance somewhere in Mexico. A warrant's still out on him for the Calexico guys, though. They haven't forgotten.''

"Hold on a second." Wil wrote a moment, then spoke. "Who's the girl who died?''

"That's where it gets interesting. Her name's Lucinda Pacheco, sister of the guy they found dead in the Colorado. Incidentally, his name was Porfirio, aka Sonny. He and Zavala were pals. According to the police it was Sonny first got Zavala into the people business—Zavala did the runs to L.A. while Sonny collected the pigeons, sometimes vice versa. Sonny Pacheco had a sheet as long as your arm down there and no shortage of enemies. Finally moved his family up here.''

Mo stopped to clear his throat, started again.

"Anyway, Lucinda. It's secondhand, but the Mexicans think she fell for Zavala and he responded by getting her hooked. Up here she got in deep and died in the usual squalid way. Sonny took it hard. According to police records, he tipped off the locals about when Zavala was making a run, and they notified our people. Sonny must have known Bolo would try to shoot it out but didn't figure on his getting away. Bolo did and Sonny paid.''

"Any Pachecos left in L.A.?''

"Just ask. We tracked a sister, Donna. Her name's Ybarra now. Lives in East Los Angeles, address 542 Hibiscus Place. Horrible neighborhood, more like East Beirut.''

Wil finished writing. "Sounds like you've been there.''

"Such a dick. The good lady suggested a way we could get to know each other better.''

"Must be your way with women, Mo. She know anything about Zavala?''

"Yeah. Said he died in a knife fight.''

Sunday traffic was light until he hit the Valley, the overcast breaking up as he parked in front of the house and went in. To his relief, Paul seemed to have forgotten their conversation, although Wil knew he'd have to bring it up again. The feeling of walking a tightrope was hard to ignore.

Paul drove. On the way, Wil briefed him on the calls from Gilberto Reyes and Mo.

"So where's that leave us?" Paul asked. "Any closer to a motive?"

"I can't see how. If it wasn't for money, that leaves sex. But nothing's turned up in Zavala's background, at least that Mo found. And people like that generally have histories."

"What about the people he sold the boy to?"

"Benito would have been an investment for them, something to keep around. The medal indicates he was killed right away."

"So who'd murder seven kids—devil worshipers? Great talk for a Sunday, huh?" Paul signaled a left, then waited to turn.

Wil said, "Yeah. I'm no expert, but it seems pretty clean for those types. From what I've read, they leave symbols."

"Sheeit."

They turned and followed a line of cars down an unprosperous street into a crowded parking lot. Sun glinted off numerous luxury automobiles. Doors thunked, feet step-shuffled. As they joined the walkers, Paul noted the Mercedes and BMW nameplates.

"Damn," he said. "That kind of sheet metal in a neighborhood like this? Unreal."

Wil nodded. Ahead of them St. Boniface rose up; he stood, taking it in as Paul went on ahead. The church was newish, sandblasted concrete giving it a miniature-cathedral look, oversize doors curving Gothic-style to meet at the center. Recessed in thick walls were stained-glass windows. Thirty-foot deodars stood sentry along the walk.

At the foot of the stairs, a tall priest in a purple vestment with gold brocade was smiling at the people milling around him. Silvering hair framed a tan face and white even teeth.

He looked familiar somehow and very much in his element. Sixty, Wil guessed—until he caught up with Paul, who was shaking the priest's hand.

Few wrinkles showed in the priest's face, the effect slightly disconcerting. Paul was saying, "Father, you remember me, the Ortegas' cousin? We spoke the other day about Hermosillo."

"Mr. Rodriguez, of course. Isabel got you your list?" The voice was rich and softly accented.

Paul turned to Wil. "Yes, thank you. Father Martin DeSantis, my friend Wil Hardesty. We served together in Vietnam."

The priest extended a manicured hand, sun highlighting clear nail polish. He gave Wil a firm grip; dark eyes sought his. "Mr. Hardesty, welcome. It's always good to see a new face." To Paul he said, "Is this the friend in difficulty?"

"Oh no, Father. This friend is helping me help my other friend."

"Friendship is a wonderful thing," said Father Martin. "By the way, I passed your request on to Leonardo." He turned from Paul to Wil. "Leonardo Guerra—perhaps you heard he would be here today. Which reminds me, you should go in. Latecomers have to stand."

As if to confirm his point, bells sounded.

They entered, found a seat in back. The interior was at once traditional and contemporary: more raw concrete—attractive in a stark way—dark pews, metal crucifix behind a slab altar, antique stations of the cross, Plexiglas pulpit. With just over two weeks until Christmas, St. Boniface was red with poinsettias. As Father Martin predicted, an overflow gathered in back and down the side aisles.

The church had forgone Latin, Wil knew, but he was unprepared for the impact of English. As Mass progressed, he tried to be open; at least there was active participation.

Halfway through, Father Martin ascended the pulpit. His gaze encompassed them. "How privileged I am to see you," he said. "All of you know that we have done much in a short time. And yet there are so many still who need our help."

He leaned forward.

"You were with me when we fed and sheltered the homeless. You were there when we went to assist families coming here to find the dream. Together we created a network of urban resources, jobs for the indigent, legal help for the downtrodden, centers for the sick and the persecuted. You reached out beyond your own border, and the result was a program governments have held up for example."

Paul leaned over. "Some delivery—regular Charlton Heston."

Martin DeSantis went on, his voice rising. "When we stand as one there is nothing we cannot do. *Nothing!*"

There was a murmur of approval.

"Yet as much as we have given, as many sacrifices as we have made, our work calls louder and clearer than ever." He unfolded a letter.

"This is from Miguel, who has been with us since Hermosillo's inception. He says our old warehouse cannot contain all the food and clothing we send. It rots outside unprotected while all over Mexico the hungry and the sick, the neglected, go without." On "without," he slammed his hand on the pulpit.

"There is more," he said. "Our shelter there no longer is safe. Plaster crumbles, pipes burst, ceilings sag. Those who have nothing have nowhere to go. We turn them away as Joseph and Mary were themselves turned away two weeks from today, almost two thousand years ago.

"I look at you and see people who are whole, complete. Yet who is complete when others are not? Which of you will let brothers and sisters, sons and daughters, go hungry? Which of you can be happy knowing others are suffering, can live knowing others are dying?" Father Martin held out his hands.

"There was a time for our other tasks. The time for Hermosillo is once again now, the clarity of our mission absolute. Once more I ask you in His name. Give us the tools. Give us the money. Allow Los Amigos to remain a beacon for those without hope." After a final look, he descended to sit between his altar boys.

Volunteers set forth with long-handled baskets. Everywhere in the congregation was the rustle of bills and envelopes, the clink of coins dropped by wide-eyed children: "Put it in the basket, dear, it's for Father Martin."

After the collection Wil saw the Eucharist raised, heard hymns and responses, but it was the passion of Martin DeSantis that held him. The power. For a moment he projected the priest into politics. Then Mass ended, and he filed out with Paul as the choir punched up "Adeste Fidelis."

As they exited, he was there. Standing in bright sun, basking in the moment, his congregation pressing in for benediction, then dispersing.

"Father, you're enough to return strays to the fold," Wil said at length. "And your church is not what I expected."

"I tried to tell him, Father," Paul added.

Children pressed in. The priest smiled, reached under his vestments, came out with foil-wrapped candies he passed out. "That's all," he said, and after they'd left, "You expected perhaps a few old ladies in rebozos. It was like that once. But we've been building St. Boniface for over twenty years now with the help of God and these people. Are they not incredible? They come because we offer them a chance to make a difference in the real world, with its disease and hunger and suffering." Raising a hand, he shielded his eyes from the sun.

"Just now they blessed us with over twelve thousand dollars."

Paul's eyes widened.

"You might appreciate, Mr. Rodriguez, that our operating budget was over six million this year." He waved at a well-dressed family.

Wil was about to ask how the money was distributed when a man stepped up behind Father Martin. Aviator-style glasses emphasized eyes the dull color of zinc; slim fingers smoothed a thin mustache. The aroma of citrus cologne hovered around him. With him was a Latin-looking young man, similarly dark-suited and silk-tied.

The man cleared his throat.

Father Martin turned. "Ah. Gentlemen, this is the man who made St. Boniface possible. Everything you see here he built. Leonardo, this is Mr. Rodriguez, whom I told you about, and Mr. Hardesty."

They shook hands. Leonardo Guerra introduced his foster son, Julio, as the youth lowered his eyes. Guerra then dismissed the young man, who headed toward the parking lot.

"He is doing very well, Martin," Guerra said. "We talked—he wants to be an altar boy. I told him I would ask you."

The priest smiled broadly. "Classes start Thursday, four o'clock. And now, Mr. Rodriguez and Mr. Hardesty wished to have a word with you, so I will get about my business. Gentlemen, I leave you in excellent hands. Leonardo Guerra is a true friend of St. Boniface."

They sat at the end of a long row of folding tables, the hall crowded with people socializing over post-mass coffee and doughnuts. Sunlight streaming in high windows flared in the diamond on Guerra's right ring finger.

"There is talk of the Nobel Prize, you know." The speech was Spanish-laced, the inflections arresting. "I have been here from the start, seen what he has done—the missions, the centers, the programs, these buildings. All since he came."

"When was that?" Wil asked.

Guerra thought. "Christmas sixty-six. I had just moved here. He was simply—incandescent. Filled with what he had to do. Like Jesus to Peter, he beckoned, I followed."

Wil ignored the comparison. The man had an odd, vain manner, smiles that stopped short of his eyes. "Leonardo—" he began.

"Lenny, please. Only Father Martin calls me Leonardo."

"Lenny. You built St. Boniface?"

"My company did, yes. Before coming to Los Angeles, I was in construction, so it was logical for me to help Father Martin with his new home." He looked around the room. "The labor of love, you might say."

"You moved your business from Hermosillo?"

"Father Martin must have told you. Yes, but I don't do construction anymore." Guerra noticed Paul's quizzical look. "Import-export. Latin American antiquities primarily."

Paul nodded. He bit into a doughnut, wiped his lips with a paper napkin. Wil said, "Did Father Martin tell you we're trying to locate someone?"

Paul swallowed hurriedly. "For a friend. He'd be very grateful for any help you can give us."

"The man we're looking for used to live in Hermosillo," Wil said, throwing Paul a look.

Paul flushed and returned to his doughnut. Guerra stroked his tie.

"So Martin said. You know, gentlemen, Hermosillo was not a small place even then, and my memory gets no better with age."

As Guerra spoke, Wil was struck by the absurdity: Hermosillo was a city, and this man hardly seemed the type who'd know about someone like Zavala. Still, this was what you did—asked somebody who knew somebody else who knew something, and somewhere along the line you made something happen.

"The name is Zavala," Wil said. "Antonio Zavala, Bolo he was called. Stocky, reddish hair, mottled complexion. Among other things, he did some boxing."

Paul finished a bite, used the napkin on sugared fingers.

Guerra leaned back, hands coming together as though in prayer.

"Mr. Hardesty, Mr. Rodriguez, this is a remarkable co-incidence." Smiling, he opened his palms.

Isabel Diaz, who happened to be working Sunday, brought them fresh coffees; at Leonardo Guerra's suggestion they had moved to quieter quarters, a paneled office in another part of the building. After Isabel returned to her desk, Guerra removed a silver case from his coat pocket, offered cigarettes around, lit one with a filigreed lighter. He exhaled smoke.

"I saw him fight. Not more than nineteen, he was—no style, but a ferocious puncher. The night I was there, he nearly killed his opponent, wouldn't stop even though the man was clearly finished. Finally the other cornermen jumped in, and Zavala threw both of them out of the ring. From then on they refused to let him box."

Guerra smiled. "After the bout I asked someone about this bantam rooster and was told the young man worked slaughtering pigs. I was also told a story. His father was a drunken ex-fighter who used to spar with the boy, wanted to make him hard to hit in the ring. To do so he had him put a razor blade in his mouth. The father would get mean on tequila, land punches and cut him. One day Bolo was fast enough. He spat out the razor blade and sliced his father's ears off, as a bullfighter would, told him he would kill him if he ever saw him again." Guerra paused. "I don't know if the story is true, but not many laid a glove on him. Even fewer wanted to fight."

Paul stirred sugar into his coffee. "Some story."

"And after that?" Wil asked.

Guerra began polishing his glasses with a handkerchief, first fogging the lenses. "After he left the ring, I lost track. Occasionally I'd see him at a match, then not at all. Someone told me there had been trouble with the law, that he had been killed, although I don't know when or how."

"You remember what kind of trouble?"

"Guns, I think, Mr. Hardesty."

"Did you ever hear of him running families out of Mexico?"

"No. But again, I didn't follow him closely after the boxing." He drew on the cigarette. "I know people down there. I could put you in touch if you wish."

Paul sat forward to speak.

"Thank you," Wil said, "perhaps later. One more question if I may. Have you ever seen Bolo Zavala at any time in Los Angeles?"

Guerra crushed the rest of his cigarette in an ashtray on the desk. His tone was patronizing. "That would be most bizarre in a city this size. No, Mr. Hardesty, I have not seen him."

Julio sat patiently in a black Mercedes; Wil could see his profile through the tinted glass as they walked to Paul's car. The lot was nearly empty now.

Paul said, "Some lead, huh? Not bad for an over-the-hill gunnie." He steered the Chevy wagon out into traffic. "Thoughts?"

Wil slipped a loafer, rested his foot on the dash. "Interesting man, Guerra. Had a good memory after all, didn't he? The razor blade story works with Gilberto's tattoos, everything else with what Mo found out." He rubbed between his eyebrows. "I don't know. Everybody on the same page—makes you wonder a little, maybe."

Paul looked at him.

"Sorry, man, you did well. By the way, you want a free tip? Never give out more than you have to, even on something as small as a client's gender. I learned that once the hard way."

Paul stared straight ahead. "You concerned about Guerra?"

"Not even sure he caught it," Wil said.

Paul nosed the wagon up the on-ramp. For a while they

drove in silence, then he said, "Damn, that's some operation out there. Twelve thousand—in that neighborhood? Raeann won't believe it."

"We're not the only ones impressed with Father Martin, are we?"

"I haven't seen that many furs since the zoo." Paul thought a minute. "Antiquities been bery-bery good to ol' Leonardo, from the looks of that suit."

Wil regarded his friend's blue polyester. "Maybe you should go talk to him."

"Sheeit."

At the house Wil phoned Mo Epstein and got an earful about a break they'd gotten in the Lynwood hooker killings, some woman whose husband had contracted AIDS from one and passed the virus on to her. Wil mentioned the coincidence of Zavala-Guerra and then described the man with the gray eyes.

"Just a wild hair, Mo, but I'd be hard pressed to recall what he did about some boxer I barely knew twenty years ago." He let a few seconds pass. "Look, it's probably nothing. You guys can't be checking out every Leonardo Guerra coming down the pike." After the expected profanity, he hung up, promising to call Mo again Monday. By then Raeann and Paul were off on errands.

Wil strapped on the .45, put on his coat, and left for East L.A.

ELEVEN

Hibiscus Place was a pothole-scarred orphan that dead-ended at the freeway, surrounded by a neighborhood in full retreat.

Wil got out of the car to a barrage of traffic noise and looked around. Tired weeds waved surrender through split sidewalks; dirt long ago had overrun the lawns. Wood siding on the houses begged for paint. Eaves and porches sagged.

Five-forty-two was just up from the dead end, its exterior a faded urine color, the molding a long-ago eggshell. On the porch a child about two gnawed a *chicharrone* that had been dropped more than once. The child eyed Wil suspiciously as he approached.

Wil knocked, waited, knocked again—this time louder than the game show playing at high volume inside. In the gloom past a dusty screen door, springs creaked.

"Told you people I don't talk to no fuckin' cops."

"Not a cop," said Wil.

"The fuck you want, then?"

"Justice for Sonny Pacheco."

Somebody won the bonus round, and a large shape became just visible through the screen. Yellowish shirt over worn jeans, part of a bulging stomach the shirt refused to cover—a woman, about thirty-five, Wil guessed.

She said, "What do you know about Sonny, asshole?"

"One, that he was cut by a man named Bolo Zavala. Two, that Zavala is still out there."

A foot kicked open the door, nearly hitting him. Instinctively his hand went under his coat, relaxed as the door banged harmlessly.

"Donna Pacheco Ybarra?" He could see her better now: big and gone to seed; pretty perhaps, in a coarse way, with deep dark eyes. Some of her hair was up in pink rollers. She held a pistol-grip spray bottle as though ready to shoot him with it.

"Maybe. Who the hell are you?" Despite her bulk, her voice was raspy, asthmatic almost, reminding him of gravel being raked around.

"Name's Hardesty. I was in the neighborhood."

"Yeah, just like the cops. Funny how everybody's all of a sudden taking an interest in some guy I used to know." She picked up the baby, who had made a beeline for her legs. "What kind of justice you talkin' about? My brother's been dead a long time."

"We talk in there? Might be quieter." Wil gave her his card.

She sized him up a moment, then grunted and turned away. "Shut the screen behind you," she said.

He took a seat on the couch across from a patched recliner; a TV tray held more pink rollers. Under a painting of the Sacred Heart, fiesta dolls in ruffled skirts pranced on a table surrounded by orange-and-chrome chairs. In the corner was a scattering of toys that the child went for; charging full-tilt, she fell and began to howl.

Donna turned off the TV, put the sprayer on the tray, bumped it as she sat down. A roller fell off onto the floor. Getting no attention, the child shut up.

"One more time," she said. "What's your interest in my brother?"

"I'm looking for the man who killed him, Donna. For a friend of mine who believes Bolo Zavala murdered his son."

"So?"

"So he wasn't much older than your baby. Maybe you heard about it: six other kids found with him, buried in the desert. Their throats cut."

Donna shifted in the recliner.

Wil went on. "I need your help. Everybody says Bolo Zavala is dead, but no one's seen a body. I think he's out there laughing at us."

She slipped out of red plastic sandals, moved her feet under her. "I told the cops. He's dead, stabbed in a fight."

"You mean you heard he's dead. What if he's not? What if that's just a story he wants you and everybody to believe so nobody will look for him?"

A cuticle caught her interest, and she picked at it.

"That would mean he's still out there, Donna. Still killing." Wil gentled his voice a notch. "Look, you knew him. What would it hurt just telling me about it?"

She chewed the nail. "Bolo Zavala didn't kill no kids."

"He killed Sonny, and you're Sonny's sister. How can you not help me find him?"

Wil waited for her reaction; at first he thought it was a cough. Her laugh rumbled around her throat, then died.

"You're real good, Mr."—she checked his card—"Hardesty. 'A' for effort. But you're full of it. My brother deserved what he got. Yeah, that's right, Bolo Zavala did him, so what? He ratted on Bolo, nearly got him killed."

Wil sat silent, not moving as she began to warm to it.

"My brother was *pinche cabrón,* no-good trash. Dumped us up here and left us. The cops said Bolo hooked my sister on drugs. That's shit. Sonny hooked Lucinda, then when she died, used her as an excuse to turn on Bolo because he wanted Bolo's share of the business." She glared at him, her eyes and tone defiant. "Not how you heard it, huh? Listen, Sonny was the devil. Bolo just sent him on back to hell."

As she glared, he thought about it: She was a grenade with the pin pulled, ready to go off and blow something out. "True enough," he said. "That wasn't how I heard it."

"Goddamn right. What do you think now?"

He shrugged. "Still leaves me with no Zavala."

"I told you he was dead. And I just know, that's all."

"When was the knife fight?"

She gathered a clump of hair, sprayed it, began to wind it around a roller. "Years ago. Eighty-three, I think."

"What happened?"

"They were Colombians. The dealer's bodyguard pulled a knife. Bolo must have been juiced, or the guy would never have got him. He was real good with a blade." A thin smile crossed her face, then was gone. "He cut the other guy, but it was too late. They dumped him somewhere."

"Where? Who told you about it?"

"*Fuck you.* What do you care—you have no idea what he was like. Didn't kill no kids, I can tell you that."

She was all defenses. A thought came to him, and he went with it—nothing to be gained by silence. "You loved him, didn't you?"

"That's none of your fuckin' business. He wasn't nothing like you say. Bolo was kind to me even though he was with Lucinda and I was young. He was nice. Not many were."

"Donna, he killed people in Mexico. He shot up three border patrolmen. Now it looks like he murdered seven children. Help me understand how nice he was."

Instead of answering, she went to the kitchen, came back with two cans of malt liquor, and handed one over. She popped the tab on hers, gulped some down.

Wil eyed his, conscious of an ache spreading in his throat.

"Nobody ever gave him spit," she said, "just beat on him. Then he got fast and hard and people stopped beating on Bolo Zavala 'cause he beat back harder." She raised her eyes. "Yeah, maybe he's done bad. And maybe they had it coming."

"My friend's boy was six."

"No way. Bolo Zavala may do a lot of things, but he ain't no child killer. You tell your friend that." Her eyes began to fill in frustration.

"How can I tell my friend that, Donna? How do you know?"

"He'll kill me," she said finally.

"Who will? Zavala?"

Her eyes darted to the door and back. "My old man. He'd be here now except for his overtime. Frankie's all right when he's sober, but—" She put a hand on her throat. "He gimme this voice—among other things."

"Look, I'm sorry, Donna. He's bad when he drinks. But why would your husband want to kill you?"

"Not husband, old man." She sighed. "Bolo's why. About three years ago at Angel's Bar. We went out a couple times. Frankie never knew."

"So Zavala didn't die after all?"

Her head moved side to side as if it might fall off. "He came to my house, back before Frankie. I didn't recognize him at first. Been twelve years, but there he was. Like I said, the Colombians tried." She stopped for another swallow.

"I didn't think he was gonna make it. His gut was split and his face—hell, surprised me he got here at all. In time he got well. Then he left."

"And three years later you saw him again at the bar."

"More like four. Frankie was working late, and I was out with a girlfriend. We'd get together once in a while after that." Her eyes dropped. "Friends, he said."

"He *is* alive, then."

"You leave him alone. I told you, he's not like that. Bolo Zavala don't kill no kids, no way. Couldn't of, I know."

He tried to ask, but she cut him off.

"You don't get it, do you, Mr. Smartass? You don't get

nothing. Now leave us alone.'' Suddenly the can was off the arm of her recliner and on the floor, malt liquor foaming at her feet. As he watched her scramble for it, his eyes drifted across the braided rug to where the answer hit him. It was playing in the corner with a pile of Legos, chewing some, snapping some together. The answer had freckles and a shock of curly orange hair. Unlike Donna's. Wil glanced from child to mother.

Donna saw him looking. ''He's good with her,'' she said without sharpness. ''Rough with everybody else, me included, but good with her. It's how I know.''

Wil handed her his untouched malt liquor; she took it but barely noticed.

''In Hermosillo, Bolo used to hang out with my brother, but sometimes we'd come along. I remember this walk once. A man was beating his kid with a switch. Bolo freaked and knocked him down, told him the only reason he didn't kill a worthless piece of shit like that was because he was the boy's father, and if he ever hurt him again, he, Bolo, would find the guy and finish the job.''

Wil said it quietly: ''Donna, if Zavala isn't dead, where is he? Have you seen him?''

Her face flushed. ''No, and I'm not telling you no more. You leave him alone, you and your stories. You tell your friend that Bolo Zavala maybe killed his share, but he don't kill no kids.''

They'd brought out the Christmas tree, a green-needled artificial one, and were decorating it when Wil walked in.

''All the poinsettias today got me in the mood,'' Paul said. He took a gold ball from Raeann. ''How'd it go?''

Wil went through it. ''She's Ybarra now, has a kid— with red hair and freckles.'' He watched Paul's eyes widen. ''You got it, amigo. She said Zavala'd seen the baby, which puts him in L.A. within the last two years. And she mentioned a bar, Angel's.''

Paul got a pile of phone directories from the den and

thumbed through them. "At least we're not looking for a ghost anymore." He made notes on a pad. "Four," he said at length. "The Valley, East L.A., South Bay, San Gabriel. Start with East L.A.?"

Wil saw Raeann's look. "Paul, I'm going this one alone."

Paul straightened.

"You know this guy, what he's done," Wil said. "Let me take it from here."

"Man, I was shootin' and gettin' shot at before you knew which end of the gun the goddamn bullets come out—*if* you remember." He jabbed a finger at Wil. "This bozo's bad as they say, you're gonna need the help."

Raeann went to him, rigid and glaring. "Listen to him, Rodriguez. I didn't spend thirty years with you so you could run around after some hoodlum in your golden years. We know you can handle it, baby, we're just asking you not to."

He pushed her out to arm's length. "How many baskets, Rae? How many little chores we make sound important?" His tone relented, but still he held her. "You're busy, hon, but I'm making work. This is my life, too. I'm not ready for it to end yet."

Tears came. Paul drew her in; over her shoulder he said, "Look, man, I'm not trying to make trouble here. But this Angel's probably a Mexican place—even if they speak a little English, they'll stop the second they see you. *No comprendo.* Then what?"

Wil said nothing.

Paul said, "Trust me: You go to Angel's, I stay in the car. When you're ready, you signal and I read these guys like a book. What do you say?" He smiled hopefully.

Feeling like shit, Wil said it. "I'm sorry, amigo. We're a long way from the Mekong Delta."

The Christmas tree stood abandoned; Raeann was lying down, Paul self-exiled to the garage. Incompletion hung in the air like the haze after a burn. Wil used their phone to reach Mo Epstein, ran through the Pacheco-Ybarra visit, the Zavala connection, Angel's Bar.

"Fuck," Mo said, "all she gave us was bad language. Probably looked in those Irish eyes of yours and couldn't help herself. Real sweetheart, huh? The yellow rose of cactus."

"Yeah," Wil said absently. "This Angel's might be something. Are you in?"

"Lemme check with Vella, but I don't see why not. Should have an answer by late tomorrow."

"Reach me at home, then. And see if you agree: East L.A., South Bay, San Gabriel, then the Valley—assuming it goes that far."

"Such an organizer."

"Just tell Freiman I'm cooperating like crazy." He hung up, decision made; cops or no cops, he was going. In the garage, he found Paul at his workbench, struggling with a broken lawn chair.

"Thanks for everything, *Jefe*," he said. "I'll let you know what's going on."

Paul kept working.

"Look, I love you for trying, man. I'd do exactly the same thing. Friends?"

Paul looked up, forced a smile. *"Por supuesto,"* he said. "Of course, friends. Sheeit, this is me, remember? Whatever you need, you got. You want me to stay out of the way, I stay out of the way."

Back late, up early, his breath preceding him in the morning cold.

Wil eased down the stairs and headed for one of La Conchita's tunnels—four feet high, eight feet wide, half a football field long—that ran under the railroad tracks and the highway. He stooped his way through, pausing on the rocky revetment that shored up the roadway on the ocean side. At high tide, water came almost to the base of the rocks.

Sometimes when the waves were big, he and Lisa would come watch. Once, during a storm, blanket-wrapped, they'd made love.

He clambered down to packed sand, started an easy pace toward the Rincon—with the tide out, there'd be beach most of the way, the sea calm and flat and slate-colored under overcast. He passed only two people, a girl in sweats like he was and an older man running a pair of black Labs. Gulls fought over a dead man-o'-war. A flock of pelicans skimmed the water.

Wil smiled at how much Devin used to like this run. Just the two of them dodging incursions of surf, Dev laughing delightedly when they misjudged it and the foam surged over their feet. His son was turning—had turned—into quite a runner. Couple of ten-K's completed; youngest entrant in a half-marathon Wil encouraged him to enter.

He'd taken to surfing, too, Dev had. Better coordinated than his pals, better certainly than his father had been starting out.

Fearless.

Wil watched the Labs chase a stick into the water and realized he'd slowed to a walk, conscious now of the stitch in his side. The whole thing with Dev was like a movie. Beginning, middle, end—a little slice out of your life and afterward not wanting to leave the theater because the story moved you to tears. What he desperately wanted was to change the ending from what it had become back into what it should have been. Get it on course again, fix how it all came out. Especially his role in it.

Hero to fool.

Wind chilled the tracks on his face. The beach was deserted now. Identifying with Ignacio Reyes, another fool who by his own hand had lost his son and whose sorrow would never cease, Wil started back toward the house.

Lisa was just coming out of the shower. Wil followed her in and afterward joined her in front of the window where she'd set a tray with the carafe and their mugs on it. He filled his, stirred in half-and-half.

"Penny?" she said.

"What?"

"For your thoughts. You're wearing out the spoon."

"Sorry, Leese. This thing with Bolo Zavala," he lied. "What I told you about."

"Like what specifically?"

"Like why he'd murder seven kids younger than Devin. What's frustrating is knowing that he's out there somewhere. Alive and with the answer."

She was quiet so long it prompted him to ask why.

"I was just thinking," she said. "About how incredibly distant all that is from what I do. From what most people do." She sipped coffee. "Then there's Gringo. You know that he and Pam split up?"

"No. When?"

"I don't know exactly. They were talking about it at the store."

"Not hard to see that one coming," Wil said. "The guy just has an awful time committing." He poured them more coffee, saw her look. "Christ, Lisa, you're not serious."

"You're right," she said. "It's not as though you aren't committed. It's that I don't know what you're committed *to* anymore."

He felt a familiar tightening in his throat. "Loving you is what I'm committed to."

"That's what hurts, Wil. You remember how long it took to conceive Devin? The goddamn endless tests, the things we tried? Then the doctor telling us to quit trying so hard, maybe it was that?"

He nodded as she went on.

"Suddenly there he was. You remember how it felt? Like all the Christmases you'd ever had rolled into one. Well, that's what I want again. And it's tearing me apart thinking you don't want the same thing."

He saw her tears forming, put down the mug, and held her.

"I know."

"I don't understand," she said into his robe. "You loved Devin—"

Gently he held her away from him. "I did, I do, and I will, Lisa—every day as long as I live. But you know how I feel."

She choked back an angry sob. "Still blaming yourself. Goddamn godlike Wil, no accidents allowed in his life."

"Look," he said, "maybe what we need to do is what we did before. Quit trying so damned hard." He held her again until she broke from him and got up off the couch.

"Being with you made me want a child, Wil, something I lost when Dev died. But if you understand nothing else, understand that feeling is back for me—no matter how much I try to rationalize it away." She turned and walked into the bedroom, shut the door.

He could hear her cries. Words that echoed and stung: *No accidents allowed in his life.* What the fuck was he doing—playing God, like she'd said? Wounding her to beat down his own pain? All his promises began to sound hollow and spin around him like mosquitoes eager for blood. Landing on him, sucking at his resolve—threatening to upset the delicate balance he'd created for himself.

No!

To be doing something, Wil hit the free weights in the basement, but they felt twice as heavy as normal and after half an hour he quit and showered again. The rest of the day he and Lisa gave each other as much space as the house permitted, not angry so much as not talking. After Lisa left for a meeting, he called to update Reyes, leaving out the part about Zavala having a child, for no better reason than gut feel.

At four Mo called, breathing hard.

"Exercise bike, smog'll kill you out there," he said.

"Okay, Vella bought in, so I'll meet you downtown tomorrow at eleven. We take your wheels?"

"Pick you up on the Broadway side," Wil said.

"Freeway close and a rose in my teeth. *Mañana*."

He waited awhile then phoned Paul, the feelings from yesterday kept fresh by his sense of guilt. After talk that bordered on trying too hard, he tried a peace offering.

"Papa Gomez, my treat," Wil said. "Tomorrow after the last Angel's so you can hear what we found out. Six o'clock, tell Raeann."

The voice on the telephone was no longer calm. "What cops?" It was shouting now. "When? *Cuénteme!*"

"They were at her house," Bolo Zavala said. "Asking about me. Luckily she told them nothing."

"God*damm*it," Leonardo Guerra exploded. "Sheep, you said, not to worry. Yet someone has involved the law—who else but her?" His fury subsided somewhat, replaced by thought. "Unless one of your sheep involved Hardesty and Rodriguez, and *they* informed the cops. That would explain—"

"Maybe the real problem was telling them you knew me."

Guerra's tone became impatient. "To live a long life you must love your friends but sleep with your enemies. Meeting them, I learned two things. The first is that they know nothing."

"And the second?"

"Their client is a man—not much, but something."

Zavala was silent. He unwrapped a cheroot, lit it, tossed the burnt match into an ashtray. From the uneven buzz, he knew Guerra was pacing with the portable phone.

"Think again," Guerra said. "About the sheep, about some father or brother. You must remember something. What about the name on the medal?" The anger was rising again.

He exhaled blue smoke. "How many times must I say

it, the names meant nothing, Benito means nothing. They were ignorant peasants. As far as I was concerned they had no names.'' On the other end, the buzzing stabilized; there was the creak of a chair, a glass set down.

Guerra said, ''Then we have no choice. We must assume Hardesty and Rodriguez talked to the law, Hardesty hoping for some kind of deal for his client. We must assume also that his client's afraid to come forward, whoever it is could have done so without them. They are middlemen, these two, between your sheep and the cops. When we sever the link, the cops will have nothing, only hearsay. It is time for you to act.''

Zavala took a long drag on the cheroot, passed the smoke through lips drawn tight. ''My time for that is over, *patron. Terminado!*''

Guerra's laugh was without mirth, a snake hissing. ''Poor Bolo. You have forgotten how many men there are still anxious to find you. Men who remember and wait, who oil and sharpen—men I know. Not stopping this foolishness now would be most unwise.'' He paused.

''And, Bolo? Do something about the woman.''

TWELVE

The man in the ragged fatigue jacket sidled over to the white car and eased in. "Classy," Wil said. "Explains the naked vagrant I saw back there."

Mo Epstein eyed Wil's stained bomber jacket, jeans, and scuffed boots. "Go ahead," he said, "spend all your money on clothes." He examined the interior of the Bonneville. "Nothing sadder than a concours without d'elegance."

"You'd fit nicely in the trunk. What are those?"

Epstein showed him a stack of photocopies: sketches of Bolo Zavala with an inset of the razor blade tattoo, his description, and a phone number. Wil glanced at one: odd seeing Zavala for the first time. The eyes looked right; mean eyes, Gilberto Reyes had said.

"You packing?" Mo asked.

Wil showed him.

"Jesus, not the forty-five. Even the army's retired that old warhorse." Epstein rolled his eyes. "Bad enough to feel like Ahab inside Moby Dick. Now I'm in a time warp." He unsnapped his hip holster, extracted the gun. "Beretta 92F—handles nice, shoots good, holds fifteen rounds. Name of the game these days."

"Will it stop a jeep?"

"Forty-fives stopping jeeps was always more myth than fact."

Wil patted the bulge under his jacket. "Yeah, but mine doesn't know that."

Epstein stowed the nine millimeter, shook his head. "Goddamn dinosaur," he muttered as Wil grinned.

The East L.A. Angel's was glass-brick-fronted and smelled like cigarette butts and Lysol through the open door. Wil entered, felt the place enter him. Bleary patrons sat hunched over their drinks—the usual numb morning crowd working up to post meridiem oblivion. Looks he'd seen before in the mirror. They nosed around, passed out flyers.

Ahng-hell, the man tending bar, spat on the floor as they left.

Forty minutes later, on Pacific Coast Highway, they located the second Angel's, a sandblasted brick place with polished oak floors. "Watch out, or you'll catch it," Epstein whispered, looking around.

"Catch what?" Wil said.

"The yup—what these people got." They left a life-guard-looking barkeep named Wesley examining the flyer and shaking his head.

Afterward they ate at an open-air fish and chips restaurant near Ports O'Call. Sun glinted off the water; pleasure craft of varying sizes moved up and down the channel. Mo regarded the boats.

"Doesn't anybody around here work?" he said. A blond in a large Chris-Craft smiled and waved. "Get a job," he yelled, though she couldn't hear him. Just smiled and waved some more.

Wil waved back. "Lighten up, will you? Somebody has to enjoy all this."

"I'm gonna order surveillance on the East L.A. joint," Epstein said. "But I can't see Zavala sipping banana daiquiris with Wesley." He crunched something battered and deep-fried. "By the way, your Leonardo Guerra is an interesting guy."

Wil looked up from his coleslaw.

"Came to L.A. from Hermosillo when you said, but what's interesting is why. Turns out a hospital his company built there collapsed, killing a goodly number of people. Quite a scandal when the authorities found out Guerra's company'd shaved the specs. Guerra blamed his foreman. The foreman said he'd split the profits with Guerra. Guerra denied it, and the case got sent up for trial. Guess who turned up dead the day before the case was due in court."

"The foreman."

"Somebody'd cut his throat—sound familiar? We cross-checked, and sure enough it was one of the murders they thought Zavala had a hand in. Of course Guerra had an alibi, and Zavala'd split, so a firm link was never established. Case dismissed. Little while later Guerra emigrated. He is now a citizen, thank you, and yes, we're checking into his L.A. background."

Wil looked up from watching an incoming boat luff its sails. "Damn, if Guerra and Zavala did know each other in Mexico, could be they're still in contact. Zavala might even know we're looking for him." He washed down the last of his lunch, thinking he'd better alert Paul, no sense taking chances. While Mo phoned his office, Wil used the next pay phone.

Strange, he thought, how much he was used to answering machines. And how noticeable it was when there wasn't one.

Paul left the house at two, headed the Chevy up Hazeltine, took a right at Victory. It was early, he knew, but he was going anyway; Wil hadn't said, but the only thing that made sense was hitting the Valley Angel's last, especially when he was coming by the house afterward. If Wil was due at six, he'd be at the bar when? Five, probably. That would mean, to be safe, Paul should get there at four. Piece of cake, then: park out of the way, observe, then go in; be there when Wil needed him. He knew what these places were like. Dumb looks and *no hablas*.

Not with Paul Rodriguez there.

With time to kill, he'd swing by St. Boniface first: couple questions he had for Father Martin about Leonardo Guerra. Besides, the church was in the same general direction. He drove east, then north, turning into the parking lot about the time he figured Hardesty and Epstein would be heading for San Gabriel.

Angel's number three was across from a rock-processing plant, not far from the gravel pits that once aspired to be a pro football stadium. Once a tract house, it was the first and last one the developer put up before going broke. Renters trashed it until Mel Jefferson bought it to water the motorcycle gangs with which he occasionally rode. Talk was, you could buy just about anything there—one of Mo's people had returned his call, told them about it as they drove.

Wil parked the Bonneville up from the twenty or so bikes surrounding the place and looked it over. Squat, featureless, and pink, all word-associated. "Angel's," he said as they approached the door. "I wouldn't have thought to call it that."

Mo fell in behind him. "You still own a Harley?"

"It's for sale."

"I was brave last time. You talk, I'll cover."

It took a minute to get accustomed to the smoky gloom; bikers and their women at the long bar and a few stand-up games; figures bent over pool tables beyond an arched doorway; fans struggling overhead. Thumpy music.

Epstein flashed his badge as Wil was approached by a bartender whose T-shirt read, RIDE YOUR BIKE, NOT THE HELP. Pinned to it was a black plastic name tag: MEL. I OWN IT! He squinted at the sketch, grunted, and shook his head.

"We don't get a lot of beaners in here. Try Pomona."

Wil smiled. "Mel, this guy would love to hear you call

him a beaner." He gestured with the copies. "I'm going to pass these out. You get to announce it."

"Shit, man, this is bullshit," Mel snapped. "Cops stay the fuck outta here. We're a club."

Wil continued to smile. "Can the indignation, Mel, this place is a blight. Now we need your help in locating a man who would just as soon slice you as look at you. Clear?" Cold as he could make it.

Mel nodded; behind them the room began to quiet down, which made the blare from the speakers that much louder.

"Tell 'em," Wil said.

Mel reached slowly under the counter and turned down the music. "Achtung!" he barked. "Law wants to know whether or not you seen some Essey."

Wil set out with the copies; Epstein followed, hand on the Beretta's grip. At each stop they got headshakes and glares. Moving toward the arched doorway, Wil heard Mel's voice: "—asshole cops—some fuckin' greaser— stow that shit, man."

Through the archway: four pool tables, each with a game going under fluorescent fixtures; pay phone on the wall next to a mirror next to a red exit door. The smell of marijuana. Players, alerted, stood by the tables; around the periphery, pink-eyed types waited to play winners.

Wil began laying out copies on the first table. "This man's name is Zavala—we're trying to locate him. We appreciate your cooperation."

A few bikers, and then more, collected slowly around the faces in the buzzy light. "Guy's connected to some bad shit," said Mo Epstein. "Child killings, multiple. Who's seen him?"

Vacant looks. Nobody moved except for a twitchy player in a leather vest—taller than Wil but about thirty pounds lighter. He held a longneck loosely, tossed his cue to another player as he stepped forward.

Wil could see the dilated pupils.

"This sucks," the player growled. "Why don't you two

assholes get the fuck outta here? Guy prob'ly did us a favor—too many fuckin' kids as it is, man.'' He looked to
the room for approval.

Epstein moved then. He grabbed a flyer, shoved it at the
player. "Shame your mother didn't feel that way, dickhead,
she'd have saved everybody a lot of trouble. Now, one
more time. You seen him, you know something? You do
and don't say and I'll find you. Even if I have to lift every
rock in LA. to get the one you crawled under.'' He glared
and turned away.

In a flash the player reversed his grip on the beer bottle,
brought it back, snapped it forward. Wil caught a blur of
motion just before glass exploded against bone.

Mo Epstein dropped like a gallows weight.

Wil froze, stunned by the suddenness: the crowd pressing
in, the player bending over Epstein. The jagged stub cocked
back.

Adrenaline pumped then: Wil drove his boot upward into
the man's elbow. The player dropped the weapon and
clawed his injured arm as Wil loosed the .45 and backhanded him with it across the face. The player staggered,
dropped to his knees. Blood streamed from under his fingers.

Wil knew he had to stop the action or lose it, the crowd
had the look. His eyes dropped to the Beretta, exposed now
on Mo's hip; a short, tattooed biker, seeing it also, was
edging that way.

Wil fired at his feet. Sawdust flew; in the close room,
the noise was a wall. The players hesitated, then retreated.

Seeing his chance, Wil grabbed the tall man by the hair,
yanked him to his feet, forced his head down on the table.
Zavala faces scattered. Wil touched the .45's muzzle to the
man's head and watched all fight leave him. He scanned
the room: some chains and knives were out, but the crowd
held its distance; at his feet, Epstein began to moan. Wil
risked a look: Blood had soaked through Mo's collar and
was beginning to pool under his head.

"That's it, over," Wil said with force. He gestured with the gun. "That door there. Use it. Now!"

Sullenly, the crowd passed out the rear exit.

"Mel, where are you?" Wil spotted him in the doorway. "You're gonna call in an 'officer down.' No, use the phone where I can see you."

Fixing the gun squarely on the bartender's chest: *"Do it."*

Father Martin was inside the church lecturing a couple of altar boys. Paul kept a diplomatic distance; he'd served mass and on more than one occasion blown the responses. He glanced around at high ceilings and shining wood. Without the congregation, the space seemed huge; it also smelled pleasantly of candle wax and wood soap. Organ riffs floated down from the loft.

He was enjoying the music when Father Martin dismissed the youngsters, handing them each something.

"Mr. Rodriguez," he said, spotting Paul. "You might as well have a couple, too. Hershey's Kisses today."

Paul pocketed them, shook the priest's hand. "Father, you're a regular candy store."

"My personal cross, I'm afraid." He transferred a rolled-up envelope to under his arm, peeled a Kiss, and put it in his mouth. "I meant to ask if Leonardo was any help Sunday. What was that man's—?"

"Zavala," said Paul. "And he did know the name. Quite a coincidence, said he'd seen him box."

"That sounds like Leonardo, always inviting me to some fight or other."

Paul looked at light making rosy pools through the stained glass.

"Your Leonardo's an interesting guy, isn't he?"

"I see you enjoyed talking with him."

"He must be very wealthy."

The priest smiled. "Leonardo's success in business has brought semiretirement, which permits him to spend time here. For which we are thankful.'' He began to stroll up the aisle.

"How did you meet him?"

"Leonardo attended one of my first masses." Father Martin stopped to replace missals in a pew rack, then resumed. "It became clear we shared a similar vision. Since then we could not have accomplished what we have without him."

"He have other interests besides antiquities?"

"You really should ask him, Mr. Rodriguez. I find it hard to keep up with all the things he does."

Paul saw writing penciled on the envelope—Niños de Mexico. He was starting to inquire about it when Father Martin continued.

"You seem very curious about Leonardo. Is there a reason?"

"Only that it seems an amazing coincidence he'd know the man we're looking for."

"Known *of*, you must mean. Leonardo mentioned it had been quite a long time ago."

"Certainly, Father, let me explain." Wil could hardly object to a priest hearing it, he thought. "I can't say much about what I'm working on, but the matter involves a child brought to L.A. from Mexico in the late sixties. We think Zavala murdered him."

Father Martin crossed himself. "How awful. I know Leonardo would want to help find this man—perhaps through his connections in Mexico—"

"He's already offered, Father, thanks." Paul lowered his voice and stepped out further onto thin ice: "Father, I'm reluctant to even suggest this, but do you think Leonardo Guerra could be connected to Zavala in some way?"

How thin the ice was became immediately clear: Father Martin's face clouded; veins jumped in his neck. "Leonardo Guerra is the most selfless man I know," he began. "What you see here is but a small part of what he has done for us. The world is a terrible place, Mr. Rodriguez, full of hostility and suspicion. But your words are the worst; they wound the Savior's heart and mine.'' He slapped his palm with the rolled-up envelope. ''Shame on you!''

Paul felt fire on his face, ice in his gut. Instantly he was the chastened altar boy again, averting his eyes—hoping his complexion hid the embarrassment but doubting it. Hoping nobody'd heard.

''Father— I was not accusing Leonardo Guerra. Forgive me. I meant no disrespect.''

Father Martin's ire died as rapidly as it had flared. ''Of course you didn't. It is I who ask forgiveness, Mr. Rodriguez. Misplaced indignation compounded by friendship. Please—can I offer you a cup of Isabel's tea?''

Paul gulped air, checked his watch. ''I wish I could, really, but I have to meet someone.''

''I'll bet it's your friend from Sunday—Mr. Hardesty, right?''

Paul nodded.

Father Martin put a conciliatory arm around Paul's shoulder, walked him through the vestibule and out into the afternoon. ''Business or pleasure?''

''Some of both, Father. Dinner tonight after we check out a place where Zavala was seen, a bar near here. Some name, I'm sure you'd agree: Angel's.''

''There are so *many*,'' the priest said. ''Like the plague. Good luck, Mr. Rodriguez.'' He pumped Paul's hand once. Then he headed up the path toward the rectory.

Starting the wagon, Paul was aware of how much he'd sweated, his still-racing pulse. *Sheeit*, him and his big mouth; probably deserved what he got. He remembered the writing on the envelope in Father Martin's hand. Forget it— no way was he facing the wrath of God twice in one day; besides, he'd stayed too long as it was. He picked up the notebook he'd brought along, opened it, wrote down the name, made a mental note to ask Father Martin about it later.

•   •   •

It took a while: First the law rolled up—four LASD units responding to the triple-niner—then the paramedics. After treatment, the cuffed biker was hauled off, his nose packed and seeping through cotton. Wil held an IV bag as they revived Mo Epstein.

"Napoleon'd be proud," he said. "How you feel?"

Mo answered slowly, as if thinking it over. "Woozy—dumb. Pissed mainly."

To the paramedics Wil said, "That's one of his vital signs. Nice work."

Epstein grabbed his sleeve. "On the last Angel's—wait for me. Be okay tomorrow." Then he was wheeled toward the orange-and-white emergency vehicle.

Wil watched as they radioed a nearby hospital, then closed the doors. As the siren faded, he took deep breaths, rubbed still-damp palms on his jeans. It had been a long time, something like this happening. Ever since Nam, where violence ceased to be an abstraction, he'd hated it—as much for the primal stirrings it generated in him as the fear. Participant or bystander, it was like a bloodstain on a white shirt; no matter how faded with washings, it reminded you of how it got there. And how you responded to it.

To distract himself, he walked around outside, but how close they'd just come followed him until they took his statement, the process time-consuming but grounding. At five-fifteen he was on the road. From the car phone he reached Vella, who'd heard about Epstein already, Angel's number three being county turf. For a while he cruised, then the traffic slowed around Alhambra. He dialed Rodriguez again, dismissed the feeling of unease when nobody was home.

Punching more numbers, he got an official-sounding voice that told him Lieutenant Epstein's condition was stable, that tests were scheduled for tomorrow. Wil was not surprised, but it left a decision. He could always do the last Angel's alone and wanted to, but it was tempting fate, Freiman's cooperation at stake.

The cooperation swung it. He'd wait.

• • •

Sheeit, I oughta do this for a living, Paul thought.

He reclined the seat a notch, unzipped his windbreaker, and scrunched down to wait. Half past four: Wil'd be there anytime now. He could see the bar clearly over the window molding. Across the street and up, Angel's sat hunched between a dead store with newspapers in the windows and a taco stand surrounded by a rutted parking lot.

Paul cracked the window and caught the aroma of searing meat, his stomach reminding him of the time. He remembered the chocolates in his jacket pocket, ate them, made entries in the notebook, scanned the front of the bar: scrawly gang tags, black double doors; in the circular windows, Christmas wreaths. Two painted-looking *chicas* lounged under a sign with racked pool balls marking a smaller door to the left.

Raeann'd be bent at first, he knew. But they'd have a few beers, and Wil would tell her how much he'd helped, how he couldn'a done it without him—realize how good he was at this stuff, maybe even work him into other cases. Paul shifted on the vinyl seat and nodded.

Friends didn't by-God cower at home when friends needed help.

At Pasadena the traffic ground down to stop-and-go.

On either side of him commuters picked noses and drummed steering wheels. In a 300ZX, a man spoke heatedly to someone on his cellular phone; a Plymouth full of nuns fingered rosary beads as two pickup-truck cowboys flipped each other off. Life in the fast lane, Wil thought.

Seeing the guy in the ZX reminded him to call Rodriguez again.

Raeann answered. "You gotta see the basket I made," she told him. "The Easter bunny should be so lucky."

He made small talk, deliberately unconcerned; then, "Raeann, have you seen Paul? I'm running late, a thing we had out in San Gabriel."

"I see lunch dishes, but no Rodriguez," she said. There were clatter sounds, plates on a countertop being moved. "Usually he leaves a note. Probably at the hardware—he was going to fix screens today."

Wil tried to dispel unease. "Some life you guys lead. Okay, no need for him to call back. I'll be there as soon as the traffic goes home where it belongs."

He pressed the gas, then the brakes a second later. In the west, the setting sun lit up a few scattered clouds, then was gone.

It was getting dark when Bolo Zavala showed.

Paul, stretching to loosen the kinks, stopped suddenly. It was him, had to be: older than he'd anticipated, but hell, the man must be fifty by now. Collar-up gray leather coat, dark pants; even without seeing the freckles, Paul knew the stocky build and red hair. The physical presence. He watched him banter awhile with the two hookers, look around several times, then disappear through Angel's pool entrance.

He began to sweat. Where the hell was Wil? Who knew how long the guy'd hang around.

Thirty minutes went by: fidgeting, worrying, adrenaline surges, righteous anger. If Zavala left, should he follow him? Probably—he could break this thing wide open. Go in? Probably not—Wil'd shit bricks if he saw him inside. He found himself wishing he'd brought a gun.

"Goddammit," Paul breathed. "You're blowing it, man, he's there. Hurry up or I'm goin' in."

What if he did? Zavala had no idea who he was: walk up and have a beer with the guy and he wouldn't know Paul Rodriguez from Adam. Stare him in the face, count freckles—better, sure, if Wil was there, but Wil wasn't, and the risk lay in Zavala's getting away. He took a deep breath.

Up to him.

Paul gave Wil another ten minutes, then locked the car and went in.

THIRTEEN

Despite the cold, the girls in the leather miniskirts were cracking up laughing as Paul approached. From across the street he'd watched them unwrap a square paper and snort the contents.

The bosomy one started it, calling to him in Spanish, "Hey, sugar. Want an early Christmas present?" The shorter one in the purple sweater shrilling in, "Yeah, piece and goodwill." Both breaking up again—druggy giggles just shy of losing it, their eyes nearly invisible under black makeup.

Paul pushed past them and went in.

Inside was warm and smelled of beer. From the jukebox a singer cried over *amor perdido*; men in work clothes downed Tecates. Through a cutaway Paul could see two men playing pool as a couple of bored-looking women watched. An open door showed a dim hallway with rest rooms and a telephone sign; above it, the Hamm's bear circled a faded clock face.

Six o'clock.

Zavala was not at the bar. Paul ordered Tecate, sat with it a few minutes, then shuffled over to look into the pool-room. The two men were arguing over the position of the cue ball. No Zavala.

He finished his beer and ordered another plus a shot of tequila, which he downed in one gulp. Can in hand, he moved toward the hallway, once there noticing two things. The first was that the hallway ended in a door past the toilets and the telephone. The second was Zavala. He was alone in a small game room Paul hadn't noticed, standing between the single pool table and two poker stations. He was lining up a shot, nine ball in the side.

Paul drew a breath and entered.

Zavala took no notice, fired down the nine, began racking for the next game. The leather coat was over a chair, black shirt rolled up. The man's forearms were thick; on the underside of one Paul could see a razor blade dripping tattoo blood.

Zavala glanced up, looked at Paul, gave a slight nod as Paul moved forward into the light and took a swig of beer. "Mind if I watch?" he asked in Spanish.

Zavala addressed the rack and broke with a crash. Two balls went down. He looked back at Paul, leaned over to shoot again, then stopped.

"You want to try me?" he said in English. His eyes glittered.

Paul hesitated.

Zavala said, "If you're expecting someone—" Letting the words fade, the body language deride.

Shit, why not, Paul thought; in this far, feeling good— playing him might put the man off guard. "I'll take the solids," he said, removing his windbreaker.

Wait'll Hardesty got a load of this.

Stuck now, not moving.

Wil saw signs for the cutoff about the time he'd spotted the red lights flashing up ahead, the accident bad from the looks of it. He got out and stood on the Bonneville's nose, saw the highway patrol directing traffic down to a single lane at the far right. Three cars, one overturned, piled up around a jackknifed semi; two emergency vehicles standing by; paramedics working over someone on the pavement.

As he watched, a motorcycle patrolman pulled up next to several CHP Mustangs.

Wil got back in the car as traffic began to inch forward. Six-fifteen. He'd given Raeann his car phone number, and she had promised to call him once Paul got there. He sat and stared at the receiver, willing it to ring as red light pulsed in the window glass like a racing heart.

They finished shooting, ordered more Tecates, then started another game. He was no real match, but at least he'd kept it interesting—talking had gotten him nowhere. Zavala simply responded by blasting each shot with great force, as if he had to smash Paul. Let him, Paul thought, the beer and tequila warm inside, boosting him. Even so, he began to sense the danger of the man. He was glad Zavala was unaware of his mission—and yet, as Zavala stared at him between shots, the hair rose on his neck.

Ridiculous, of course. How could he know?

God*damm*it. Where was Wil?

Midway through the second game, he remembered Wil's rolling number in his wallet. Why hadn't he thought of it? He'd use the hall phone to find out what was up. Then either wait or abandon ship. Or whatever.

Zavala called the eight in the corner pocket and struck the ball so hard it sounded like the crack of a rifle. He sniffed, wiped his nose, looked up at Paul.

"Again?"

Paul nodded as casually as he could, then said, "Gotta check in with mama first. You know how it is." He leaned his cue against the table, headed for the door, fishing for coins, turning back to ask if Zavala wanted another beer.

Zavala kept racking, paid no attention.

The alcove was a snug fit—time to lose a few pounds, Paul thought, twenty maybe? Yeah, start Monday but add ten. Fumbling for the card, he found it finally, then popped the coins in and dialed, tapping his fingers on the little shelf as he waited.

• • •

Wil jumped as though shot, picking it up before it could buzz again. "Raeann? Paul! Where are you?"

Paul's voice was low and confidential, but hearing the excitement in it Wil knew immediately where he was. "We're doin' pool and beers down here," came the half-whisper. "Real buddy-buddy. Got the tattoos and the hair and the scar, and what do you want me to do? You comin' or what?"

Wil struggled to get a grip as the traffic started and stopped. "Paul, listen. I'm gridlocked half an hour from there if everybody just vanished. Get out of there—now. Epstein discovered a possible link between Zavala and Guerra. You may be made already. Put the phone down now and get the *fuck* out!"

There was breathing on the line, and then Paul repeated, "A link?—" the way he said it both questioning and knowing, Wil thinking this wasn't at all how it was supposed to go.

"Paul, you hear me, goddammit? Get out of there."

It was so obvious Paul almost smiled: the posturing outside Angel's, the empty room, the games. Zavala had been waiting for the two of them to show, figuring he'd take them both down. Only Wil hadn't come, the fly in the ointment. Paul was alive because Wil Hardesty was stuck somewhere in traffic.

Paul looked at the receiver, rushing in his ears making the voice in it sound far away. *Get out now:* barely hearing it, staring at the buttons on the pay phone. Right, get out. Put down the phone and walk through the bar and out the door. Get in the car and go back to your life. Now!

Something against his throat then. Something very sharp.

"Hijo de puta," the voice hissed from behind him. "Did you really think Bolo Zavala would be so easy? That I would fall to some fat *pendejo* who sleeps in a room with lace on the pillows?"

Paul struggled briefly, then quieted, trying to comprehend that Zavala had been in the house—*his house*. The knife was cold fire, the pressure increasing now. He felt tiny rivulets and, by his ear, warm beer-breath. *Rae!* He stood very still, anger competing now with fear. When had the bastard broken in?

"My wife," he managed to say. "You—"

Zavala was a graveled whisper, goading. "We share a taste for dark meat, *puerco*. Maybe I don't kill that one."

Paul twisted, only to feel more pressure at his neck. Fighting to stay calm, he heard from far away Wil's voice shouting and Zavala again.

"This what you wanted, *puerco*, to hunt down Bolo Zavala? *Qué?* Now you got him, what next, eh?" He sniffed in sharply. "Tell your friend you and I are going to have a party, that we're sorry he is not here. Tell him now."

Paul raised the receiver, warnings still coming from it. "Wil," he said. The force of the blade on his throat made it hard to speak, but he heard the line quiet suddenly. "We got a problem."

"He has a knife, man. He knows about you." The voice in the phone was guttural, labored.

Fingers of ice started at Wil's groin, worked their way up his spine. *Jesus God!* Catching himself then, nothing in giving way to panic. He had the phone, not much but something. *Think!*

He took a deep breath, let it out. "Paul, we'll get through this," he said. "Hand him the phone."

He heard a rustling, then breathing; brassy trumpet faint in the background. He was conscious of his grip on the phone. "My friend knows nothing," he started. "It's me. I want to ask some questions—no danger to you, no law, just questions. We can work this out, but not if you hurt my friend."

No answer.

"I can be there in minutes. All I want is to talk."

"Liar!" The voice was bright with fury. "The truth, or your friend dies now. What questions? Who is asking them? Why?"

There was an excruciating gasping sound from Paul.

"All right, it's yours," Wil said. "Whatever you want, no tricks. Just stay loose." Again no answer, Wil thinking Zavala was considering it—just maybe. He heard Paul give a strangled gasp, then:

"Fuckin' kid-killer, man—don't—"

Son of a bitch, not now. There was a savage grunt and the receiver banging hard against something and his own voice rising to a shout. *"Zavala, wait, anything you want."* Pounding on the steering. *"Wait!"* Trying not to imagine what he was hearing.

Seconds later there was a muffled rubbing and the voice, cold now. "Sad you can't see this. No mind, there will be another time for you, Señor Hardesty. Another time."

After that there was nothing but the sounds.

FOURTEEN

It was the honking that brought him out of it, forcing him to notice the guy behind him in the jacked-up stepside. The driver was gesturing at the car's length that had opened up, leaning out now, yelling loud enough for Wil to hear.

"Fuckin' car phones. Move your ass, goddammit."

Beating back the impulse to stay on the line, Wil killed the connection and dialed 911. As he waited, he fumbled for the Angel's Bar address, then 911 answered and he told them. Next he dialed Vella, praying that he hadn't left work yet; five rings, then Vella was there, listening, questioning, promising to roll units, be there himself ASAP.

After that Wil went to work on the traffic: lying on the horn, bulling his way nightmare-slow to the frontage, breaking free then, tires riding the curb. Horns screamed back at him. As he approached the accident, the motorcycle patrolman blocked his way.

"You Hardesty? Sheriff's just radioed, said you were in this mess and where you had to get to. Follow me."

They made it in twenty-seven minutes, the CHP hanging a U-turn as Wil swung into the taco stand's parking lot in between a paramedic truck and an unmarked unit. Angel's crawled with cops: four cruisers in front, lights flashing as Valley cops directed traffic around the scene. Two white vans stood by the bar's entrance. Vella, looking tired, came out the double doors, grabbed Wil's arm.

"Brace yourself," he said, then as Wil slipped past him, "and don't touch anything."

Angel's hummed: a pair of uniforms stood with the bartender while detectives in plainclothes conducted interviews; specialists combed for evidence, one sketching the layout. A paramedic brushed past him toward a group tight-quartered in the hallway where flash equipment strobed.

Vella evidently told them he'd be coming, because they let him pass—through the door, past a game room where dusting for latents had started, past the room with the *baños* sign, to the yellow crime-scene tape, and into hell. The blood looked spray-gunned on; it patterned the pay phone, the telephone alcove, the floor. Paul had evidently staggered, hitting the walls in several places where it was especially heavy.

Wil pressed fingers into his eyes, then looked at what had been his friend. Paul lay on his side in a huge red pool, eyes and mouth open, hands at the obscene wound in his neck as though trying to pinch it together. The paramedic came over.

"You okay?"

He nodded, not risking speech.

"You knew him, I take it," the paramedic said as they looked down. "Slicer took out both carotids and the jugular—the cleanest I ever saw. Probably over in a minute."

Wil looked at the still-dangling receiver, found his voice, the sound mostly croak. "I heard it," he said. "But it wasn't a minute. It was a goddamn lifetime."

Wil found Vella leaning against the unmarked, holding a cigarette at his side. His breath rose, illuminated in the flashing lights.

"Some fucked day," Vella said. "I'm sorry about your friend." He drew in smoke. "That his car? Couple of sidewalk trade told us he got out of the wagon over there." When Wil nodded, Vella called a deputy over and briefed him; he motioned Wil inside the unit and got in himself.

"Look, I know this is tough, but what the fuck was an amateur like Rodriguez doing tracking a guy like Zavala? And how come no mention of it? We'd have had this sucker if we'd been tipped. Freiman's gonna shit."

Wil looked at him; the headache that had started back on the freeway was moving to a point behind his eyes. "Paul was freelancing, Vella. You knew about this when I knew about it. End of story."

They watched the transport people muscle a gurney toward the white van; doors opened, then slammed, and the van took off. Vella shook his head. "An amateur, for Christ's sake."

Wil said, "That amateur saved my life once—in a fucking river in a fucking war nobody gave a damn about. I was supposed to be here, but I wasn't. I could have saved him, but I didn't. Now I have to tell his wife that."

Vella kicked halfheartedly at a taco wrapper blowing by, then dropped his cigarette and stepped on it. "Yeah," he said. "Look, I'll brief Freiman. You take an hour or two, get things squared away with the wife. When you're finished, come downtown. We'll talk then."

Wil nodded. "I'll help your guy with Paul's car, then take off. When you're through, leave it. I'll pick it up tomorrow."

One of the night-duty detectives directed him to the office. As Lieutenant Vella finished a call, Wil looked out at city lights, replayed the horror on Angel's floor, the parting look in Raeann Rodriguez's eyes.

She'd known as soon as she saw his face at the door. "I lost him," he told her after trying to explain what happened. "Paul was waiting for me. I wouldn't even be here if it weren't for him."

She put aside the brandy he'd poured her, left the room, and came back with a small tight thing—pine needles with a geometric pattern woven in. At the top the basket curved gracefully in on itself.

His first thought was that she'd gone into shock.

"I finished it today," she said. "I was going to surprise Paul, hope it might get him interested in coming to class. That's where I was today. While Paul was at Angel's and you were wherever you were and that man was wherever he was." She touched his cheek. "Nobody forced Paul. You were no more responsible for his being killed than I was."

Her face hardened, and then the hardness was gone, and it was as though she were aging in front of him, her color draining, cheeks sagging. "Come back when you're through," she said. "I can't be alone. Not tonight."

Vella hung up the phone.

"Nothing I didn't expect," he said. "Freiman's ticked you didn't tell him about Rodriguez." He took an ending drag on his cigarette, crushed it as he exhaled. "Some lousy luck about your friend, but at least we know who we're after."

"Yeah," Wil said, snapping out of it. He turned away from the window. "He knew my name, Vella. The son of a bitch knew we were coming."

"How could he have known?"

"I have no idea how, let alone when. But he knew." Wil started to pace. "Paul said they were playing pool. Then the man's at his throat and calling me Hardesty— some kind of macho play, I think."

"The call—Zavala overheard him, figured it out."

"No way. Paul kept it low, never said my name. I think Zavala knew all along who Paul was and decided to kill him when I didn't show." He rubbed his temples. "You got any aspirin?"

Vella found some in his top drawer, lit a fresh menthol as Wil gulped four tablets down with coffee. He plunked the match into an empty hamburger box. "The girls said Zavala acted like he was expecting company. What I don't get is, it's been a long time since anybody was even close to catching up with this guy—how'd he know Paul?"

"Paul called some people he knew about Zavala. Maybe

one of them tipped him. Still doesn't explain how Zavala knew about me, though.''

"How about Guerra? You know we found a possible link there.''

Wil stopped pacing and leaned against the wall. "Maybe. But Paul understood that I thought Guerra's knowing Zavala in Mexico was a stretch. He wouldn't have said anything to Guerra, even if he *had* seen him before he went to Angel's.'' He thought a second. "This link between Zavala and Guerra anything provable?''

Vella tapped ash into the box. "Unlikely. It's cold trail, almost thirty years. Nothing conclusive even then.''

"Anything more turn up at Angel's?''

"Lab people didn't find much. The investigating team's still interviewing, but so far nobody knows *nada*. Bartender told them he noticed Paul but never saw another man. Same for the pool players. Local cops said Angel's is no virgin: drug busts, fights, stabbings—nothing like this, though.''

"I take it your shop's handling the investigation?''

Vella yawned, backhanded it. "We do their one-hundred eighty-sevens. We should have prints back soon, but the dusters said they found only one cue out. Zavala probably wiped his and stuck it back in the rack. Nothing comes easy, does it?'' He puffed, waved away smoke, then pulled out photocopies that were stapled together and tossed them down. "Take a look. They're pages from a spiral notebook we found in the glove compartment of the station wagon.''

Wil thumbed through it as Vella talked.

"You'll notice Paul set up his watch at a little past four and spotted Zavala at five seventeen. The last entry was at six when he went in after him. Corroborates the girls' story.''

"He must have been afraid Zavala'd leave before I got there. No bloody chance.''

Vella pointed to the inside front cover page. "What's this Niños de Mexico—any idea?''

Wil looked: The writing was separate from Paul's stakeout data. He shook his head slowly. "If it relates to An-gel's, I don't know how. Raeann made the other notes in there, I'll ask her if she knows."

"And let me know?"

Freiman talking now, surrounding him like Vella's smoke. "Sure, Lieutenant," he said. "And let you know."

Vella extinguished the cigarette. "The investigators should be back by now—through there, the long room with the desks. Stay in touch, huh?" As Wil stood up, Vella dialed an extension on the desk phone.

It was midnight before the Homicide detectives finished with him. Outside the office, the night had a clean, cold bite; cars still tore out of L.A. and over the Hollywood hills.

Spent, driving with the window down, Wil picked up Mulholland past the Hollywood Bowl, then took the rim to Coldwater Canyon. Fresh air helped chase some of the up-set he was feeling from four aspirin on an empty stomach; before descending, he pulled off at a view spot and parked. The Valley shimmered below, rivers of light moving like gaudy blood through the traffic arteries. He got out of the car, leaned against the grille, and took deep breaths.

Every cell hungered for a drink. For obliteration. He wondered what normal people were doing at this hour. Sleeping off a day full of boss and kids and not too much saturated fat. Christ! He and Epstein nearly lose it in a bar, then Rodriguez.

In spite of Raeann's absolution, he felt none of it; he should have saved his friend—better, cut off the whole thing sooner. He thought of times they'd shared overseas. Of nearly dying, the stink of river and spent rounds, Paul's grip on him in the water.

His boot touched a rock and he bent down and picked it up. For a long moment he looked at the sharply irregular shape; then his fingers wrapped around it—harder and harder until there was only the pain and a wetness in his palm and he heaved it as far as he could into the dark canyon. A faraway crashing of brush came back, the crack of dead wood, and in the following stillness the awful detached telephone sounds again and the voice: *Another time*. Tears came then, turning the Valley into a neon abstract.

Which of those lights is you, Zavala? he thought.

Stay alive, you son of a bitch.

Leonardo Guerra stood at the arched window that looked out over the arroyo. In the glass he could make out the man in the white sweater seated behind him. He addressed the reflection.

"It was fortunate that I spoke with Father Martin this afternoon, unfortunate our luck did not hold. Hardesty remains a threat, and there is still the matter of his employer." He drank from the bottle Julio had brought. "You're sure Rodriguez had no idea who you were—"

"Fuck Rodriguez," Bolo Zavala said lightly. "It's simple enough for you, isn't it, *patrón*. You just wave a finger, say make them go away."

"Which Bolo of course does," Guerra answered. The softness of his voice could not conceal its edge. "Although there have been times when even Bolo Zavala needed help."

"That was a long time ago." Zavala took a slug of his ale. "Things change."

"Do they? Perhaps you should consider all the fine things you would have missed had it not been for me."

Zavala fished in his pocket, brought the inhaler up to his nostrils, took long, deliberate pulls. The gesture was to aggravate him, Guerra knew; as always, it did. "Poor Bolo," he said, "all that cocaine, and for what? You think you can escape in it—throw your life aside like so much garbage?"

Zavala's face went taut, the mottles standing out; Guerra pressed him. "Maybe you thought it would be easy to dispose of me as well."

The smaller man's eyes glittered, fires on a dark plain.

"I see," Guerra said. "Except for a file that will reach

certain hands should anything foolish occur.''

"No fucking file will keep you from me if and when I choose. Comprende?''

Guerra backed off his anger: Zavala sober was one thing, but high and after a kill . . . at least he was right about one thing, it was not like the days when he could rein the man in with a glance, a well-chosen word.

The fucking coke.

He split a wide grin. "Such talk—what are we saying to one another? We are like this." He crossed the underside of his wrists. "Flesh and blood, twin heartbeats. You did good work tonight. Now you should go home, get some rest, and we will make a fresh start tomorrow, united as always." He handed Zavala the trash bag full of his bloody clothing to dispose of, then saw him downstairs to the narrow path that led along the edge of the arroyo to the street. As he single-filed ahead of him, Zavala took another exaggerated hit on the inhaler.

"Cuidado," Guerra said, watching the dark shape disappear into the brush. "Take care."

Walking back upstairs, he stroked his mustache, thought about Bolo, the nagging feeling he'd not told him everything about tonight. Not only that, his old sources in Mexico had reported further inquiries, this time about *him.* Not good.

He lifted a slim panatella from a cedar box and called for Julio.

It was almost 2:00 A.M. when Wil let himself in. Edith Sandoval, the neighbor he'd asked to come over, had the television on with the volume low. He saw her home, told her he'd let her know about coming back in the morning, wanting some time alone with Raeann. He tried Lisa and got the machine but left no message. He then undressed in the dark and lay down in the small room, afraid to turn on the light—imagining the photographs of Paul staring at him in silent accusation.

Raeann was still sleeping when he rolled out. Making coffee, favoring his sore hand, he saw Edith Sandoval peering over her hedge and gave an OK sign. She went back to her roses, glancing back often.

This time he got hold of Lisa.

"My God—what should I do, Wil, come down? Shit, I'm booked—I'll reschedule—who could do something like that to Paul?" Singsongy phrases, edging toward frantic and cut by tears. "God, poor Raeann."

She wasn't needed now, he assured her, maybe later. He told her about Epstein, about the nightmare on the freeway, about how he felt. There was a pause, long enough for him to think he'd lost her.

"*Goddammit,*" she said finally, more to herself than him, before hanging up.

Wil showered and shaved, then tried the hospital; at least another day of tests, and they'd tell the lieutenant he phoned. Epstein called back in a few minutes. It was no easier with him. "Shit," Mo said. "We'd have been there if I hadn't screwed up. *Son of a bitch!*"

As he hung up, he felt Raeann behind him, turned, and held her. He poured her coffee. "Paul hated funerals," she said finally, "but his family has a plot up in Santa Barbara. It's kind of far, but I think he'd like it there, don't you?" She welled up, recovered.

"Raeann, can you think about something for me?"

She nodded.

"A notation Paul wrote in your notebook separate from his bar entries—Niños de Mexico—that mean anything to you?"

She searched her memory. "Kids? I'm trying to think, but it's not familiar."

"Okay. Also, Paul's first notes started at 4:07. I called about two-thirty and he wasn't home. Any idea where he might have gone?"

"No. I know he had lunch, though, because of the dishes—he always eats at noon." She looked at her hands.

"Could he have stayed here and missed my call?"

She hesitated. "I don't think so. When I left at eleven, I'd just straightened up. If he spent the afternoon here, the place would have looked it, knowing Paul." Raeann nodded. "The house was neat. He went someplace after lunch."

FIFTEEN

Paul's phone books had no listing for a Niños de Mexico; directory assistance brought similar results. Fresh out of phone company insiders who'd risk a right-to-privacy rap to give him an unlisted, Wil called Vella, who said he'd get a warrant for the number and pursue the lead.

"How's the wife holding up?" Vella asked.

"Raeann," Wil said with more sharpness than he'd planned. "Her name's Raeann."

"Thank you, that's just what I needed. How's she holding up?"

"All right, I suppose, all things considered. I told her you'd probably have somebody out to talk with her."

"They've left already. Where'll you be?"

"Here and there—my place later. I'm not going anywhere."

"Right."

Wil hung around to be with Raeann for the LASD detectives, the man and woman who'd questioned him after Vella last night. Afterward he asked Edith Sandoval to drive him out to Angel's Bar to pick up Paul's Chevy.

Sitting there after she'd dropped him off, cramped behind the steering wheel and feeling Paul's presence, he waited, reluctant even to adjust the front seat. Finally he did, and it was then he noticed the candy wrappers jammed down in the crack between the seats. There were two of them.

Small foil squares with chocolate residue on them, as though they'd melted slightly before being unwrapped. Hershey's Kisses.

Wil started the car and drove to St. Boniface.

Father Martin was in his office in the rectory. Wil waited until he was finished with a committee meeting, then went in as they were filing out, half a dozen well-dressed men and women chatting earnestly and holding notebooks. He found the priest staring out the window at a rose garden, his back to the room.

Wil scoped out blond wood bookcases and desk, green carpet, a large crucifix like the one behind St. Boniface's altar. On the desk was a blotter, computer printouts, a pen set and clock, several mementos. The bookcases were arranged gallery-style into groupings: books, small statues and artifacts, framed photographs. Spotlights set into the ceiling illuminated a round conference table.

Wil tapped the back of the heavy oak door. "Father?"

The priest started slightly, turned from the window. "Ah," he said. "Mr.—"

"Hardesty," Wil finished for him.

"Of course. Sit down, Mr. Hardesty. How can I be of service?"

"I need to talk with you. It's important."

Father Martin joined him at the conference table. As he sat down, he checked his watch. "I'm afraid I can't spare more than—"

"When was the last time you saw Paul Rodriguez?"

"Is there some problem?"

"Would you recall for me, please?"

Father Martin cast his eyes upward in thought. "Well, let's see. Last Sunday, I suppose."

Wil tried to keep the surprise out of his voice. "He wasn't here this week? Yesterday?"

"He could have been and talked with someone else, I suppose. Would you like me to ask if anyone might have seen him?"

"I'd appreciate it, yes."

The priest moved to the phone on his desk, picked up the receiver, and pressed a button. "Isabel, you remember Mr. Rodriguez from last Sunday? . . . That's right. Was he here yesterday? . . . I see. . . . You'll let me know right away?" He hung up. "She's calling around," he said to Wil. "Is Mr. Rodriguez missing?"

"He was murdered last night," Wil answered. "At a bar not far from here."

Father Martin made the sign of the cross and sat down heavily. *"Madre Domini,"* he said as though infinitely fatigued. "I didn't know him well, but he seemed so decent. He had a family, hadn't he?"

"A son grown and gone. A wife at home."

"The poor woman. What happened?"

Wil told him about it as the priest slowly shook his head.

He said, "And you think this man Zavala you were looking for had something to do with it?"

"He was expecting us. On the phone he used my name."

"My God."

"Someone let Zavala know we were coming, Father. Someone Paul may have inadvertently told."

"Not someone here, surely."

"Not necessarily, but someone I hope to find."

The intercom buzzed then, and Father Martin went to pick it up. "All right, thank you," he said after listening a moment. He laid the receiver down. "Isabel checked with everyone she remembered as being here yesterday, even the volunteers. No one remembers seeing Mr. Rodriguez. I'm sorry."

Wil stood up; as usual, it had been too much to hope for. He fondled the pieces of foil in his pockets—little sins probably, indulgences Paul kept from a weight-conscious Raeann. Meaningless.

"Is there anything I can do for the family?" Father Martin was saying. "A mass, of course, but anything else?"

Wil was touched by his sincerity. "I'll let you know,

Father. Thank you for your time.'' He was almost to the door, his hand still in his pocket, when something occurred to him, prompted in part by hunger. ''Father, you wouldn't happen to have any more of those mints you gave Paul, would you?''

There was the slightest hesitation before the priest answered. ''No.'' He smiled, reaching into the pocket of his black suit coat. ''But maybe a couple of these would help keep body and soul together.''

Into Wil's hand he put three foil-wrapped little shapes.

Which proves nothing, Wil thought, eating the Hershey's Kisses and taking the concrete path toward the parking lot, not a damn thing. The candies could have come from anywhere, could have been there for days, could have anything: likely find a stash of them right now in Paul's garage. And Father Martin lying? Come on, Hardesty, do better.

Passing the church, he heard the sound of organ music and went in. For a moment he just listened—some hymn he couldn't place, vague notes in the shafts of sunlight flooding down on empty pews. He spotted stairs and climbed the loft.

The organist was a balding gnome with a florid face who looked as though reaching the pedals was a constant struggle. When he saw Wil he hit a sour note and stopped playing.

''Sorry to interrupt,'' Wil said.

''Don't tell me,'' the man said, ''another new request. I keep telling them, these hymns take time to learn.'' He looked as if he were about to cry.

''Were you here yesterday?''

''Here every day. You don't have more work for me?''

''Just a question,'' he said, noting the relieved look. He described Paul. ''Any chance you might have seen him here yesterday, around three to four o'clock?''

''Look for yourself,'' the man said. ''From up here I see Christ on his cross and a lot of stained glass.''

"Right. Thanks for the music." Wil was at the stairs when the man said:

"*Heard* somebody yesterday about the time you said."

Wil turned back.

"Catchin' holy hell from Father Martin, he was. Boy, can he skin 'em alive when he wants to."

"You catch a name?"

"No. But the guy was gettin' it over some question he'd asked."

"What question?"

The gnome rubbed his lips. "You notice how stuffy it gets up here? Makes a man thirsty, if you catch my drift."

Wil took out his wallet and passed the man a ten. "The question?"

The bill went into his pocket like metal to a magnet. "I didn't hear it actually, just who it was about: our illustrious financial adviser and benefactor, 'His Royal Anus'—oops, naughty me—Leonardo Guerra. Must've been something, because he really got his head handed to him."

At the Rodriguez house, Wil exchanged cars, told Raeann he'd be at home for a few days, then headed west on the Ventura toward Ignacio Reyes's place. Hugging the slow lane, he turned things over in his mind. If that *had* been Paul in the church, why had Father Martin lied? What would have angered the priest—some suspicion Paul had about Guerra and Zavala? Paul hadn't even heard of the possible link Epstein found until last night on the phone. He'd have been speculating.

Wil turned off the freeway and called Vella from a pay phone, heard that Paul's autopsy report would be ready "sometime soon." The coroner's office was swamped with bodies, Christmas holidays bringing out the best in people as usual. "You unclear how he died, Hardesty?" Vella asked, sounding like Epstein. Wil ignored him and rang off.

Clouds were moving in, deep shadow and brilliant sun striating the foothills as he parked the car in front of the white house. A gardener was making scant progress against the wind. Leaves were dropping from the Chinese elm as fast as he could blow them off the lawn.

Marta was not pleased; reluctantly she showed him in, let him find his own way to the den where Ignacio Reyes nursed a beer. From the man's eyes Wil wondered how many had preceded it. He seated himself on the couch as Marta appeared with the coffee he'd requested.

"I realize this is sudden," he said, taking a tentative sip and finding it too hot, "but I came here to resign." He watched a flush spread over Reyes's pale skin and decided the tall man wasn't refused much.

"You disappoint me, Mr. Hardesty," he said. "I had understood you to be making progress. You want more money, of course." He got out a leatherbound checkbook and began writing.

"Money has nothing to do with this. It's become personal." He explained about Paul.

Reyes's mouth dropped; he put a hand to his throat. "My son and now my friend. The miserable bastard."

"My reasoning is this," Wil said. "If I can get a crack at Zavala, I intend to take it. If I kill him, there might be talk you hired me to do it, or that I was working a vendetta on my client's time. I'm sure you understand that neither is acceptable.

"And there's another problem. If Zavala learns who hired me, he'll go after you. He has everything to lose if you identify him."

Reyes slumped in his chair. "You mean my family is in danger?"

"Potentially yes, more likely no. Somehow he knows who I am, but not about you, because he asked who I was working for. I'll tally up where we stand, and you can send a check. For now, save your money." He stood up to go.

"One thing more," he said. "You keep a gun in the house?"

Reyes shook his head as though having marginal success trying to keep everything separate.

"I recommend you look into it." Wil scribbled down the name of a gun shop he knew Paul favored. "Tell them you want to learn to use it."

Reyes got up then, but Wil stopped him as they started for the front entrance. "I'll take the back," he said, shaking Reyes's hand. "You should know also the law is now involved. They don't know about you and won't from me, but it's another good reason for us to stay apart."

Reyes took a breath as if to say something but didn't, just led the way to the sliding glass doors. *"Vaya con Dios,"* he said, then drew back inside.

Wil eased out onto the patio. Skirting the pool, he followed a fenceline concealed by laurel, then walked to the Bonneville and caught the 101 for home.

Leonardo Guerra took pride in his ability to sniff out fear the way a shark smelled blood. That it was over the phone only enhanced the metaphor. "You're slipping," he told the voice at the other end. "This is no time for mistakes."

"I am not your equal in these matters. I willingly confess to that."

Guerra felt the barb in the tone, but dismissed it. "You're lucky that no one else remembered Rodriguez," he said. "Was there some reason you had in not just admitting you'd talked to him? What would have been the harm?"

"The tree is best nipped in the bud. Perhaps if you had not been so forthcoming about knowing that murderer—"

"Useful murderer."

"Perhaps you could explain how useful it was for him to tell Hardesty he knew they were coming."

Guerra heard a rushing in his ears like water through a spillway. *"What did you say?"*

"On the phone. From that bar. Your man was even so kind as to use Hardesty's name while threatening him."

There was a narrowing of vision, a tightening of the skin. Finally Martin DeSantis said: "Are you there?"

Fearful of what he might say next, Leonardo Guerra hung up the receiver.

SIXTEEN

Wil waited until they'd finished breakfast to explain about the danger; afterward, in the silence, he took her hand. "I just think it would be a good idea for you to stay with your parents. A few days, Leese. Till Zavala's finished."

Lisa looked at him. "This is our house, Wil."

"I know. But this is different, that must be obvious."

"Nobody can find La Conchita," she joked, "even our friends. I don't want to leave. What I want to do is help."

"You'll be helping by leaving."

"No, I'll be running away. There must be something I can do."

He was in no mood. "Zavala knows who I am, Lisa—for Christ's sake, he called me by name as he was cutting Paul's throat. How hard would it be for him to find me? Or you?" He got up and went out on the balcony.

She followed, brushed back hair the breeze had swept across her face as they stood looking at the ocean. "What about your friend Mo Epstein—police protection and all that?"

"My point exactly."

"What did he say?" His hesitation was her entrée: "Have you even discussed it with him?"

"I have my reasons, all right?"

"I know you," she said finally. "You *want* Zavala to find you. You want to square this thing with Paul the hard way, kill or be killed. And what do I do, just smile while the bullets fly?'' She turned to face him. ''You're scaring me, you know. We've already lost one member of this family.''

He gripped the railing. ''Thanks to me, you mean.''

''Did I say that? If you still feel blame I'm sorry, but it changes nothing.''

He calmed down with deep breaths.

She said, ''What happened with Devin is over, but I can't go through it twice. If something happens to you, it happens to me. You think about that.''

''Look, I'm not trying to be the Lone Ranger. But I can't just leave this thing to somebody else.'' He gathered her in, kissed her. ''I'll be careful.''

''And you'll think about how I can help in this?''

''Yes,'' he lied. ''Right now, though, you can help most by doing me that favor.''

''All right.'' She moved against him and they stood a minute at the rail. Then she led him into the bedroom and they made love very slowly, forgetting the distance between them, the danger, everything—cooling off afterward in a pool of winter sunlight that lay across the tangle.

Later, as he helped her pack a few things, he made up something about his schedule being iffy so she'd take Edward. Loading the cage, he promised again to be careful and to call every night. Then he kissed her, and she was gone.

From the window he watched the black coupe shoot north past the Rincon and disappear, thinking that she was right, of course. His hunger for blood was as real as the taste of copper pennies on the tongue.

Vella came on the line after a slight delay. Not much new: Epstein was home and expected back Monday, the stitches holding, his concussion effects receding. Wil would call him later; for now he had other business.

"Who should I talk to in Lancaster?" he asked. "I want to see the graves."

"Whatever," Vella said.

Wil took down the information. He made the Antelope Valley sheriff's station in just under two hours; from there they took Sergeant Montoya's Blazer. Montoya was a big man: fortyish, two-twenty, Wil figured, tall for a Hispanic. Eyes deeply lined at the corners.

"Got the word you were in on this. How so?"

"Cost of doing business," Wil told him. "Still, I appreciate the time. Thanks."

Montoya nodded. They headed east toward Saddleback Butte, passing block after block of housing tracts in varying stages of development. "Take a good look," Montoya said. "Pretty soon you won't be able to see the damn desert. I grew up out here, watched this shit taking over. They build an airport like they're talking about, you might as well put these Joshua trees in a museum."

"Growing like crazy, all right."

"And the crime rate right along with it," Montoya said sourly.

They drove, finally escaping the sprawl. Off to the right the mountains showed a hemline of snow; where they were, the clouds roamed like tumbleweeds. Pools of sunshine darted among the shadows.

"Vella said you supervised the gravesite."

Montoya nodded, easing around a cyclist. "Till Homicide took over. Man and his son found 'em, at least the first one. As light got better, we found the second. Then another one, and another, and pretty soon seven. Eerie, like they were growin' there."

They passed the butte; Montoya found a gravel turnoff and headed north. "A flash flood uncovered 'em," he said, "once-in-a-blue-moon thing. Whoever did the burying was smart, dug where the developers wouldn't be—at least not in this century." Another turnoff and a couple of miles in, they bumped to a stop.

"Now we walk," said Montoya.

Minutes later Wil spotted the yellow crime-scene tape. Far away a storm thundered; wind blew cold off the snow; a flicker hammered at a dead Joshua tree. Following Montoya, he dropped down a shallow embankment and approached the site.

"First one was here," said Montoya, pointing, "the kid with the medal. The second was over there. I don't recall how the rest went. Somethin', huh?"

Wil nodded. The scene looked like a mining operation, gridded out with stakes, lines, and fluttering markers. The top layer of soil had been lifted off; graves, enlarged in the search for clues, were now just depressions. At the perimeter, among creosote and sage, debris lay piled on stony ground.

He kicked a rock, imagining the killer here: digging, a small form lowered, earth replaced, footsteps leaving. One by one he wandered the graves, wondering who the other children were and why. He asked Montoya and got a question back.

"You have kids, Mr. Hardesty?"

Simpler to say no, so he did.

"This must seem bad to you, but it's worse with kids. I've got four—can't imagine what I'd do if something like this happened." Montoya picked up a piece of quartz and chucked it, following its flight with his eyes. "I bleed for the parents, whoever they are."

He turned back to Wil. "As to your question, I don't know. Sex maybe, pedophiles kill sometimes. Pretty clean, though, for sex murders." He lifted and resettled his hat. "What worries me is what's been goin' on in the meantime."

"Meaning?"

"Serial killers usually don't stop—they keep at it, like an addiction. How many more, I wonder, since these?"

A dust devil formed, stinging them with sand. As they watched it whirl away, Montoya said, "I'd like to get my hands on the sucker. What's a kid ever done to anybody?''

Wil blew on his hands. "Could somebody with kids do this?"

"Yes and no. Sometimes a parent does his family and makes a run for it. More often it's murder-suicide, breaking-point cases. Personally, I can't see anybody who's had a child killing one, let alone seven. Especially like this.'' Montoya shook his head. ''Fuckin' thing's scary, it's so cold.''

They poked around a while longer, then Montoya was out of time—the sun would be down in another hour, and he had reports waiting. Wil was reluctant without knowing why, but he followed, turning back once. Shadowed now, the graves looked grim and sad and overwhelmed by the vastness of desert.

"God," he said to no one.

Mo Epstein was on the couch with his feet up, full of game shows and ibuprofen. His head was shaved in back, exposing an ugly line of black stitches.

Wil opened the pint of Jack Daniel's he'd picked up leaving Lancaster and poured Epstein a snort. "Nice place," he said, looking around the condo.

"Better living through pressboard," Epstein said. He watched Wil pop open a 7-Up. "Can't tempt you, huh?"

"One's too many, a hundred not enough. Thanks anyway."

"How's Raeann Rodriguez?"

"Thinking about visiting her son in Texas, who should be arriving today. Be good for her to get away for a while. The house is full of Paul."

"Just retired, hadn't he?"

"Couple of years ago."

"Shit. I sent flowers—anything else I can do, you let me know." Epstein raised his drink. "He was a good man. I'd like a piece of the guy who did him."

They drank to that.

"Anything on Zavala from your end?"

Wil shook his head, told him about the threat, of packing off Lisa.

"Vella know about it?"

Wil tilted the soft-drink can.

"Jesus Christ," Mo said. "You are *not* thinking what I think you are."

"He'll come and I'll be waiting," Wil said.

"Just you and your bird and that goddamn warhorse gun."

Wil looked at him. "Bird's gone. Just the warhorse."

"Don't be stupid. That's why God made cops, remember? Let me order you some extra firepower."

"I'll let you know."

"Well, fuck me," Mo said. "Never mind my ass is on the line, never mind you made a deal. You're already one strike down with Freiman, you know. Vella told me how he felt about Rodriguez." He knocked back a gulp of whiskey and had to hold his head. In a moment he recovered.

"I suggest you reconsider, pal. By the way, Vella said to tell you that Niños de Mexico is an office in West L.A." He consulted his notebook, copied a page, handed it over.

Wil noted the West Olympic address, thinking it must be almost to Santa Monica or close.

"Vella had some people over there today," Epstein said. "They do adoptions, homeless kids from Mexico. Referrals only." He rubbed the glass on his forehead. "Somehow it wasn't on the list of agencies the team checked out after the Innocents broke. None of the directories had it, he said."

"Legit?"

"Apparently. Vella said they turned over files from sixty-six, -seven, and -eight—what the investigators have been asking for."

Wil downed the last of his 7-Up and stood to go.

"Wait, you'll miss the most interesting part. Guess who owns Niños de Mexico?"

"C'mon, Mo, I'm fucking beat."

"Yeah? Try Leonardo Guerra on for size."

SEVENTEEN

New questions, old ones rephrased, panning for gold in worked-out tailings: The truth was he didn't know where else to go this early. Besides, it was relatively close to the motel where he'd stayed after locating the Niños building last night.

Five-forty-two Hibiscus Place hadn't changed. The porch still drooped, the paint peeled, the garbage stank, and the freeway traffic tore by as though trying not to notice. Next door, a boy of about five pulled his screaming sister in a battered wagon. Seeing the tall man, brother stopped pulling and sister quieted to a sniffle. They stared a moment, then the boy yelled at Wil. *"Hey!"*

"Hey, yourself, kid." Wil said, grinning. *"Lo mismo a usted."* Slowly the boy turned the wagon around, began pulling his sister up the block. She looked around a final time, then began to yell halfheartedly.

Wil stepped up on the porch and knocked, waited, knocked louder. Eyeing the street, seeing no one, he tried the screen and found it hooked. He peered inside: dust hovering in a shaft of morning sun, shapes beginning to form through the dirty screen. Wrong shapes. He slipped a knife blade into the crack, lifted the hook out of its eye, and opened the door, hand under his leather field jacket.

The house looked hurricane-hit: chairs tipped over, fiesta dancers with their petticoats torn. Lamps were broken, pictures floored, drops of blood spattered like obscene rain. He drew the .45, moved slowly to the kitchen, found it similarly trashed. The back door was deadbolted; whoever had been there had likely gone out that way. Or was still inside. From the kitchen he could see into the bathroom: empty. Past a couple of the dancers, the bedroom door was open a crack.

Wil crossed the room on the balls of his feet; worn flooring squeaked. At the bedroom door frame he listened intently.

Labored breathing, ragged snores.

Flat against the frame, he pushed open the door from the hinge side, glanced, withdrew, ducked, looked again. She was lying faceup on the bed—at least he assumed it was Donna Pacheco. There was caked blood around her flattened nostrils. Her lips were huge, her eyes purple and swollen. She had a cut above her eyebrow and another on her chin.

Wil checked the closet, holstered the gun, got a glass of water and a towel; when he returned, she was starting to make quiet hurt sounds. He wet the towel from the glass and dabbed her forehead.

She jerked awake.

"Hardesty, Donna. I was here a few days ago." He propped her up with pillows, dabbed the worst of the blood off, covered her with a robe from the closet. In a cupboard he found budget whiskey with a dreg left and managed to get some down her.

"You have a doctor?" He looked around for the phone.

"No 'octer," she attempted. "I be hine. Hy you here?"

Wil remembered about her throat. "Frankie do this?"

She laughed—a gurgled cough. "Hrankie's hawn."

"Gone?"

She nodded, tried again, frustrated and struggling with it: "Got hrunk—drunk. Left. Huk 'm."

He held the bottle for her again, saw the eyes were focused beneath their puffiness. Apart from the bruises, her color was returning.

"Who, then?"

She turned her head away; tears started down, pinkening as they progressed. "He hook—took her. He took my—baby. Took—Yessica!"

"Who took Jessica?"

She eased her head back. "I hawt he loved me, but he took my Jessie."

It was slow and painful, and he felt for her as she told it: about Frankie Ybarra always suspecting the baby wasn't his—making it easy when he lost his job to steal the money they'd saved and split. Bolo coming then. Telling her he was taking the baby, going back to Mexico, that L.A. was no place to bring up a kid. Donna begging to go along; Bolo saying no way in hell, that he had a matter to settle first, but he was getting out and then nobody'd find him. Laughing when Donna said she thought he loved her. Beating her when he went for Jessie and she'd put up a fight. Bolo Zavala, the ex-fighter.

Wil let himself out and backtracked to a drugstore, where he cashed a check, bought bandages, aspirin. Another stop for a pint of bourbon. He fixed her up the best he could; it must have hurt, but she said nothing. When he finished she looked like a war casualty.

"Donna, think hard about where they might be, something he might have told you. A name, anything."

Seconds passed; her head moved side to side.

"All right. You have my card. If I'm not in, leave a message, okay?"

She nodded.

"I'll need a photo of her."

Another nod, this time at the dresser. Wil pulled a drawer open, found snapshots, jotted Donna's phone number on the back of one and put it in his pocket. Then he dialed Vella and laid out what happened.

"There'll be photos here," he said, "but the girl's—?"
Donna held up V'd fingers.

"Two years old, smallish, red hair and freckles." He covered the receiver. "You remember a car?"

She looked at him as if nothing mattered anymore, spoke haltingly as he relayed it: "Dark blue Camaro, Vella. She doesn't know the plate."

Vella asked him again where he'd be, and he said at home, then cradled the phone and stood up. "They'll be here in a little while, Donna. I'll be in touch." He peeled off five twenties and laid them on the dresser, watched her eyes widen.

"Thing I have for women and kids in distress," he said. "It goes back a long way."

It was nearly one-fifteen when he left the house. The wagon was on the sidewalk, no one in sight on the street. Cops, he knew, would knock on the neighbors' doors, ask who'd heard anything, noted times, seen license plates, but the results would be the same as always. *Nada.* Frightened looks or angry silence. People in the barrio knowing when not to know things.

He started the Bonneville and drove west, thinking. Zavala wanted out—of Los Angeles, obviously, but beyond that what, some deal with Guerra? He drummed the steering wheel. Jessica he did *not* understand; Zavala didn't seem the type, and traveling with a two year old he'd be spotted, where he could be nearly invisible alone. Yet he'd risked it. As for the someone Zavala intended to settle up with, Wil could only hope.

Diverting to uptown, he found the Japanese place near the Wiltern that had good sashimi, then took in a movie, timing it so he'd be at Niños de Mexico about five. At that, he missed his turnoff, having to backtrack to Olympic Boulevard and the brick building fronted with reddish granite that he'd cruised past the night before. It was five-twenty when he parked and put on the Shetland sport coat he'd brought along in case he had to look respectable.

The office was two stories, U-shaped around the parking lot and some liquidambar trees. Stairways led upward at the wings. Niños had the second floor—climbing the stairs, he could see its windows faced the courtyard. He pulled open the oversize door and went in.

Soothing colors met him; big-eyed brown kids smiling from lacquered frames made him think of Dev at that age. The room was divided into glass-walled offices where half a dozen people worked. As he looked around, a receptionist smiled decorously.

"Is someone expecting you?" she asked.

Wil eyed white metal files, a dark wood door at the far end of the room. He smoothed a wrinkle on the Shetland. "I was referred by Leonardo Guerra."

The receptionist regarded him. "Mr. Guerra isn't here right now. Would you like to see one of our counselors?"

"Please."

She spoke into the phone, and a severe-looking woman he pegged as late fifties appeared from a forward cubicle. Handkerchief points rose like alps on her gray suit; graying hair was tidily upswept; rimless glasses bit the bridge of her nose. She introduced herself as Mrs. Contreras, then motioned him inside the enclosure and gestured to a seat opposite the black lacquer table she was using as a desk. On the high-gloss tabletop was a yellow tablet and a silver ballpoint.

"You're seeking to adopt, Mr.—?" She picked up the pen.

"Hardesty," he said, seating himself. "My wife and I find the concept of adopting very, um—appropriate."

Mrs. Contreras wrote on her pad, then looked up. "Mr. Hardesty, I'm sure you're aware our children come from Mexico. They are generally from mothers who cannot support them or from families for whom another child would be an extreme hardship. As far as age is concerned, they are newborn up to perhaps twelve." Her words had the staccato ring of ice cubes dropped into a bowl.

Wil said, "If they look anything like the posters, I'll take a dozen."

Mrs. Contreras managed a weak smile. "They are beautiful, aren't they? And so loving. I must reiterate, however, that these are not Anglo children, even though most of our adoptive parents are. Sometimes there are difficulties. I will take your continued presence to mean that a child of Mexican ancestry is not a problem for you. By the way, what nationality is your wife?"

Operating by feel now: "Mexican is not a problem, my wife is Japanese, and we have no children." He closed an opening. "But artificial means are so impersonal."

The thaw was noticeable. "I *am* glad to hear you say that. Our way gives you choice without the risk of childbirth, plus the assurance that you have given existing life a chance."

"Mrs. Contreras, your receptionist said you'd acquaint me with the requirements."

"Jennette, please," she said. "First, you must truly want a *niño*. That we ascertain in a series of interviews. Second, you must be referred by someone who has adopted one of our children. Then there is a financial requirement. I must warn you it is no small sum, yet it will complete your life in a way mere money cannot."

He said, "Would a referral from Leonardo Guerra suffice?"

"I'm sure you know the answer to that, Mr. Hardesty."

"Well, then," he smiled, "the interviews are no problem. What about the money?"

Mrs. Contreras narrowed her eyes. "Our adoptive parents express their thanks for our confidentiality and response in the amount of fifty-thousand dollars—most equitable, all things considered."

Equitable for whom? Wil thought. "Confidentiality, Mrs. Contreras. Tell me about that."

"I'm sure you can appreciate what that means to prospective parents merely by looking at recent events. Birth parents suing to reclaim their rights, countersuits from those who have, in good faith, adopted. Hearts broken, emotions trampled in the media. Even worse, children played like pawns in some awful game.'' She sighed. ''Such unpleasantness is not our way, Mr. Hardesty, you may be assured.''

''You also mentioned response. I assume you mean fast?'' Through the glass walls Wil could see staff members putting on their coats.

Jennette Contreras removed her glasses, leaving red indentations where they'd been. She began polishing them on lens-cleaning paper. ''Most adoptions are long, dreary affairs; some take years. Ours do not, and we find our clients most appreciative.''

''One happy customer after another,'' Wil said. ''How is it you can succeed where others can't?''

''I'll just say, Mr. Hardesty, that we know our business. As yet no one has been disappointed.'' From a file cabinet she withdrew printed materials. ''Under the terms, we require half the fee in advance; with that we begin the process. The final half is due upon delivery.'' She handed the paperwork over. ''The completion of these forms and your initial payment indicate a desire to proceed.''

As he took them, she tore the top sheet off her notepad, then checked her watch. ''Forgive me, but I must prepare for an appointment. Next time, perhaps, your wife—'' She thrust her chin up expectantly.

''My wife certainly will be part of this. Thank you, Mrs. Contreras, we'll be in touch.''

She saw him to the door. ''Mr. Hardesty, your relationship with Mr. Guerra . . . You are fortunate, he takes an interest in very few individual cases anymore.''

''Some kind of guy, isn't he? I can't wait to thank him in person.'' The door eased shut behind him.

Six-forty and dark outside, stars showing through broken clouds; a cold breeze searched the liquidambars for dead leaves. Wil backed the Bonneville out, drove a block west on the boulevard, turned left, and circled around behind a coffee shop that afforded a view of the brick building.

Stan's Café was humid and uncrowded and smelled of things frying; across the windows holiday greetings unfolded like paper dolls. Wil nodded to the cashier, found a window booth with a relatively clean Formica top. A brown-eyed waitress moved in.

"What's good?" he asked her.

She winked. "Besides me? Well, the meat loaf ain't too bad, kinda fifties style with mashed potatoes and stuff. You wanna give it a shot?"

Texas, Wil guessed from her accent. "My life's in your hands."

"Not yet, but it could be." She poured him coffee, winked again, left to put his order up.

He adjusted the window blinds; with the ground floor empty and the staff gone, the white Camry had to be Jennette's. It was still in the lot when his food arrived.

"*Voilà.* A work of Stan." The girl waited for him to appreciate her humor. "Not a work of Art, get it?"

Wil cracked a grin. "You bring joy to meat loaf"—he checked her name tag—"Cindy."

"Bet your buns," she said, moving off.

He scanned the materials Mrs. Contreras had given him, recalling a cousin who'd adopted a Korean boy. The whole thing had taken forever, driven them crazy. Niños circumvented that, if he believed their literature. He stuck the paperwork back in his jacket and focused on dinner; as he was finishing, Cindy brought him a slice of pie on the house.

"There's more where that came from," she said.

Thanks, Stan, he thought. Watching her take away the dishes, he almost missed the black Mercedes pulling in and Leonardo Guerra getting out of it. Guerra stretched, moved unhurriedly toward the stairs, passed out of sight, then reemerged on the balcony. He was heading for the oversize door when Wil lost him behind the corner of the building.

Working late—so what? Still, he felt a tingle of anticipation.

"What's caught your eye there, sugar?" Cindy said, refilling him. "You are glued to that window."

"Afraid I'd lose all control if I didn't distract myself."

"Well, at least you're a cute liar. They come in here sometimes."

"I'm sorry?"

"The people from that building over there. The gals are pretty nice, except for this weird one I call Ice Maiden. Comes in with a guy looks like Ricky Ricardo." Her eyes narrowed. "You some kinda undercover type?"

Wil smiled. "How about another piece of that pie?"

"I love it when y'all say that. Hang on to your fork."

This time the pie came à la mode, the mode on Stan, Wil figuring Stan was going to go broke unless he left soon. Nibbling made it last thirty minutes; at nine, two people showed on the balcony, reappeared downstairs, walked to the cars. Guerra opened his trunk, lifted out a suitcase and put it in Jennette's trunk. Jennette drove away. Guerra unwrapped a cigar, lit it, smoked awhile, then got into the Mercedes. Wil could see the glowing tip as the black SEL cruised past the coffee shop.

He gave it till nine-twenty, laid two tens on the table, then made for the cashier, feeling awash in coffee and leaden with Stan's cooking, which was precipitating a culture war with the sashimi from earlier. Cindy blew him a kiss, then he was outside.

After a stop at the car, where he changed back into the dark leather field jacket, Wil angled across the street. To shake dinner down, he took in an extra block, was feeling better as he entered the alley that ran parallel to Olympic. Save for some leaves the wind had rustled up, the lot was empty. Luckily it was poorly lit, and he was able to make the exposed patch in relative darkness. From there it was up the stairs and a crawl along the balcony to the big door, feeling around for burglar alarm wiring.

Nothing.

He extracted his B&E tools from a zippered inside pocket and rationalized the risk. Paul-Zavala-Guerra, gut-feel connected: deadly coincidence bolstered by an old murder—Guerra's foreman—and a name in a notebook. After a few sweaty minutes the big door clicked open, and he edged his way inside.

No buzzing, ringing, blinking. He got out a small flash, mouthed it to free his hands, then started on the file cabinets—locked but easy to breach. Not exactly sure what he was looking for, he picked through files dating back to 1980, found forms, client statements, documents issued by Mexican and American authorities. Each file held snapshots of white ecstatic couples holding brown bewildered children. After a few minutes of looking, he found the older files, minus the '66 through '68s Vella's team had taken. Wil scanned them, found nothing different from the ones he'd rifled. This time, he jotted down a few of the names with addresses and phone numbers.

Thirty minutes gone.

Discounting the cubicles, he went straight to the main event, began working with the picks. This one was a bitch, but after ten minutes the dark door to the private office yielded and he stepped inside: white carpet and couch, rosewood desk, framed masks lining one wall. On a pedestal, a contemporary sculpture reflected the flash.

Old-looking statues about ten inches high regarded him from a display case. A closer look ID'd them as similar to one he'd noticed in Father Martin's bookcase, leis of cowrie shells the common element. Antiquities, Guerra'd said. He was making for the desk when he saw the red eye of a motion sensor blinking at him from the ceiling.

Shit. The question was, how long had he got? Upstairs, hemmed in by two easily blocked exits, dick for hanging around. Still, he had to try—if there were anything here to find, Guerra would almost certainly move it after a break-in. Praying someone had fallen asleep at the monitor, Wil checked his watch: ten minutes, no more.

He was through the three drawers on the left in four: Guerra Imports stationery, drawer phone, directories—one for Hermosillo—an unopened package of computer disks, a box of cigars.

The right side was locked but worth the gamble, he decided; after an anxious minute the lock gave, releasing both drawers. The deep-bottom one contained various dividers: Niños de Mexico, Amigos de Hermosillo, miscellaneous names. Concentrating on Niños, Wil found files similar to the others: Guerra's personal interest cases. He wrote down the names of three: Toluca Lake, Bel Air, and Pasadena. Another three minutes gone.

The top right drawer seemed to be for things awaiting filing. Faceup was a nine-by-twelve envelope that had been rolled and smoothed out, ''Niños de Mexico'' penciled on the front. One edge was sliced cleanly off; inside were stats of twelve baptismal certificates, three of which matched the last names of the three files he'd noted.

They were signed by Father Martin DeSantis, Pastor, St. Boniface.

He slid them back, shuffled through the rest of the drawer, hit bottom and a Metro section of the *L.A. Times*— which could have been saved for any number of reasons except for the date, the morning after the night Paul Rodriguez was murdered. Wil remembered the section, confirmed it with a quick look inside.

Ten minutes gone: a what-the-fuck glance into Guerra's rosewood trash basket, empty except for a tangled wad of register receipts stuck to the bottom, which tore as he lifted it out. Shoving it in his pocket, he replaced everything, hurriedly wiped the desk, then backed out past the blinking light. Twelve minutes after entering Guerra's office, he was outside as a car pulled up and doors slammed.

Seconds from a bust: If he jumped from the middle of the balcony, he'd land directly in their line of fire; if he waited, they'd cover him where he stood. Getting shot was out of the question. So was getting nailed—Freiman would have his ass and his license and the whole enchilada.

Wil mounted the wrought-iron railing, leaped for the overhang: quietly up and over the eave and onto the roof, thankful for tar paper without rocks. He lay there barely breathing as the two converged on the big door below. There was a jangle of keys, whispered commands. The door opened, he could hear them moving inside. He rose and made for the right stairway; outer office covered by now, he guessed, just opening the inner door. With nothing tossed and nobody there, they might blame a short—another electronic gremlin, check it out in the morning.

From the shadows at the edge of the building, Wil dropped to the outside rail, to the stairs, then down past the car: a security firm—scrambled from home base, which explained the time. As he tracked the dark safety of the alley, he could see the beams of their big Magnalites stabbing out through the trees.

EIGHTEEN

The day had been *mierda*, the aroma of soiled diapers well suited to the degenerating tenor of their confrontation. First there was Bolo's incredible macho stupidity in revealing himself to Hardesty—something Bolo insolently shrugged off, but which may have doomed them all. Then this new thing with the child. Leonardo Guerra sank back in the leather chair, thirty-year-old Funtador offering scant solace for Bolo's insufferable strut, the words that still rang in his ears:

"Whose do you think she is, goddammit? Find room!"

He felt like a man sinking inch by inch into quicksand.

He drained the brandy, was feeling nothing from it when the security company phoned. Yes, they had responded. No, they'd found no one. Yes, it could have been a false trip— even the best devices were subject to hiccups. Nothing disturbed, nothing to worry about; they'd be by in the morning to check it out. Sorry to bother him.

Son of a *bitch*—would this day never end?

He started to pace. If there *was* a breach, it would have been right after Hardesty had been by the office asking questions and using his name, the intrusion too close to be coincidence. Assuming the worst, he wondered how long the man had been inside his office.

On the other hand, what would Hardesty have found? Guerra thought about possible compromises, rejecting each, knowing the weight he gave such matters, concern that accounted in no small measure for his success. He unwrapped another cigar. This evening, he deserved a second.

He lit it and blew a smoke ring. Very soon now, Hardesty would be old news. But that damn Zavala, his nose leading his head around . . . then the idea hit. For a moment he puzzled with it, adding form and substance. Could it? If it did, even the child might not be the liability it first seemed. Perhaps, rather, a blessing in disguise.

Savoring the symmetry of his thought, Leonardo Guerra laid down the unsmoked half of his cigar. Moderation in all things, he reminded himself. Except, perhaps, in certain areas. He drained the rest of the brandy, and with quickening pulse set off down the hall toward Julio's room.

The burning started at Wilshire. Heading up the San Diego freeway toward the Ventura, Wil flipped open the glove box, palmed a pack of Di-Gel and popped two, waiting for his stomach to calm after a night of coffee shop meat loaf and illegal entry. Around Whitehurst he began to feel better. Under his sweater, the damp T-shirt stuck like Saran Wrap.

Friday night traffic was comforting, a moving blanket after being so vulnerable. Past the Valley, however, it began to thin, reminding him of what he faced at home. He could rig the house to prevent surprise, but outside he'd have no such advantage—Zavala could pick the spot and the time.

He steered his thoughts back to Guerra's office, devil's-advocating what he'd found: nothing really, a piece of newspaper. If Guerra'd clipped or highlighted the article, perhaps. But there was nothing unusual in his saving an entire section—not that he could prove. Not yet.

The baptismal certificates were curiously single-sourced, but again, hardly damning. He wondered how many of the files contained St. Boniface paper, found himself wanting another crack at them. Enough to break in again? The thought made him pop a third antacid.

Despite it, Wil felt a twinge as he slowed past Mussel Shoals for the turnoff. He unsnapped the .45, gripped it on the seat beside him, every familiar ditch, tree, parked car now threatening. At the driveway he maneuvered the Bonneville, probing the unlighted carport with its beams. He hit Park and slumped down; opening the side door, he rolled out onto damp gravel and came up sweeping an arc with the gun.

Ten seconds, twenty, thirty. Nothing. Pulse thumping, he ran for the stairs and inched across the landing to the door. Anyone looking must love this, he thought. He'd explain in the morning: just practicing.

Stupid not to leave lights burning—or had he? He unlocked the door, pulled it open to still air and silence. Tossing his keys into the dark interior for diversion, he slipped against an inside wall, then pushed off, seeking cover from better-adjusted eyes. Seconds passed, the house dead quiet. Wil crawled to a light switch and flipped it on. All seemed in order until he saw himself on the floor.

The photo was the torn half of a snapshot he recognized from Paul's den, Wil and Paul at Cam Ranh Bay. He aimed the gun at the dark hall, knowing instinctively he'd have been dead had Zavala been there. With manic intensity he checked bedrooms, den, bathrooms, returning finally to the photograph, this time spotting the other half under the table.

Reuniting the pieces, he studied the poses, their confident looks. That's how Zavala had known Paul—busted into his house, made him from the snapshot. Paul had walked right into it. Now Zavala was spelling it out for him: *Fuck you, I'm here. Close.* Wanting him to know it was coming.

After a while he remembered the Bonneville and moved it into the carport. Then he killed the house lights that were making him an easy target and slumped down in a chair. *Another time*. Fine. He'd get the bastard. Here was where it stopped.

He made coffee and settled down to wait.

• • •

Lisa caught him early, before she left for a client meeting. Her parents were glad for the company; she was busy, curious about Zavala, missed him, wanted to come home. Hold tight, he told her—nothing about the torn photograph.

He made a pot of high octane, drank it while staring at the Saturday overcast, then showered, put on jeans, sweatshirt, holster, and started on the house: slats positioned in the rails of things that slid, wood wedges under things that opened. He wired electrical cord to door handles so that anyone trying them when they were plugged in got zapped. The remainder of the wire he'd zigzag around the stairs before turning in. Finally, he hung a couple of trouble lights at spots not covered by the outdoor floods.

It would have to do.

At eleven Staff Sergeant Tommy Rodriguez of Lackland Air Force Base called from Raeann's: They would bury his father's ashes Tuesday and wanted Wil and Lisa there. As Wil confirmed it, his eyes dropped to the patched-up snapshot. He asked about Raeann.

"She's okay, Mr. Hardesty," Tommy said. "Pretty close to going back to San Antonio with me." He said good-bye and hung up.

Around two Wil slipped outside, cut through yards to the mini-market where he bought basics and a half-dozen burgers to go, back in about forty minutes. Halfway up the stairs, someone was leaning against the house. Black pants and shoes—tapping, restless.

Wil set down the bag, pulled the .45 from under his jacket, thumbed off the safety, and crept to the corner of the house. On the stairs the pants shifted position slightly. He got a two-handed grip on the gun, then whipped around the corner in a police crouch. Mo Epstein just looked at him.

"Fort Hardesty, I presume," he said.

He was thin in the face and pale. Wil backed off the hammer, said, "How can someone look so shitty and so good at the same time?'' Unlocking the door, he told him about Zavala.

Mo zeroed in on the Cam Ranh photo.

"I just got off the phone with Paul's son," Wil said. "Everything's fine at Raeann's. No reason Zavala'd go back."

Mo picked up the phone and requested surveillance. "You never know," he said. "Might figure he'd catch you down there." After the call, he reviewed Wil's homemade security system. "Nice thought, anyway. Any idea when this creep's coming?"

"Tonight or tomorrow. He'll give me time to burn out a little, get careless."

"Real *mano a mano* guy, Zavala."

"It's why he's vulnerable, Mo."

"We'll talk about that. My being here doesn't mean I approve."

As they ate burgers, Wil rehashed details of Donna Pacheco's beating and her daughter's abduction, most of which Epstein knew. He leaned back, the eyebrow lifted. "The woman's lucky to be alive. You told the good guys about Zavala's little visit here?"

"No."

"Freiman hears the hard way, he'll shit."

"That's his problem."

"Listen to yourself. *High Noon* is a movie, pal. This is real life, and you agreed to Freiman's deal, remember?"

Wil's temper slipped before he could jam it. "Zavala nearly cut Paul's head off in a goddamn bar while I listened. Fuck Freiman." Cool it, he told himself. "Mo, it's way beyond that. It's our best shot."

"Sure, and what's to lose? Only you, Jessica, the Innocents bust for certain."

"We can stop him."

Epstein snapped his fingers. "Like that I can put a shooter in every closet. Tell me why not."

"He won't hurt the baby," Wil said. "But he will bolt

for Mexico with her the second he spots a trap. Smart says we take him when he comes for me. Then save Jessica.''

"And you'll have taken out your man. Very neat. What does Lisa have to say about it?''

Wil turned on him. "This thing has to play itself out, and you know it. Are you in or not?''

Mo Epstein stood and paced across the room; his voice was glacial. "You'd better hope you're right on this. Because if you're not, we're both going in the shitter.'' He picked up his burger. "Where's the nearest supermarket? I ain't livin' on these all weekend.''

Mo Epstein dumped grocery bags on the counter, his hair and jacket glistening from the trip out. From the window Wil nodded, then turned back, seeing only gray where the oil platforms and the Rincon had been. Christmas strings threw colored halos; cars already had their headlights on.

"Now wouldn't be a bad time for it,'' Wil said.

Mo put a couple of frozen dinners in the microwave, tossed Wil a soda, paper-toweled off. "How you want to play this, *mon capitan?*''

Wil thought. "Split the watch, front and bedrooms, rotate posts. It'll keep us awake.''

They ate, then loaded clips and checked pistol actions. Wil cut the house lights, opened the blinds; they split up and settled down to wait. Outside, drizzle sparkled in the floods.

"By the way,'' Mo said from darkness, "the lab turned up an unsmudged thumb on one of the pool cues and a partial palm on the table. Matched the prints we got from Mexico and the Feds. They're turning cartwheels.''

"No more doubts, huh?''

"You know what I mean.''

"Sure.''

Steady drip metronomed the hours; at eight the drizzle became rain, making it harder to detect foreign sounds. Wil broke silence. "Mo?" A low grunt from the gloom. "This may sound odd."

"What could be more normal than this?"

He hesitated. "It's not adding up for me—Zavala, I mean, and the kids in the desert. At least not Zavala alone."

There was a sigh. "Are we talking about the same guy? Where's this coming from?"

"Something Montoya told me: Nobody who fathered a child could kill this way."

"Old murders," Mo came back. "He's only been a father for two years."

"So far as we know," Wil said. "But it's a good point, and I don't have an answer, just instinct and Donna Pacheco. She swears he's no child killer. Even after Zavala took Jess, she never mentioned thinking the kid's life was in danger, only that she was gone."

"From what you said, she was pretty spaced. I know the feeling."

"She's still the kid's mother, Mo. And she told me most of that before he beat her up."

"Sorry—what seems to be is usually what is, the blinding flash of the obvious. Or maybe it's that this guy's got a bead on me right now." After a moment of quiet he added, "What do you mean, 'at least not Zavala alone'?"

Wil told him about Paul, St. Boniface, Father Martin. "I think Guerra fingered Paul for Zavala," he said. "Nothing I can prove."

"Then you think this priest lied?"

"I don't know. But Paul slipped up once before, and if Guerra did pass it on, he got it from somebody."

"You wanna relate that back to the Innocents for me?"

"Would if I could, Mo."

"Yeah—our strong suit right now."

Wil drew in a breath, listened to not much of anything: night noises, dripping sounds. "Dev used to like the rain," he mused. "Funny how I keep expecting him to come padding down the hall. Even now." Suddenly he felt the need to say it: "You remember when I poked that deputy, Mo. He was right about me letting Devin surf there. It *was* dangerous."

"Come on, living is dangerous. He'd surfed there before. He was good—you wouldn't have taken him otherwise."

"The bottom line is I didn't protect my son."

"Because you couldn't protect your son and let him have a life. That's at the heart of it with Lisa? No more kids because you can't ensure their safety?"

"I can't go through life terrified for them, Mo, it won't work. For a kid *or* for me."

"Terrified—"

"Of it happening again. You get that? Lisa doesn't."

"It's your call, man. I ain't been there, but—"

"I have."

"So what happens now?"

In the dark, Wil rubbed his eyes. "With Lisa? I don't know—play it by ear, I guess."

At dawn they agreed to spell each other sleeping. Later the wind freshened and the rain stopped, cloud cover breaking into fast-moving cumuli. Neighbors did Sunday things; kids played with dogs. By evening they'd finished the last of the frozen entrées.

"Guerra," Mo said suddenly, "I forgot to tell you what we found out, probably because he's been a very good boy up here. Even the Niños files checked out. Guy's a pillar—active in service clubs, helps the church, pays his taxes."

"You left out clever," Wil said. "Wives or relatives?"

"Never been married."

"Any chance that someone at your place might have tipped him about Angel's?"

Mo gave him a skeptical look. "Vella did notify the other police departments that we'd be in their jurisdictions—you know, protocol. Seems a hell of a stretch, but I can nose around."

"Probably nothing," Wil said, tossing his paper plate in the trash.

"You figure this guy for tonight?"

Wil nodded.

"Yeah," Mo said, looking out. "Me, too."

Too much caffeine and too little action, three to five had been especially tense. But now light was showing in the east and their piranha snappishness was easing. Zavala would have hit by now if he were coming—chased, they figured, by too much heat and too little time.

Wil stood a last watch while Mo readied himself for L.A., then Epstein stayed on duty while Hardesty slept. At eleven Mo woke him with, "Great weekend. Especially the food." He jammed the last of his things into his duffel bag. "Keep in touch, chum, and I'll do the same. What Freiman doesn't know won't hurt him."

From the window, Wil watched Mo's car turn southward, lost it past the Shoals, then cast an eye north. Not bad conditions. He checked the scope, thought he saw Gringo out there. After three nightmare days and the sun out and Zavala in flight, he was ready.

Deliberating whether or not to pack heat, he rolled up the .45 and four clips in a spare towel, put them in his beat-up ice chest, and locked the door behind him. The fresh air tasted clean and big and salty and it mussed his hair. Taking it in, he felt like a convict loose after hard time.

NINETEEN

Bolo Zavala watched the white car cross the tracks and swing north. First the other man and now Hardesty, no telling how long he'd be gone. Follow or break in and wait? Two days already shot thanks to the other *cabrón*—a cop probably—not that he hadn't had his chance. He'd fucked up leaving the photo in there. By now Donna'd probably given him up. Should have done her when he had the chance.

A snort of cocaine snapped his head back.

It was getting crazy: Donna, the baby, Lenny. Where else did Lenny think he'd take his kid? The thought reminding him he had to get back. *Fucking time!* He hit the other nostril and it all came into focus. Lenny didn't know it, but his time was up; soon as he came back for the baby, he'd settle up with Lenny. Fuck Lenny's file and his threats and his contacts, there were places he knew.

Vida nueva. Almost there.

His eyes followed the white car and its driver. The knife would have been so much more satisfying. But he had the Llama with the silencer and an AK-47 he was pretty good with.

Passing the banana plantation: now or never.

With a shower of mud and gravel, Zavala shot the IROC out of hiding and onto the freeway. Distance melted; he saw the white car pull off and cautiously followed it into the parking lot marked Rincon. At the opposite end, Hardesty nosed into a space next to a rusty pickup; Zavala watched him unload a longboard and a cooler and make for the trail.

It hit him like a jolt of the flake: The *cabrón* was a surfer—better still, a bird in a shooting gallery—thinking he was safe, that Bolo Zavala had gone slinking away like a dog. *Guess again.* He stuck the pistol under his jacket and started for the trail, minutes later spotting groups of spectators watching the action, but no Hardesty.

He was in the water. It would be the rifle.

Too public where he was, however; around the point a creek offered cover, but it was too far from the action, though it did lead back to the parking lot. A clump of bushes faced the surfline; behind them, green lawn and a house. He cased the property. No one there—maybe his luck was back.

He approached a group of young men in bright wet suits waxing their boards. "Which is Hardesty?" he asked. "I was told he is one to watch."

They ignored him, so he asked again, sharpening his tone this time. One, expressionless in iridescent wraparounds, pointed out to a group of surfers waiting for a wave. "Longboard, red stripe crossed by blue. Dude's wearing a black wet suit. You can't miss him."

Got that right, *chico*. He felt like turning the pistol on them. Never worked a day in their worthless fucking lives—at their age he was bleeding in smoky arenas for pesos. He started to go, stopped. Curious in spite of himself.

The figure caught the wave, swept down it, let it curl over him, then burst free. Casual moves, a flip, and the board was pointed back toward the line of incoming breakers.

Bolo Zavala spat, turned toward the IROC and what was in the trunk. Picking his way over the streambed, he noticed the jet trails pointing north. They were like white tracers, sharp contrast against the sky's depthless blue.

They'd finished a run when Gringo brought it up.

"Crankin' out there," he said. "Think you could handle this baby?" Grinning at Wil, "Nah, I guess not."

Wil swung wet hair out of his eyes. "That popgun? Come on, get serious."

They were sitting on their surfboards, feet dangling in the water. Catching their breath as the surge rolled past beneath them. "One way to find out," Gringo said. "Deal is, whoever has the most dumps on the other's board buys the brew—winner's choice."

Wil looked at him. "Your brew against my cheeseburger?"

"Oh, right. You ever get a yen for the old days?"

Closing too many bars with Gringo came back like the mornings after. "Fall down and throw up, you mean? Listen, I'm sorry about Pam's leaving."

"Yeah. So what's life without barf? We on here or what?"

"You must like taking gas," Wil said.

Gringo's expression twisted to a smirk. "Fall off something that big? Give it up, Kahuna."

"Don't say I didn't warn you."

Wil handed him his leash, took Gringo's, and they headed out. First runs were dicey, the waves radical overheads that started early and finished late. Wil found the thruster much quicker than he anticipated and oversteered, then watched Gringo having control problems with the longboard. They wiped out here, bailed there, before getting the hang of it. At length Wil kicked out of a wave near Gringo and paddled over.

"This thing's wild, but I'm gonna feel it tomorrow," he said. "One more, then swap back."

"If I can borrow the barge again sometime."

"You passed. C'mon, rock and roll." Muscles complaining, Wil paddled toward the point.

Bolo Zavala wrapped the assault rifle in his jacket and made his way back down the creekbed, cutting in this time at a secluded path between houses. So far he'd been lucky. Spectators crowded the beach, nobody leaving or arriving; to his right and through a gate he saw the patch of green, the bushes beyond. He entered, prepared now to kill anyone who got in his way.

The foliage was good cover—luxuriant growth six feet high. The only drawback was he could be seen from the house, something he'd deal with if it happened. He unwrapped the rifle, settled in, turned his attention to the pointbreak, for a moment panicking, realizing then his target had taken a previous swell. He used the time to line up another rider, watching the black suit raise up, gather momentum, angle right to left. Damn, he'd have to be quick. It was in his field of fire only briefly, then was gone, too distant for a sure kill. Crucial to anticipate.

Off to his left he saw the big board slicing back out.

Gringo beat him but waited, letting a couple of half-baked ones go by. Wil caught up and they sat facing the incoming sets, wanting picture-perfect, dream-session water. Three passed, then four, and there it was: forming out beyond the others, keeping its shape, promising the moon. They bellied down, and then it was on them.

Gringo, up the line, took it first, glancing back to hoot-salute.

Two seconds behind, Wil saw the bright bloom, saw Gringo jerk upright and pitch forward off the longboard. Hearing the pops, seeing the flashes and the waterspouts, he dove for the safety of the water as the big wave heaved away to spend itself.

He gave it thirty seconds, then surfaced. The shooting had stopped; from the beach came frantic scattering, thin screams. He twisted back, scanning, scanning, seeing Gringo then, facedown in a trough, arms out as though conducting some underwater orchestra. A few yards away, the Southern Cross tugged at Gringo's leg. Urging him on.

Sonofabitch-sonofabitch-sonofabitch—

Wil made up the yards between them in seconds: The exit wound had blown away half of Gringo's forehead; he lay sprawled on the surface, his long hair a red jellyfish in the rising-falling water. Wil shouted to the beach, to the others, anyone who'd hear. *"The fuck was that?"* said the first surfer to reach him. Until he saw Gringo.

With difficulty they got him up on the longboard and headed in, coffin-carried the board ashore. A crowd formed around the body. Gringo had the vacant look of someone wondering where everything had gone.

Wil stood a minute, fighting nausea, doubled over from the exertion, then found his towel, placed it over the shattered head. Some time later—he wasn't sure how long—four sheriff's deputies picked their way over the rocks. He put a hand over his eyes, feeling enraged and responsible and despondent in no particular order.

"You know this fella?"

He looked up at a hawk-nosed man with a dark crew cut and non-committal eyes, the tag reading Sgt. Jim Dietrich. Unlike the uniforms, he was dressed in corduroys and a windbreaker.

Wil nodded.

"He got a name?"

"Adams . . . Jared," Wil said, struggling to remember it. "Goes by Gringo. He's an occasional carpenter, odd jobs. Lives in La Conchita—he has a trailer there."

Dietrich began penciling in a small notebook. "And who might you be?"

Wil told him, waited for Dietrich to quit writing, said, "My ID's in the cooler there cabled to that log." He fumbled for the key.

Dietrich handed it to a deputy, who undid the lock and

brought it over. They went through it, then Dietrich looked up. "Not everybody surfs so well armed. You expect this?"

"No, Sergeant, but I am on a case." He rubbed his temples, weary of knots in his gut.

"Don't overwhelm me with details," Dietrich said. "For instance what this guy did that made somebody take him out like that. And why you really came to the beach with a .45, extra bullets and all. We can do this easy or hard— your choice."

Wil looked past him. By now the deputies had pushed the crowd back from the body and were examining the ambush site. A siren growled down, a gurney bumped toward them; nearby a flash unit went off. At the eye of it, Gringo looked oddly neglected.

It was getting all too familiar. "Easy," Wil said.

They sat in Dietrich's sedan as the deputies reported. No one got a look at the killer, the gallery freaking at the sound of gunfire, although a couple in the parking lot did spot a guy running for a dark blue Camaro/Firebird/One-of-Those. No reason to remember the license, just that he'd wasted no time leaving. A deputy went to radio the CHP.

Sunlight danced on restless leaves.

Wil ran through the whole thing, after which Dietrich contacted Vella and Epstein for verification. A sticking point was Hardesty's judgment. "Wonder nobody else was hit," Dietrich griped at him. "You got a killer on your tail, and you not only play it alone, you bring your grief here. Jesus Christ."

Wil said nothing; there was no arguing the point. Freiman doubtless would come to the same conclusion. And Lisa. "You need me here?" he said.

"Don't go far," Dietrich said coldly. "And don't forget your artillery."

Halfway to Santa Paula, Bolo heard the scanner's first calls. The net was forming; no surprise there, he knew he'd been spotted. Already he'd ragged down and tossed the AK-47 into a drainage ditch; if found, it was untraceable and no great loss, plenty more around. A more serious problem was the car. The IROC was out of time.

Nosing off 126, he began to scout for wheels. Downtown Santa Paula was busy with holiday shoppers, so he cased side streets until he found it parked by a restored bungalow. The old Dart was perfect, the For Sale sign meaning it probably ran. With luck it wouldn't be missed until the owner got home; couple of hours to L.A., then he'd switch again.

He parked in the alley behind the Dart house. Grabbing his jacket and the nine millimeter, he was ready to do it when the car phone buzzed.

"Where are you?" The tone was impatient.

"Safe enough," he said. "There were problems, but it's done now." In the earpiece he heard an expulsion of breath.

"Bolo, Bolo—it was on the radio. You got the wrong man, a friend or something. Come in. *Now.*"

"Que—?" His head felt light; heat started in his gut like a boiler firing.

"I said you missed, goddammit. Open your fucking ears."

He barely heard. The *cabrón* was dead. He'd seen it— the board, the figure in the sights, the hit. He twisted the key, thumbed in AM, flipped around until he hit a newscast.

"—occurred about forty-five minutes ago. Dead at the scene was a twenty-five-year-old part-time carpenter, identified by another La Conchita resident, Sean Wilson Hardesty. Authorities are searching for a late-model dark blue Camaro seen leaving the Rincon. No motive has been established yet for the slaying—"

How? The lightness became a roaring that blocked the newscast, Lenny's voice, the car, the need to flee. The heat went acid, stabbing his diaphragm. *How was it possible?*

"Going back," he managed to say.

"Bad enough you let the woman live, Bolo. Don't make it worse."

"Bolo will not be made a fool of."

"Too late for that, my friend."

He found the inhaler, two hard pulls. "La Conchita," he said. They'd never look for him there, so close. "I will finish this thing and be back tonight."

Guerra softened his tone. "Listen to me. They're watching the roads, they know the car. Now is not safe. Not smart."

Motherfucker: Lenny was a dead man. "*You* listen," he said. "I will kill this bastard and then I will come for my *niña. Comprende, patrón?*" He heard Lenny say something else, but it made no difference, there would be no more listening. He wiped down the IROC, left it with the keys in. Somebody stole it, so much the better.

Two minutes to swipe the Dart, roughly the time it took to backtrack west, orange trees blurring as he gained speed. Fucking luck—losing his touch if he didn't know better. Hardesty he'd fix—sever the link, erase the threat. But a flood, for Christ's sake. And the medal. If only he could remember: *Benito-Benito-Benito-Benito*—as usual, nothing. Slowing for the turn north; sure enough, black-and-whites tearing east. Restaurant on the left, Hungry something. Hungry, all right—enough to scarf the menu with room left over.

Smoke poured from the Dart's tires, and it slewed sickeningly before he controlled the skid. Stopped there on the fringe, heart pumping, he hit the inhaler as he'd hit the brakes. *The goddamn menu.* It had been there all along at the fat one's house, the name on the note: Reyes, the family who owned the restaurants. Ignacio Reyes. He tried to picture the man, came up with tall and gaunt-looking, nothing much else. No matter—Reyes was as dead now as *el cabrón.*

What to do? No phone in the clunker and no time to find

one. In a short while, however, all the time in the world.

Finally he would finish it with Leonardo Guerra.

Wil leaned against the Bonnie, tilted the bottle, and knocked back another slug of Jack Daniel's. *Fuck it!* Below where he'd parked, waves boomed, their constancy reminding him only of broken promises.

Fuck 'em!

He took another belt, conscious of the fire in his upper gut and a spreading shame fed by guilt and his failures. The bourbon made his mind loop: Paul, whose ashes they'd bury tomorrow; Gringo, who had nobody much to care what happened to him; himself, casualty of a battle he hadn't yet figured out. Some detective. Just don't stand too close.

He thought about calling Lisa, decided to tell her at home. Around five he slowly backed the car down the bluff, turned it around, and pointed it south. Still in the wet suit, he ached for a hot shower, ached to scrub it all off, settled for more whiskey.

He passed the Rincon, feeling Gringo. Beyond the presence he'd miss, there was what Gringo represented—freer times, if there were such things. Wil looked at the waves curling around the point. Just before sunset the light was gold, the water translucent as it foamed up the beach and rolled back. As he made the left turn, the setting sun blazed from La Conchita's windows.

Pretty some other time.

In the carport he capped the bottle, raised the trunk, lifted out the Southern Cross. Among the scratches and dents from rocks was a shallow groove from a stray round and traces of red. He hosed it off, replaced the board in its stirrup. Grabbing the bottle of Jack, he put the ice chest under his arm and started for the stairs.

The first fusillade hit the Bonneville broadside, making a *punk, punk, punk* sound he knew at once. He scrambled for cover around the front of the car to the back, tore open the chest, and racked a round into the .45. The flashes were coming from the drainage ditch near the entrance to the tunnel. The faint coughing noise told him silencer; little doubt who was pulling the trigger.

He flattened as more rounds hit, spanging and clanking in the wheels, blowing out both rear tires. Wil squeezed off five himself; he needed better cover, but where? Everyplace he looked would put a neighbor in jeopardy. Some already were appearing on balconies and lawns.

He yelled at the closest one, saw her duck back inside. Then he dove behind the corner of the carport—still not good enough. He had to direct Zavala's attention away from the houses. Rolling to his right, he expended his remaining shots, shoved in a new clip, angled a frantic sprint toward the ditch.

Rounds sang past his head, then he was in the weeds, the line of fire now parallel with the highway. He could see the man's position, pumped his entire clip toward it. Dirt flew. Zavala slid down the ditch and ran under the railroad tracks toward the tunnel; seeing him for the first time, Wil felt a wild surge of adrenaline. Crazy, he thought—the man cutting himself off like that. Unless he had a car on the other side.

Zavala opened up from the mouth of the tunnel. Exposed now, Wil scrambled to where he could cover his advance. With the third of his clips, he drove Zavala back, firing as he ran toward the entrance. Feet pounded inside: Wil flattened and rolled, warhorse pointed toward the retreating sounds.

There—silhouetted against the sunset down the tunnel's length, halfway across, stooped over running. Wil fired all seven rounds, saw the figure stagger and fall, get up and lurch forward. Two clips left, his odds dropping: He could bang away from where he was, hoping for another hit, but if he missed, Zavala would make the other side, hold him off, counterattack, or split. Crossing above the tunnel was out, more lives put at risk in a firefight across four lanes of traffic. Wil reloaded, bolted after the stumbling figure.

He nearly made it.

Ahead, the tunnel suddenly emptied and then an arm extended back toward him. Flashes came again; bullets ricocheted. Wil hit rough damp concrete, fired to drive the arm back, then rose up zigging, making slim progress before the bullets drove him down again. Slowly he cut the distance, his shots raising acrid fog, their noise savaging his eardrums. Ten yards from the tunnel's mouth, on his last clip, the firing stopped.

Meaning what?

Wil could picture Zavala scrambling up the rocks, tires burning rubber, his own rage. Worse, the man waiting in ambush. In the sunset's afterglow he'd be an easy target.

Shit.

Wil launched himself toward the opening. The surf was loud, his breath came in gasps. Five yards, two—still no flashes; the knife, maybe: happy thought. He pressed against the south wall. Traffic jammed by overhead, and he could see shapes of the boulders supporting the roadway. He darted to the opposite side. The man was either gone or tempting fate; by now someone had to have called in. Assuming no unit was already close, a black-and-white could make Ventura-to-La Conchita in about ten minutes, fifteen at most. As if to confirm it, *reeirr-reeirr-reeirr* became audible rounding the Shoals.

Wil leaped for planking that served as a small platform outside the tunnel; twisting, he landed in a crouch facing the upslope. Zavala was there, but not the way Wil expected. He lay spread-eagled, eyes shut and head to one side, gun in his left hand. There was a hole above his left eye; another wound darkened the shirt under his open leather jacket. Wil flipped the gun away and felt the neck for a pulse.

The eyes opened.

Wil jerked, then steeled himself. Reflexes—had to be. And yet he knew the unpredictability of head wounds, believe-it-or-not survivals from Nam. He'd about given that up when the lips began to move. The voice was faint but distinct, a scratchy tape playing over and over.

"No mate a la niña, no mate a la niña, no mate a la niña, no mate a la niña—" The tape stopped.

"Who killed the children?" Wil said. "You?"

There was a cough and a struggle to speak, a focus now in the eyes. *"No más,"* Zavala said *"No más—"*

"Who, goddamn you?"

Another attempt without sound, then the eyes rolled back; this time Wil found no pulse. Slowly he stood over Bolo Zavala, over the orange hair, spotty complexion, scar. He was close to the composite, and yet he was different— less imposing somehow. Menacing the way a troublesome adolescent might be.

And then Wil locked in on the Llama automatic, the razor blade tattoo where the leather sleeve had pulled up, and he had no further illusions. All that remained were the voices of the victims of Bolo Zavala, crying in the night above the sirens closing in.

Wil laid the .45 on a rock and stepped up onto the fringe, his hands clasped over his head.

TWENTY

The cemetery lay on land a developer would die for; oaks grew there and cypress trees and, beside the bluff overlooking the ocean where the five were gathered, purple-flowered succulents. Wil parked the Harley on the downslope and walked the rest of the way, gloved hands in the pockets of his overcoat.

Worse places, he kept telling himself.

He shook hands with the caretakers and the two longtime friends of Paul's who still lived in town. After a few attempts, small talk ceased as they waited for the family to arrive.

Lisa kept her eyes on the ground.

He felt like shit. Parts that didn't ache were cut and scraped; bone-weariness and the alcohol had him floaty. Last night had been an onslaught of questions, accusations, fraying tempers, Dietrich hauling him into the Ventura County sheriff's office. Lisa waiting when they finally let him go.

Starting bad, it then got ugly. She'd heard about Gringo on the radio, been frightened, hadn't been able to reach him, didn't know if he was hurt or missing, and then the shoot-out at her own house and the not knowing until he called her from Ventura. *Goddamn him for putting her through that.* She went into the bedroom, slammed the door; he could hear her banging things. Then the banging stopped, and when she came out she was icy calm.

He'd *lied!* What had they talked about? How did he expect her to go on like that, and she didn't think she could, and she was going back to her folks until she could sort it out. He hadn't helped by lashing back at her. On her way out the driveway, she'd dug ruts in the gravel.

Gulls squealed in an updraft.

Having her look stunning today only made it worse. Her hair shone in the flat light; she carried a bouquet. He wanted to put out a hand to her. Instead he shifted his stance to ease an aching tendon, then regarded the rows of headstones, confirmation that life was short—one of the things you never quite appreciated, he thought, like a gift you couldn't take out of the box.

Paul's Chevy came over the rise and down.

What there was was over quickly. Tommy Rodriguez, in uniform and reminding Wil of a darker version of his father's Cam Ranh photograph, read something from the Bible. Lisa put the flowers down; Wil stuck a small flag he'd brought in the soft earth. The old friends, in their plaid coats and hopsack pants, embraced Raeann, then moved off. Tommy shook hands, then headed for the Chevrolet as she came over.

"Put it behind you, honey; he'd want that."

"I know, Raeann, thanks. You okay?"

She managed a smile. "Praise God for Tommy and the letters that came. I've decided to go back to Texas with him for a while. Did you know that?"

"I had a feeling," he said.

"You're welcome to use the house if you want. The key's where it always is."

"Thanks." Guessing it might comfort her, he said, "You might want to know, Zavala didn't make it."

"Later on that may mean something," she said softly. Her dark eyes lowered to the patch of grass. "He was a good man, my Paul, always stood up for me. I'd like to think you two'll come to see him once in a while." She paused. "Funny, isn't it—how you have to lose something to really appreciate it?"

She walked away without looking back.

Wil and Lisa watched the station wagon curve around and disappear. For a moment they said nothing, then she turned on him, her eyes flashing. "What's sad, Wil, is that maybe—just maybe—I could have helped. Guess we'll never know, will we?" She spun around, ran for her car, and drove away.

For a while he fixed on the spot where the black coupe had been, then he walked up the rise to the motorcycle, kick-started it, and glanced back. The scene was different from the graveyard in the desert, but the same: lonely as hell and hard to leave. He thought of Paul and the final strangled defiance coming from the car phone. Then his eyes stung, and he packed it in and left.

It came as it always did, with too much bourbon and too little sleep.

Bits and pieces out of sequence: Devin laughing, water flying off long hair he liked to swing forward and flip back; rust on aging I-beams; the sound of flatline.

Then, as though the projectionist took notice, the dream settled in at the beginning. Picketline. Named for the chest-high picket of decaying oil pier supports running out into the surf—their spot when the Rincon got crazy. Like Rincon, a right break with a rocky bottom; swells approaching in tight, regular formations. Forming up and breaking sweetly.

A succession of quick cuts then. Dev and Wil surfing together; hours later the warm sand feeling good; eating sandwiches Lisa'd packed; watching the hotdoggers get radical as the swells begin picking up; Dev wolfing his lunch, chafing to go back in until Wil relents. Them hitting the water again, everything fine until the big set hits.

"Stay here," Wil says. "Wait for me."

Dev nods. Dissolve to Wil taking the breaker in, special

moves to impress his son, looking back then, expecting to see Devin bobbing up and down where he'd left him. Suddenly the dream projector slows from twenty-four frames a second down to twelve, to Dev mouthing "Waaaaatch meeeee, Daaaaad," slow-motion distorted, him paddling to catch the biggest wave of the day in half-speed. Wil trying to shout him off it.

At first Devin makes him proud with the obvious emulation, father recognizing himself in his son's form. Then something wrong, the wave carrying the boy directly toward the picket, Dev not cutting out where he should, nobody but Wil noticing.

"NOOOOOO!" Zoom-lens close: Dev transfixed, attempting a last-second bailout. The big wave crashing through the picket, sending pieces of smashed surfboard beyond it, leaving a limp form draped over a rusted beam like overalls hung out to dry.

Here the film races, collage scenes of his frantic paddling, of taking a surge into one of the beams himself, noticing the blood only after they'd gotten Devin onto the beach and into the ambulance. Of Lisa, grim-faced, holding Dev's hand, the tubes coming out of him, of them praying. Of doctors shaking their heads. Slo-mo again: ten days, near-sleepless watches, little eternities until the machine's monotone, worse than any words telling him his son was dead.

Wil sat up drenched, snapped off the alarm, and touched the scar between his eyebrows where he'd hit the beam. Dream images decayed, his racing pulse came down slowly. He showered, put on jeans and a sweater, stuffed necessities and the Shetland sport coat into his black leather backpack. Hungry despite the hangover, he wolfed down cold leftovers as he replayed Dietrich's phone message.

On the way out, Wil's eyes took in the Bonnie: rear wheels scrap; six rounds in the right flank alone, ugly holes inside raw metal rosettes. He mounted the Harley. Five trys and a kickback later, he was headed south in cold overcast,

Devin's image forming and re-forming out beyond the windscreen.

Wil found a Styrofoam cup—glad even for coffee that smelled like asphalt—and dumped in powdered creamer. After two gulps the mix had ambushed breakfast and last night's bourbon. He put it aside and took a chair beside Mo Epstein, who for some reason was in Ventura.

"Nine o'clock," Wil said. "As requested."

Dietrich leaned against his desk. "Go back to the ambush, Hardesty, the house one," he started. "How many rounds did Zavala get off?"

Wil felt like heaving. "This has to be the fourteenth time. You don't like my answers, how about multiple choice?"

Dietrich turned red and said something about memory improving in the lockup, which was where most private dicks belonged anyway. Epstein cut if off with, "Wil, cool it. How many?"

"I don't know, as many as I fired back—about thirty. Maybe a few more, since he shot first."

"All right," Dietrich said. "Once more—he let loose from the ditch in front of the tunnel. Then what?"

"I set up in the weeds about twenty yards south and chased him with a clip. He took cover in the tunnel."

"Any reason to believe you winged him there?"

"Outside the tunnel, no."

Dietrich began to pace in the small office. "Okay, then what?"

"I could hear him running for the other side. Must have figured his ambush was trashed and wanted out." Wil leaned back; despite his acid stomach, he sipped the coffee. "He'd stolen a car, right?"

Dietrich nodded. "We found the Camaro in Santa Paula. Keep going."

"By the time I got there, he'd made it about halfway."

Mo Epstein said, "He was running okay then?"

"Like Walter Payton—at least until I fired—that's when

I saw him fall. I reloaded, he got up and ran again.'' Wil tried to get a read from Epstein, couldn't and kept on. "I pursued. We had a firefight, him from cover, me down and praying.''

"Until he stopped shooting," Dietrich said.

"Until I shot him in the head. Maybe you recall the wound.''

Dietrich stopped pacing. He began flipping his ballpoint pen—flipping it, catching it, flipping it again. "You recall seeing anybody, any parked cars?''

"No.''

"Hear any gunfire?''

"Zavala had a silencer.''

"What did you do with the other gun?''

Wil sensed a joke. "You mean the one I had up my rectum?''

"No, wiseass, the one that turned out the lights on Zavala.''

Dietrich watched the color leave Wil's face; he started pacing again. "The M.E. did the autopsy last night. Pretty obvious what happened, you got him once in the body then finished him with the head shot. Only it turned out to be not so obvious.'' He stopped pacing to pick up a file off his desk. "They found your lead under his ribs all right, would have killed him eventually. But not right then. The other bullet took care of that.''

Dietrich slapped down the file. Epstein said, "It wasn't yours; tests confirmed it. Not unless you brought along some reserve firepower.''

Wil felt a throb in his temple. "Like what, Mo? You know my forty-five.''

Dietrich waded back in. "Lieutenant Epstein already told us about that, Hardesty. What we don't know is how come Bolo Zavala had a nine-mil slug in his head.''

They spent a few minutes together outside before Epstein left to brief Freiman and Vella. Mo eyed him. "You've been busy the last couple of days," he said. "You doin' okay?"

Wil grimaced. "Beginning to think there's a nice surf shop with my name on it." He took a deep breath. "Zavala talked, Mo—not much, but some."

"You are fucking something."

"The first part was Spanish, kind of frantic and unfocused, like he thought I was someone else. *'No mate a la niña'*—Don't kill the girl—over and over."

"His kid?"

"My guess, too. This new thing with the bullet—I think he mistook me for the one who shot him. Whoever it was had to be close enough for him to recognize from the edge of the road."

Epstein cocked the eyebrow. "Makes me wonder if whoever shot him doesn't have the baby. Somebody Zavala left her with—or who took her."

"He'd have killed anybody who tried that. I like the leaving part."

"But if he left the kid, why the sudden concern for her life?"

"Yeah. The only thing I can figure is he wasn't worried about her as long as he was alive. Makes sense if he was going to pick her up and split for Mexico after he took care of me."

"Anything else?"

"I asked him who killed Benito. What I got was, *'No más'*—no more."

Mo's eyes widened. "No more dead kids?"

"Sounded that way to me."

"Like whoever killed Zavala is our child killer, then."

"Maybe. Or his partner in it."

"And whoever got him meant for all of it to stop right there with him."

Wil watched a flight of birds veer and disappear into a tree. "If they came together, the killer would have left in the stolen car; somehow he or she followed Zavala or knew where he'd be. Odd—he'd be a hard one to surprise, even wounded, unless he knew who it was."

"We got lucky finding the bullet, maybe we'll get lucky with the gun. By the way, Dietrich didn't bring it up, but this guy had a ten-foot-tall coke habit."

"Might have pissed somebody off, you mean."

Epstein shrugged. "Could be Sonny Pacheco gets some credit after all. You be around?"

"I think I'll renew an acquaintance. You?"

"I *was* hoping to go back to something simple like gang warfare. Incidentally, Freiman's mad as hell, talking about busting your ass when I left there, said you withheld about Zavala coming. I told him you asked for my help and that settled him down some, but it's real iffy." He rubbed shine from his forehead with a handkerchief. "Before you got here we agreed not to spill the second bullet to the media. Same'll go for Bolo Zavala's immortal words. Maybe we can find whoever popped him more easily if they think the heat's off."

They walked to the Harley. Wil straddled the bike and kicked; the motor hiccuped and pooped out. "Thanks for coming, Mo. Maybe you should leave before I draw blood."

Mo waved. "Be kind to the ass that bears you. Call me."

Wil watched him leave the lot. After two more tries the SuperGlide fired up, and he gunned it into the flow, down Victoria Street onto 101 South, his mind grappling with the second bullet. Who knew Zavala was coming back to La Conchita—somebody with him at the Rincon? An old enemy? Vengeful drug dealer? The question was, how? Until Zavala found out his mistake with Gringo, even he wouldn't have figured he'd be coming back.

Wil cut off the freeway at Woodland Hills, turned onto Ventura Boulevard, caught the magic of Christmas full-tilt: lights twinkling competitively, decorations vying for attention, windows shouting holiday bargains, shoppers prowling for parking spaces. Off the boulevard it was somewhat less spirited.

He eased the Harley sotto voce through the expensive neighborhood and parked at the edge of Reyes's property. Across the street a couple of well-dressed women disapproved. Wil stowed his helmet and the pack and started up the walk. More leaves had fallen; midway to the door, he nearly stepped in a present left by something that wasn't a reindeer.

Reyes surprised him by being in the living room watching TV, the gleam in his eye transcending the glass of white wine he was sipping from. He looked ten years younger. "You got him," he said. "It's all over the television." He turned off the set.

"Marta, lunch for Señor Hardesty—*ahora, por favor.*"

In a few minutes Marta left a microwaved cheese sandwich, colored toothpick in each half. As Wil ate, Reyes leaned forward, asking him over and over about it: the gunfight, the wounds, how Zavala looked in death. Finally he drained the wine and sat back.

"You have lifted this man from my heart."

Wil removed a toothpick. "I want to be very clear, Señor Reyes, this was not an assassination. Trying for me, Zavala killed my friend."

"I am sorry for your loss. Bring your food, I have something for you."

Wil followed him, closing the office doors behind them at a nod from Reyes, who then wrote him a check for $5,000. As Reyes spoke, he traced a finger along the checkbook's edge.

"This is in addition to your fee, for which I expect a bill shortly. Gilberto came to see me last night. We wept together, found each other again. You did that for us."

Wil went to the window; afternoon sun entered through open shutters; outside, a grapefruit tree was blooming and fruiting at the same time. "There is something you need to know, Señor Reyes, something the media doesn't." He turned. "When Zavala died, my bullet was in his gut. But he was shot in the head and killed by someone else. The bullets don't match."

"I don't understand," Reyes said.

"Someone else wanted him dead. And that's not all— Zavala was alive when I found him." Wil told him the words, his interpretation of them.

Reyes said, "You're telling me someone else is involved in the death of my son?"

"I'd feel better giving you answers instead of speculating. At the moment I have none."

A flush appeared around Reyes's neck and spread upward. "A few days ago you quit, Mr. Hardesty."

Wil said nothing.

Reyes glanced at the wedding photo in the bookcase and rubbed his neck. "Stopping here is not an option," he said finally.

"Then I would ask two favors. First, don't mention this to Gilberto; you can tell him later if something turns up. Second, someone I know needs work—dishwasher, food prep, serving line—and, if possible, a small advance." He paused. "She lives in East L.A. She's the one whose daughter Zavala kidnapped."

Reyes shook his head, plucked one of his business cards from a brass holder, and wrote on the back. "The Montebello Papa, have her see Humberto." He gave Wil a sharp look. "And if you are thinking what I think you are, don't. Gilberto was here with me two nights ago. Assuming you give him credit for knowing where Zavala was." He pushed the check across at Wil.

"It's yours," he said. "Bolo Zavala is dead and I take comfort in that. Now, where did you learn about food prep and serving lines?"

"My father had a restaurant, a small place at the beach. Hard work, but it never hurt me." He stood to go. For the first time since Wil had met him, Reyes smiled.

"I would hope not. Take your check, Mr. Hardesty."

• • •

Wil shut the car door: thirty-five hundred cash for five-digit mileage, treaded tires, and a six that ran better than it had a right to. After a final nod, he told the salesman to fill it with gas and gave him the address. Two hours, the salesman assured him.

The lot at least was close; minutes later he was tapping on the door frame as paint flaked off under his knuckles. There was a shuffling from inside, then Donna, black and blue and other colors. Apart from a nose still swollen, her face had receded. The stomach, too, he saw.

"Did you have to kill him?" she said, seeing it was Wil. Her enunciation had improved, but the tone was wrung-out. She turned, sagged across to the chair, and sat heavily. Wil pulled one of the dinning chairs over, straddled it, leaned into its back. Around the room, the table had been righted, surviving dancers reinstated, the Savior rehung.

"There was shooting going on, Donna. His choice."

"Some reason, I thought he'd be back," she said, looking at her hands. "Even though he did this, I thought he'd calm down and figure he'd need me—take me along." Her eyes rose to his. "They said my Jessie wasn't in the car."

"Donna, listen. It makes sense he would have brought her someplace safe before he came for me. For what it's worth, I believe she's okay."

A tiny spark flared in her, then died.

"Look at me. We'll find her." He drove the hope in with his eyes, waited while she blew into a tissue. "You're looking better," he said to distract her.

"Am I? I keep seein' him in Hermosillo, walking the strip with Lucinda past the orange trees. He was some'n then."

"I need your help," he said, "a name. Did Bolo ever mention a Leonardo Guerra? Lenny?"

She shook her head. "We weren't together that much, and he never said names. This one time I heard him on the phone, real low but respectful, like it was somebody who made him nervous. Afterward he slammed the receiver down. I figured he hated whoever it was.''

''Someone he worked for?''

''*No sé*. But I think so.''

''Why?''

She made a snorting noise and swallowed hard. ''*Patrón*, he was calling this guy chewin' him out.''

''Over drugs?'' Wil asked.

''Bolo always had drugs, but I don't think so. Anyway, that's all I remember.''

''All right. How's your money holding out?''

She touched a scab and shrugged.

''What about a job?'' he asked.

''Right. Beauty queens like me get hired every day of the week.''

He fished out Reyes's card, watched her read it. ''They know about Jessie, so if something breaks and you need the time, they'll understand. Job's yours if you want it. At least you'll eat.''

She turned it over several times, her eyes taking it in. ''Papa Gomez,'' she said softly, then looked up.

The keys were dangling from his fingers; he lowered them into her hand, saw her eyes get like plates. ''You'll be working late,'' he said. ''The car's clean and it runs— good as it gets with most of us.'' Wil pulled the papers out of his inside coat pocket and laid them on the table. ''It's being delivered later. It's yours.''

She sat there, eyes on the keys in her palm. Silent tears began tracking down her nose.

He cleared his throat. ''It's no Rolls Royce, Donna.''

Her ''*gracias*'' was so soft he could hardly hear it, but she said it more than once, reminding him of small victories in big wars.

The smog was twice as bad on a motorcycle; by the time Wil got to the Federal Building, he felt ready for a lung transplant. Inside, lines of long-sufferers waited and shuffled. At five to closing a relieved-looking INS employee handed him a packet regarding Mexican adoption.

He sat on the steps and read. Among the papers was a copy of a letter from the U.S. Consulate General describing legal requirements. First it was necessary to complete an INS application for advance processing. Then you had to find a Mexican child who qualified as an orphan—one removed from the custody of its parents by Mexican authorities and housed in an orphanage, or one released voluntarily by its birth parents. The child then had to be legally adopted in Mexico in a Mexican court, after which a Mexican passport would be issued for the child's departure. This would clear the way to bring the child into the U.S. via immigrant visa, which had to be applied for, then issued by the consulate. Along the way were home studies, field investigations, petitions, releases, certificates, statements, translations into Spanish. Hard time.

The system, he thought, protecting everyone, serving no one: Put your heart in the hopper and hold your breath.

Or you were rich and let Niños de Mexico handle it.

Wil checked his watch and struck off toward the Hall of Justice until thinking better of it and finding a street pay phone. Only three blocks, but there was no point in risking a run-in with Freiman. After a few minutes the Homicide desk found Vella coming out of a meeting.

Vella picked it up in his office. Wil heard him shut the door.

"We were just talking about you," he said, slightly out of breath. "Captain was, anyway."

Wil waited, hearing it coming from Vella's tone. A little flush began to spread. "Is that right?"

"Sorry to tell you, but the thing with Zavala did it. As of now we're not supposed to give you the time of day." He chuckled without humor. "Actually you're lucky. Captain wanted to bring you up on obstruction charges. The freeze-out is a compromise."

"That's terrific. Tell Freiman to keep up the good work."

Vella's voice went suddenly cold. "Kill your own messenger, Hardesty. And thank yourself for this one. Cops don't like it when you renege, especially big cops like Freiman. You played it your way—that's the price."

Right enough, Wil knew. "Vella, look. If Freiman thinks I broke faith by not telling him Zavala was coming, tough, there was no guarantee. At that, I managed to get a friend dead for the pleasure of taking Zavala down, and even then I didn't kill him. Talk price to somebody else."

"Hey, at least the FBI and the Border Patrol are happy," Vella said, his tone softening. "Can't say having the media off our necks is bad news either."

"And the second bullet?"

"We're exploring it, all I can tell you. A word, though, steer clear of Freiman. He wants your license."

A siren screamed by going up Temple Street. Wil held his ear.

Vella said, "I'll tell the captain we had this little talk—Epstein, too."

"Goddammit," Wil said.

"Between us I think you deserve better, but what the fuck, I don't make policy."

"What about the Pacheco girl—you got anything new?"

There was no response. Wil heard the siren ghosting in the receiver as it passed by the Hall of Justice. "Christ Almighty," he said.

Vella let out a breath. "What the hell, plenty of wacko calls and false sightings, everybody running around. Nothing substantive." He described their efforts: APBs, neighborhood sweeps, interagency networking, media appeals. Doctors they'd notified for new patients matching the girl's description, hospitals, pharmacies, daycare centers, on and on. "Something'll turn up," he concluded.

"Yeah," Wil said, thinking of the graves in the desert. "Thanks. You ever get the coroner's report on Paul?"

"Good-bye, Hardesty."

"He was my friend, Vella. What harm?"

After a pause, a rustle of paper. "All right, but this is it. Official cause of death listed as desanguination—some blood in the lungs consistent with the nature of the wound—blood alcohol .06—not legally drunk, but getting there. Partially digested tuna sandwich in the stomach."

"Anything else?"

"Traces of chocolate—your friend ate some candy just before he was killed. So long, Sherlock. Don't say it hasn't been fun."

The rush-hour traffic was a distant hum, a blur of sound and motion. Wil was conscious of dial tone and hung up, the DeSantis-Guerra-Zavala connection firmed yet indefinable, a will-o'-the-wisp floating there just out of reach. Gut feel: Paul stopped by St. Boniface to question DeSantis about Guerra, questions that angered the priest and were overheard in the organ loft. Which meant Father Martin had lied. To cover up involvement he suspected Guerra of having in Paul's death? Or something more sinister?

Come on, Wil thought, picturing the crowded church, the sermon, the man's life work. Who he was, for God's sake! Wil would confront him, he'd explain, and that would be that. On toward Guerra. Somehow.

He fumbled for coins, called the Shigenos: Lisa was out but had left a message to please not call, she was deciding what to do next. Wil was congratulating himself on his control until he noticed white knuckles replacing the receiver.

TWENTY-ONE

St. Boniface glowed softly in the light from two banks of spots on either side of the steps; off to the right a waxing moon showed over the San Gabriels. Wil swung the Harley into the church parking lot and turned off the motor. Stiff from the cold ride out from downtown, he loosened up with bends and proceeded up the walk.

At the rectory they told him Father Martin was working late in his office, try the back entrance to the administration building. Wil headed that way; as he passed by the window he could see through a crack in the curtains two figures bent over papers on the conference table. He found the entry and knocked at the priest's oak doors, heard "It's open."

The voice was Guerra's; they were poring over a set of spreadsheets.

"Mr. Hardesty," the priest said. "Come in." He rose to his feet as Guerra leaned back in his chair.

Wil's eyes met Guerra's. "I don't mean to interrupt, Father. Should I wait for you?"

"No, no. We're finished here—aren't we, Leonardo? Enough bad news for one day."

"Of course," Leonardo Guerra said. He folded the print-outs and put them in a black leather briefcase, snapped it closed.

"Leonardo's been acquainting me with the funds we're

going to have to raise to rebuild our mission in Hermosillo. *Madre de Dios.*" He looked closely at Wil. "Mr. Hardesty, you look flushed. Do you feel all right?"

Wil was aware his face still throbbed from the ride. "Just night air, Father," he said. "You probably heard my motorbike in the lot."

Guerra put his hands behind his head. "Judging from what I saw on television, Mr. Hardesty, you were lucky not to have been killed." He turned his head. "Did you know of this, Martin?"

The priest turned from where he was pouring the last of a glass pot of coffee into a molded white cup. "Know of what?" He handed Wil the cup, his expression echoing the question.

"Thanks," Wil said. He tried the coffee, found it bitter but warming.

"The good padre leads a rather structured life," Guerra went on. "Mr. Hardesty was involved in a fatal shoot-out with that man Zavala he was asking us about, Martin. On the news, they showed the body being taken away. Someplace near where you live, wasn't it?"

"Yes," Wil said, searching Guerra's gray eyes.

"But that's terrible," the priest said. "Thank God you're all right."

Wil admired the shaken expression, then questioned himself: Father Martin's sincerity would be hard to fake. "Thank you. Lenny's right, either one of us could have died."

"So much killing these days, so little regard for life. And for what?"

Guerra rose and began pulling on fur-lined gloves. "Well, Martin, I have obligations—as you know."

Father Martin blinked as though coming awake. "Of course. Thank you for staying late. Tomorrow again with the finance committee?"

Guerra shot the priest a look. "It never ends, does it, Martin, the need for money. Mr. Hardesty—" Briefcase in hand, he nodded to Wil and slipped out the oak doors. Wil could hear the exit door bang and reverb down the hall.

"I'd be lost without him, you know, my head for figures," Father Martin said. "Before he came we were lucky to have paper clips."

"What about support from the archdiocese?"

Father Martin sighed, pushed back his chair, and crossed a polished black shoe over his knee. "It's like everything else—too many demands on too few resources. Cutbacks and prioritizing and squeaky wheels getting the grease. Church politics that I have no use for."

"Father, I've heard you. If anyone can get the grease, it's you."

"To keep the doors open, perhaps, altar wine in the cruets. But it's Leonardo who makes the real work of St. Boniface possible. The charitable missions and—" He was about to add something when he stopped. "Forgive me, you didn't come all the way out here for a dissertation. What can I do for you?"

Wil sipped his coffee, buying time to collect his thoughts. Remembering the organist's description of Father Martin's blowup, he decided to start simply and work obliquely.

"Paul Rodriguez's widow asked me to express her gratitude on behalf of the family," he said.

"Please tell her one mass is very little in light of her loss."

"Did your secretary find anyone here who might have talked with him the day he was killed?"

"Not to my knowledge." He frowned slightly, as if the subject were distasteful. "Mr. Hardesty, your friend's killer is dead. Is there a reason to continue with this?"

"Two reasons, Father. One, I'm convinced Zavala did not act alone. And two, someone other than me killed him." As he explained about the second bullet, Wil watched for reaction, saw none beyond curiosity.

"But who, then?"

"Father, are you familiar with the Innocents case?"

The priest nodded. "The children that Zavala murdered—yes, unfortunately. I don't live in a complete vacuum, Mr. Hardesty, though at times I wish I did."

"What's been frustrating about the killings is the motive—before Zavala died, and especially now in light of the second bullet."

"There is no absence of evil in this world—I'm sure you don't need me to tell you that. Evil exists."

Wil began to feel live mines around him, trip wires. "I think Zavala was procuring children for someone else. Someone who killed him. . . ."

Father Martin's eyes held Wil's. "Mr. Hardesty, are we dancing around something here? If we are, maybe you should just tell me what it is."

"Before he died, Zavala abducted his two-year-old daughter from her mother, ostensibly to take the child to Mexico. Jessica wasn't found with him after the shoot-out. No one knows who has her. But every minute would seem to increase her chances of ending up like the others."

"Jessica— The poor mother. Is there a way I can help?"

"It's a long shot, I know, but in your studies of religions I was thinking you might have come across one—"

Father Martin cut him off. "Exactly what are you suggesting?"

"I'm not sure. Some sort of ritual?"

Incredulity blossomed in the priest's expression. "You can't be serious. Religions regard human life as sacred. Besides, Christ's sacrifice made all others pointless."

"I wasn't thinking of Christianity."

"What were you thinking, then?"

"I don't know. No stone unturned, I guess."

"Surely there are other explanations for this tragedy. Now, if you will excuse me." There was an edge to the priest's tone.

Defuse, Wil thought, getting to his feet; he looked around, spotted the collectibles in the bookcase. "Interesting display," he said. "Isn't Leonardo Guerra in the antiquities business?"

Father Martin followed him to the bookcase. "That's right. He's always giving me little things—clay animals and whatnot."

Wil focused on a sculpted male figure with a strand of cowrie shells draped around it. "This one, for instance?"

"Among others."

Wil was sure now: The statue was the same as those he'd seen that night in Guerra's office. For the priest's benefit, he spent another moment admiring it: bearded figure with bulging eyes and broad nose, smaller figures bent over in supplication, the wood cracked in places. "Looks old," he said. "Would you happen to know its origin?"

He caught it just before it vanished, the look in Father Martin's eyes: faint ripples in a deep pool, a cloud across the moon.

"Someplace in Latin America. Now I really must ask you to leave me to my work. Good night, Mr. Hardesty." He moved to his desk and sat down.

"Good night," Wil said. At the door he turned back, cherry-picked the words. "Father, I need your counsel. In Catholic school, I learned that someone who is pleasing to God always tells the truth."

The priest looked up sharply from his desk. "What makes you say that?"

"Being lied to in my work, I suppose. Maybe it's just me, but there doesn't seem to be much premium on veracity anymore."

"And that troubles you?"

"What I want to know—at least understand—is whether the virtuous man is still responsible for the truth."

"I see." Father Martin's eyes held a distant look, as though he was poring through an album of old photographs. "It would help me if you were eight years old, Mr. Hardesty. Then I'd simply insist that a virtuous person—one who would be with God—is always truthful. That lying is wrong.''

It was not the answer Wil expected. ''Then you do understand,'' he said.

''What I believe I understand, Mr. Hardesty, is that it is still possible to be a good man, if not a virtuous one.''

''A good man?''

''Someone who strives for the greater good in what he does and prays every day for forgiveness.'' Father Martin got up from the desk and stood facing the window, hands clasped behind his back. ''Drive safely,'' he said.

Wil eased out, letting the door click shut behind him.

Father Martin was still staring at the rose garden when the door opened and Leonardo Guerra entered. ''Goddammit, can you not give a simple yes or no answer when it's called for?''

Martin DeSantis said nothing.

''You might just as well have told him you were lying, for Christ's sake. Where is your head?''

''So much killing . . .''

''Don't forget, *presbitero*, if I go down, all of it goes down. You, this, everything.''

''You have her, don't you? His little girl.''

''Just keep in mind what I said.''

''You think I don't? Every day—every minute? How do you think I keep going?''

Leonardo Guerra lifted the lid on the briefcase. ''Save the self-righteous shit for your flock, Martin, it's wasted on me. And calm down. Sometimes I think you're losing your mind.''

''He knows about Zavala.''

''So I heard.''

''And?''

''And we have work to do. Yours and mine.''

•   •   •

Wil found a frame place open late on Ventura Boulevard and a sub shop near it where he put away a wilted salad and a meatball sandwich. Another stop and he was at the Rodriguez place at eleven. He fumbled for the key in the fuchsia planter, let himself in, opened the pint of JD he'd bought, and poured himself a stiff one, which he carried to the den along with the newly framed photograph. He opened the door, went to the spot on the wall. The photo fit fine in the space. For a minute he looked at the two friends with the torn seam between them, him and Paul at Cam Ranh, frozen in time. He poured in a slug of the Jack Daniel's, hoping to flood the guilt-voice and the one yelling about what the bleeding hell he was doing with a drink in his hand—clashing, incessant voices that led to mumbling into the bathroom mirror at 2:00 A.M. and thinking about the razor blades in the cabinet behind it.

Tightening his grip on the glass, he turned and left the den.

The pint didn't help. He slept like crap—tossing fitfully in Raeann's small guest bed, trying to jam together pieces of a puzzle that wouldn't go. Finally at four-thirty he gave it up, showered and shaved, then left the house and chased the moon west over Topanga Canyon to the beach. Cold light saw him walking on sand like wet pavement, accompanied by foghorns, the *ka-whump-hiss* of surf, the salt-rot smell of low tide, his own breath. Groups of sea birds stood hunched as though they were trying to disappear into their feathers; mist obliterated the horizon.

The hangover made it hard to think, but his general take on last night was that Father Martin was a strong man hiding something. Resigned to it as though it was a price to be paid. To whom—Guerra? Had to be: Guerra-Zavala, Guerra-DeSantis followed. Niños de Mexico: kids adopted, kids dead—nothing definitive except for Guerra smack in the middle of all of it. His take on Guerra: smart, smooth, deadly dangerous. Could he have ordered Zavala killed? In a heartbeat, but why? Easier to let father and child simply disappear into Mexico, right? Not if Zavala dead was where the investigation was supposed to stop. Wil was reasonably sure his mention of the second bullet to Father Martin would get passed on. That had been his intent: unnerve, trigger a mistake.

Wishful thinking.

He picked up a stone and skimmed it off an incoming line of scud.

Curious that DeSantis didn't bring up Niños last night when talking about Guerra's contributions to St. Boniface. Then there was the shell-draped statue, more on that definitely unsaid. Which left him—where?

Wil crossed the bikeway and passed a scattering of sleeping homeless people, shapeless lumps backed up to the public rest rooms. He searched his jeans, came up with a couple of dollar bills, which he handed to a young woman with an old face who looked up as he went by. She said nothing, but he felt her eyes on his back. Up on Ocean Avenue, the traffic signals blinked red.

At a breakfast spot near the Santa Monica pier, he drank most of the owner's first pot of coffee and polished off a not-bad Denver omelet. As he ate he scanned the Thursday morning *Times*. Toward the back of the first section was an article taking issue with the lack of progress by the Innocents task force: shakeups loomed, according to unnamed sources. Wil put it aside and thumbed through his notebook to the names taken from Guerra's files the night he broke into the Niños office.

Something there maybe.

Following the café owner's directions to the library, he used the pay phone outside to try Lisa again. This time her father hung up. Donna Pacheco at least talked to him: the cops had been okay, the job was fine, the car ran—the deadness in her tone said more. Be patient, he told her, and then the library opened and he was inside cruising through the phone directories. Of the names from the old Niños files, none were still listed. Faring better with the personal file names from Guerra's desk, Wil checked out the addresses in the detail street-map books and plotted his route: Bel Air, Toluca Lake, Pasadena.

Next he searched the periodicals subject indexes under DeSantis, Martin, and found twenty-two stories, fourteen newspaper and eight magazine. Each was accompanied by photographs: Father Martin at the St. Boniface groundbreaking, passing out food to a crowd of immigrant families, sorting mounds of clothing destined for Latin American outreach, balancing a child on his shoulders as he talked earnestly to reporters at a mission opening, leading a candlelight parade down Wilshire, shaking hands with the Mexican consul-general, signing his book *The Clarity of Absolutes*, clutching a bullhorn at an AIDS rally, on and on—roughly twenty years of photo-op passion and commitment. Later articles, the more rapt ones, placed the priest's lifetime of service in the Schweitzer-Sheen-Mother Teresa category and hinted at international honors to come. Wil sifted for facts: born 1931 near Portillo, Cuba, arrived Key West, Florida, 1945, studied for the priesthood in Baltimore beginning 1949, served in North Florida, Louisiana, and Texas parishes before assignment as assistant pastor at St. Boniface, then a tiny dot on the Archdiocese of Los Angeles map; took over eight months later when its pastor died suddenly. From then on a welcome and rising star, as though the questing root had struck fertile ground.

Bleary from reading, Wil left the library. As he drove up Sunset, the chill left the air, replaced by sunshine. Houses got bigger and began receding behind whitewashed walls. Lots spread out under sycamores; hedges rose up; poinsettias flamed under arched windows. Hibiscus Place came to mind.

Parker Henry was an investment banker who worked out of his Bel Air home, a raw white Monterey style with new plantings of purple lantana and lines of black drip hose. Over coffee served by Mrs. Henry, Wil told them he'd been referred by Father Martin, admired their round-faced baby girl, Alyssa, asked what they knew of the baby's origins, the process, Lenny Guerra, money, snags to be aware of—things that might smack of fraud or worse. If so, they were artfully concealed: The Henrys couldn't be more pleased. Despite the cost? Emphatically.

The Lawrence Briscoes of Toluca Lake were equally forthcoming. He was a literary agent, she ran their office; weekends they served meals to the down-and-out at Gentes de Ciudad. Their boy, Steven, was a dream come true. Sure they knew the facts—he'd been left on the steps at Los Amigos de Hermosillo—but they couldn't care less. Elaine Briscoe told him they were behind a group promoting Father Martin for the Nobel.

Wil kicked the SuperGlide toward Pasadena.

The air was thick now with valley inversion layer; above the stinging haze he could make out the tip of Mount Wilson, hovering there with a lone patch of snow. Twenty minutes later he found Orange Grove Boulevard, started looking for the Warren Sumner place not long before he spotted it. Palms lined the drive; on a broad expanse of green, a man in a straw hat guided a sit-down mower around flower beds. From the sidewalk a golf pro could clank the portico with a five iron, but only just. A large gold crest was split between the two halves of open gate where Wil left the Harley.

Diane Sumner was about his age, blond and attractive and dressed in paint-smudged work denims. At first she was reserved, then opened up about Martin Scott Sumner, their new addition, the baby named after Father Martin, whom she considered a near-saint. Warren, her husband, was an activist lawyer and legal counsel for St. Boniface; would Wil like to wait? He was supposed to be home by four. Even before he checked his watch, Wil could see where this was heading and excused himself.

From a street pay phone, he dialed Mo Epstein, gulped aspirin as he waited for Epstein to finish a call. On Colorado there was a squeal of brakes, then angry horns blaring, making his head hurt worse. He ached for a six-pack, the thought both consuming and revolting, notice that this was where the alcoholic craziness ended or there *was* no end. Just a spinning, grinding carousel of demons and twelve-step programs and falls from grace, how it had been for his mother before her Corvair crossed the line and smashed into a bus full of El Toro marines in 1967, taking his father with her. Christmas week it had been. Somewhere he still had the watch they were going to give him, the day/date crash-frozen on December 21.

"Hey," Mo said into his ear, "persona non grata. What's happening?"

"Just a great day so far. How'd you like to live dangerously?"

"I already am, talking to you. Sorry about the freeze."

"My luck. Speaking of which, I just spent five wasted hours with some big fans of Niños de Mexico. You remember it?"

Wil heard the creak of a chair, then Mo: "Guerra's operation, sure. You spoke with some of the adoptive parents?"

"Yeah."

There was a pause. "Why do I doubt that he just handed you the contacts?"

"Ask me no questions, Mo. You able to help without totally compromising yourself?"

"No, but fire away."

As Mo wrote them down, Wil gave him the names from the old list that hadn't been in the telephone directories. "If you can manage, see if these people still live in L.A.," he said. "They weren't listed, but if you score, I'll follow up. Who knows, maybe it'll lead someplace."

"Don't trust us, huh?"

Wil paused. "Thanks, Mo. I know what it means."

"Horseshit. You gettin' anywhere?"

"Don't ask. You?"

"Nothing more on the second bullet. Dietrich's men

scoured the site and found zip, not even a cartridge case. As for the Pacheco girl, nobody's seen her. Drop by the casa some time, you know where it is.'' Epstein hung up then, the broken connection underscoring Wil's sense of futility.

Walking toward the Harley as cars fumed and chased each other down Colorado Boulevard in the late-afternoon sun, he felt as distant and insubstantial as the shadow cast by an airplane.

UCLA was as he remembered: sprawling, wooded, comfortably academic. Two years he'd gone to school there, played intercollegiate volleyball, and partied around before transferring north to Santa Barbara. Time-capsule days and nights. At an outdoor table by the bookstore, he finished noting everything he could remember about the Guerra-DeSantis statues, wishing it were more, then crossed a broad expanse of treed lawn. The air was cool now and smelled of watered grass. On the way Wil passed three coeds in Bruin sweatshirts, pretty babies who smiled boldly at him, making him wonder where twenty-four years had gone.

The anthropology department was in a Romanesque brick building with olive trees by the entrance, just where Lindeman had told him on the phone. ''Thank you for staying,'' Wil began.

''No problem. A break from grading, actually.'' Professor Lindeman was thin and tanned with a shock of flyaway hair. He wore khakis, Top-Siders, a pilled navy polo shirt, hornrims that made him look studious. He studied Wil's page of notes. ''You don't have a photograph—a Polaroid or something?''

''No,'' Wil said. ''Unfortunately.''

Lindeman took down some reference books.

''Then unless you find something similar in these, I can only speculate. Holler if you do.''

For twenty minutes Wil flipped through pages while Lindeman graded papers. At a photo in the last book he stopped. "Like this, only cruder and older—more weathered."

Lindeman took the volume, studied the page. "Yoruban," he said at length. "Anything else?"

"Yeah. The central figure was larger relative to the supplicants. More strident."

"These figures are orishas, deities," Lindeman said, reviewing the pictures again. "The Yoruba religion comes from Nigeria, where it's still practiced. Cowrie shells are part of their ceremonies. Where did you say you found them?"

Wil made up something about verifying origin and authenticity for a dealer client; Lindeman's eyes narrowed, wrinkles appearing at the corners. "I really should see a statue or a photo to be certain," he said, "but there are a number of similar elements. You checked the rest of the book for an exact match?"

"That's as close as I found."

He rubbed the back of his ear. "One of the anthropology journals had an article a while back. As I recall, some deities like this were found in Cuba. I'll try to scrounge up the publication and have a look."

Wil asked about the connection to Cuba.

"Yoruba came to the New World with the slaves," Lindeman said. "It blended first with local tribal customs, then with the religion of the occupying countries. Cuba belonged then to Catholic Spain. Unlike the Spanish, though, the Yorubans were a flexible sort. They found a way to coexist."

Something clicked. "Santería?"

"You've heard of it."

Wil nodded. "Read something. Please go on."

"Well, if you've read about it, you know Santería literally means 'worships of the saints.' Basically they meshed—syncretized—their orishas with the saints: lots of orishas, lots of saints. For a while everything was fine."

He offered Wil a Perrier from a cooler beside his desk and chugged from his own.

"The Spaniards weren't altogether blind, though," he went on. "Santería's fundamentally a worship of natural forces, full of magic. They came to realize their slaves were into the magic more than the Holy Ghost. So they tried to kill it." He rested his Top-Siders on the desk. "The religion went underground. To this day the Santeros are secretive, even though the threat has long since passed. Hell, there are millions of them today, but who'd know?"

"So what about the figures?" Wil asked, rolling the bottle slowly in his hands.

"You want me to hazard a guess?"

Wil nodded.

Lindeman took another look at his notes, then the book. "Not very academic, but here goes: The slaves arrived with nothing, so unless the figures were smuggled in somehow from Africa—which I doubt, because of the workmanship you describe—they would have been carved in Cuba sometime after the turn of the century." He looked up. "Sorry, seventeenth century—when the Yorubas began arriving. Some slave priest probably carved them from memory."

"Couldn't they have been brought in later from Nigeria?"

"They sound too old for that. Figures like yours would have been used in rituals around the time the two faiths were syncretizing. Besides, Spain didn't permit Cuba to trade with other countries until the late eighteen-hundreds. By then, different images would have replaced this kind of thing." He picked up a pencil, pointed to one of the photos in the book.

"The strung cowries here represent this gentleman's wealth-gathering powers. On the left is another heavyweight—he controls thunder and lightning, fire. Your deity's not familiar to me, but that doesn't mean much. Shall I go on?"

Wil nodded as he drank.

"You're remarkably thorough, Mr. Hardesty." Lindeman's eyes became slits through his bifocals. "Especially
when I've already told you what you said you came here
for."

"My nature. Everyone says so."

"Then consider my class." He removed his glasses, began polishing the lenses on his shirttail. "All right. Santería
believes there's an orisha-saint for everything in life. Different ones control different things. Everybody gets a personal one they make offerings to for favors or
empowerment, although any may be propitiated."

What he'd read was starting to come back. Still he asked,
"What kinds of offerings?"

"Flowers, candles, fruit, food. Rum sometimes. On matters of importance, a chicken or goat. Which doesn't exactly endear them to our humane societies and animal
activists."

"Human?"

"That's Hollywood bullshit mostly."

"Mostly?"

Lindeman resettled his glasses. "There are related sects
that rob graves and use the bones for spells—Palo May-
ombe does that, witches. And there are myths about blood
sacrifice in every culture. But Santeros are a well-behaved
bunch, by and large. Some of the violent drug elements
have used Santería as an excuse for murdering the com-
petition, but even that's infrequent."

"I think that's the part I read. The article was about
cults."

"The price they pay for secrecy. People are scared of
what they don't know. Santería's no cult, it's a religion."
He put his empty in the cooler. "Your collector should
know all this."

Wil drained his bottle, rose to leave.

"Mr. Hardesty, please take something else into account." He stood up, hands in his pockets. "As I said, what
you describe sounds to me like the genuine article. How-

ever, if it *was* one of the ones found in Cuba, I would question its availability."

"Meaning?"

"Meaning it almost certainly would have been stolen." He spread his feet slightly, folded his arms. "You might warn your client."

Wil met Lindeman's gaze. "Thank you, I'll do that." He offered his hand. "You've been very helpful. What do I owe you for your time?"

The shake was firm, the expression unwavering. "Nothing," he said. "Bring me a photo if you can. Meanwhile I'll look for that article. What the hell, maybe your guy'd give me a deal."

The place was one of those that came on softly, like an old lover with nothing to prove. Even so, he circled the blocks around it several times. He'd spotted it after leaving Lindeman's office, anxious to walk off the formless apprehension that had settled into his thoughts like a silent creeping fog.

It was almost seven now, darkness making the Fox Theater tower stand out against the sky. Westwood Village boutique and bookstore windows were invitingly crowded with shoppers, colors, life. Things that only intensified the empty, detached feeling that always dogged him this close to Christmas. Two well-dressed couples passed him, chattering about dinner at some Italian restaurant they were headed for, cuddling up as they made room for him on the sidewalk. One of the girls had hair like Lisa's. She left a hint of jasmine that flirted briefly before it vanished.

Jaycee's, the neon sign read. Cocktails.

The inside was comfortably dark and leather-quiet. On the tube over the bar, a Lakers game was starting. Clint Black sang about what would happen when his ship came in. "Would you like me to keep a tab?" the waitress asked him.

Wil realized he'd been staring at the double Jack and

beer chaser she'd put down on the booth table. "What?" he said absently. "No—thank you." He reached in his jeans and came out with a dollar bill.

She smiled patiently.

He was about to pull out a credit card when he stopped. Lisa would see the receipt and call him on his backslide. Or worse, say nothing, her silence heavy artillery in a war that would wound them both—self-inflicted pain that came with the territory. "Wait a second," he said, reaching down on the banquette to rummage through his leather field coat—usually he kept a twenty in the flap pocket. It was there all right, the folded bill mixed up with something else, a tangle that came out with it.

After the waitress left, he poked through the tangle of stained paper strips that smelled of cigar smoke: the stuff from Guerra's trash, jammed in hurriedly and forgotten. Cash register receipts. Carefully, he separated them: several FoodMarts first, long curls that had torn in his haste. Then a wadded-up Stan's Cafe, Wil picturing Guerra there with Cindy. Finally a mottled SaverDrug, the kind of computer ticket that printed out the names of items rung up—good for silencing the shopper stunned at how a few things could have come to that much. Baby things, for instance.

Bottles, lotion, baby aspirin, food, powder, toys. A play-pen and multiple purchases of the same item: Pampers, over and over to the bottom of the tape. The printout was dated December 13, the day Zavala busted in on Donna Pacheco. The day he took Jessie.

Beer slopped into the whiskey as Wil banged the table on his way to the bar phone.

TWENTY-TWO

"She's at Guerra's, dammit. What more do you need?"
For an hour they'd kicked it around, Wil thrusting, Epstein
parrying.

"You know damn well," Mo came back. "Even if the
DA likes it, we have to convince a judge to sign a warrant.
And you want Freiman, one of your big fans, to kick it
off?" Mo took a swig of High Life. "Terrific. You ever
think that maybe Guerra has grandchildren?"

"Hard without a wife, Mo, remember? Besides, a grand-
father might buy toys. A playpen maybe. But the rest—all
at once like that? Give me a break."

"So we check it out."

"And two days later, the little girl turns up dead. *'No
mate a la niña,'* sound familiar?"

"Take us a morning, max. It's a task force, for Christ's
sake."

"He could kill her tonight—at the least make fifty thousand dollars off her. It's a risk and you know it."

Epstein looked at the ceiling. "What's risky here is doing
Guerra. This tape proves shit."

"You don't believe that. Sure it's not all wrapped up,
court-of-law perfect. But you've got the same instincts I
do. Trust 'em."

"Indulge them, you mean. I'm a cop. I got rules, answer

to people—not like you. We can't break the law gathering evidence.''

"The tape came from his Dumpster, Mo, not his office.''

"You'll swear to that?''

"If necessary.''

"It's too big a stretch.''

"And maybe down is up.'' Wil sat forward, tossed off the last of his coffee. "Maybe Bolo Zavala didn't bring the kid to Guerra's so he could come after me. Maybe he didn't work for Guerra at all. Maybe Lenny's the man of the fucking year.'' He pressed the mug into his temple. Racing the Harley through the Santa Monicas and out into the Valley, he'd felt it. They had a chance. Now *this*.

"Looks mean something in these cases, Wil. You know that.''

He recalled the article about shakeups: "Mo, your guys are holding an empty bag. If this is more than they've got— and it is—why not give it a chance? Screw it if Freiman doesn't look good.''

"Easy for you to say. Even if Freiman goes along, there's no guarantee the other guys will.''

"The girl could die, assuming she's alive. All I'm saying is it's worth upsetting some people to find out.''

Mo Epstein sank back farther against the couch. "They'll never buy it; it's too circumstantial. On top of that, Freiman won't hear it coming from you.''

"So tell him you had a hunch and played it. Anything. Tell him *Vella* found the tape.''

Mo rubbed his neck, went to the phone. Checking his book, he dialed and ordered a home delivery pizza. After that he called Vella—then Freiman.

The pizza arrived, was cooling by the time Freiman agreed; it was only then that Wil began to let go. He moved to the kitchen, divvied out combo wedges. Cracked himself a 7-Up and drank half of it.

Morris's eyebrow went about halfway up. "Freiman's putting it out there, I didn't think he would. Shows you what he's up against." Staring at the soft drink can, he said, "Stick around if you like. It's on for tonight if we can set it up."

Two drinks down, the pounding in her head quieting. Finally the kid was out. It had been a real screamer this time, nothing working: toys, apple juice, aspirin—mothering even, the child immediately sensing Jennette's aversion and using it for fuel.

Valium ground up in her applesauce. That had worked.

Jennette Contreras poured herself another brandy, walked the white living room, paused to look out a shuttered window. At least the house was out of earshot, the neighbors' tennis courts closer than the neighbor's houses. Oleanders would muffle sounds that escaped, not that any would. She released the shutter, checked the playpen again. Soon. No one had to say it, the moon did.

She twisted a length of hair that had fallen.

Niños at least was under control: checking in mornings while the child slept, Sofia handling her clients. As for the detective, Hardesty, she'd never believed him in the first place, him and his talk about wanting to adopt. The man was a phony, the break-in suspiciously close to his leaving. Of course Lenny was still bothered about that, though he didn't let it show. Jennette smiled at how well she knew him: Lenny had his own kind of *cojones*. He would deal with Hardesty.

Everything, really, was fine.

She looked out again. Beyond hedges, the street was quiet.

Nothing matched the late hours for being alone with her thoughts. Feeling his closeness. What a man he'd been then: handsome, full of fire. True, he had chosen a different path, but to her he would always be the way he'd been.

Again they came back, the memories, hot and sweet.

Swimming naked in the shallows; knowing he was watching her every movement for one purpose. Rolling in the green warmth, diving, standing finally and looking toward shore, toward *him*, crystal drops falling from breasts and arms and softness. Then he was there and coming toward her: plunging in, taking her in the water, her joy overwhelming, as though all the power of Yemayá's oceans had entered with him. And afterward, carrying her to a spot among the mangroves where they loved again more slowly, reverent to forces newly unleashed. As sunset faded, lighting candles from his satchel. Placing them in a circle around them.

Sea snakes they had been, coiling and writhing in the light.

More memories: not lying with him again, her marrying.

Jennette put down the glass, aware of a sudden bitter taste at the back of her throat. A marriage of convenience it had been, as surely as gulfweed grew: Fredo Contreras, the fisherman, Jennette's aunt and Fredo's mother the matchmakers, aware of the incident on the beach and of Fredo's shyness with women. She and Fredo going through the motions for a while. Hearing later that he'd tangled in a net off Marquesas Key and drowned.

By then she had been far away.

Jennette turned off the lamps around the living room and went upstairs. Closing the door, she fired a match, touching it to black wicks until the room was aglow. In seconds she was back within the circle. The space warmed, drew in around her; standing before the mirror, she loosened her robe, let it fall.

Candlelight danced again on pale skin.

Her eyes appraised the glass: nearly the figure she'd had then, fuller in the hips. The breasts were almost translucent, nipples seeming to float. She cupped her hands around them and closed her eyes. Lips pulled apart. Soft cries rang in her head across forty years.

Her fingers had begun moving when the phone rang.

Flush fading, she crossed the room. Her tone was cool as she answered—unlike Lenny's.

"Cops were here tonight," he said in a voice that crackled with tension. "Here. *In my goddamn house*."

It was textbook, letter perfect. Mo nursed bourbon and described it, shaking his head. They'd gotten the unlisted number and address, arranged for a telephone warrant to search the house. They'd even obtained a warrant requesting printouts of Guerra's phone records.

At 2:00 A.M. they'd hit.

Following the initial shock, he'd been the soul of graciousness. Of course he would cooperate: open any doors, answer any questions, provide any background. Guerra had the boy make them coffee then, and after it was over it was Freiman apologizing and Guerra excusing it as nothing and the two of them having a cigar while Guerra entranced the captain with the house and the art and himself.

The yelling had started in the car.

Mo looked pale with something worse than fatigue; their talk drifted away, replaced by leaden silence. Mo broke it finally. "He knew nothing about Jessica Pacheco, was sympathetic to any effort to find her. Far as the register tape goes, he had no knowledge of it—no surprise there. When we asked about the statues, he said he'd gotten them from a collector. No reason, just liked them. Even offered to hunt for the receipts."

"Of course," Wil said, pouring himself a straight shot from Mo's bottle. "Was the boy any help?"

"His foster son? Kid might as well have been mute." He watched Wil down the shot, pour another. "You're hoisting the flag again, maybe you ought to go light on that stuff."

"Just stick to the subject."

"All right. We lost tonight, big-time. Don't expect Lenny Guerra to make the captain's most-wanted list between now and when hell freezes. I may be sending you a card from Siberia, and don't laugh, Freiman'd find a way."

Wil threw down the second shot. "My fault. I'm the one who pushed."

"Just what I need, all right, his finding out you're involved. You like the sound of shit hitting fans?"

Wil's fuse was just as short. "Mo, goddammit, Guerra's up to here in this thing. We're talking about a two year old." He tried glaring, but couldn't; he'd been wrong, and Epstein had paid.

"I'm sorry," he said. "What about the phone records?"

Epstein jerked himself away from the kitchen counter, his face no longer pale. "What about you shutting the fuck up and leaving me alone while I contemplate having to make Lieutenant again." He tossed off his whiskey, rattled the ice cubes in the sink, then stormed down the hall. Wil glanced at his own empty glass, then drank directly from the bottle.

False dawn was silhouetting the San Gabriel range by the time Wil pulled the SuperGlide into the Rodriguez driveway and killed its rumble. The damp air felt like cold rain. For a moment he just sat there relishing the silence and letting his shoulders slump. Then he noticed the black Acura.

She was in the guest bed he'd been using. Her suitcase was up on the chair. He watched her sleep for a while, envying her peaceful state, wondering at her coming. Wanting her. Then the why of it made him want to wake her up and ask, so he slipped out of the room and lay down on the too-short couch. Mo's whiskey still churned; thoughts flooded his mind as if pouring from an open spigot—Jessica, Guerra, how sure he'd been about him having her— until sleep took him.

The smell of coffee: Wil opened his eyes and waited as the lines and planes and colors came together, then propped himself up on one elbow. Lisa sat in the chair with the antimacassars on the arms, her feet pulled up under her. Watching him. Steam rose from the mug in her hand.

"You're awake," she said quietly.

He smiled, tried to read her but couldn't. "Hi there. Time is it?"

"Almost ten. When did you finally get in?"

He blinked, ran a hand over his face. "I don't know. Late."

"Must have been a hard night. You don't look so good."

"You look terrific."

There was a quiet moment while she looked at him, then she said, "You're drinking again, aren't you." Her voice was flat.

"Nothing to worry about," he said, attempting to mask the residual buzz with a smile that stuck partway.

"I see."

"How about if I shower, then we talk?"

She nodded, and he stood up stiffly. Gray light showed through half-drawn blinds; rain murmured lightly against the windows. Raeann's mantel clock chimed twice and resumed ticking. She handed him the coffee mug, then backed away from him.

"Thank you," he said, taking a sip. "This mean we're friends?"

"Partners is what I had in mind."

"Uh-huh. You mind if I ask in what?"

She stood there in the pink silk robe he'd bought her last Christmas, saying nothing, revealing neither warmth nor ice from her look. "Finding Paul's killer," she said, clear from her tone that she'd spent time thinking about it. Then she turned and moved off into the kitchen, where he heard her setting things down on hard surfaces.

In the bathroom he washed down aspirin, forced himself through a drill of push-ups and ab crunches, then spent a long time under shower water as hot and then as cold as he could stand. Toweling off, he looked as though he had sunburn, but at least he felt better despite the red in his eyes. He dressed and entered the kitchen, where she'd set out bowls of hot cereal. They ate in silence, a talk show on the kitchen radio filling the void. A weather update predicted day-long rain, heavy at times.

"So that's what made you come?" he said at length. "Paul?"

"I pried it out of Mo a few days ago, what you're up to, what happened to your deal with his department. Other things."

He rose and set their bowls in the sink, then sat down, sipped coffee now cold.

"So you thought you'd come and do what—help me out?"

Her eyes moved slowly across his face. "Work together, yes."

"What was it you said once about all this being a long way from your world? This isn't about some self-righteous dodger looking for loopholes and you plugging in the right numbers to make the IRS go away."

"That's not only bullshit, it's unfair. I've learned things from you. Over the years."

"Well, that's just great, but the answer is no."

"I wasn't asking permission." She let a second pass. "I'd rather not, but I'll go it alone if I have to."

"You will, huh? Fucking terrific." The aspirin had chased the pain in his head to a spot above his right temple, which he rubbed. Rain binged metallically inside the vent above the stove.

"I'll manage," she said.

"To do what, Leese? The man who cut Paul is dead, remember? Bolo Zavala's dead. Look, I can appreciate how you feel, but—"

"No, you can't," she interrupted. "You haven't a clue how I feel."

"He was my friend, goddammit."

"He was my friend, too, did you ever think of that?" Her dark eyes flashed. "And I happen to know you believe somebody else ordered him killed. That's the son of a bitch I want."

"Listen—"

"No, you listen, Wil. When you were wounded, Paul was there for me. He told me stories about you and how it was. He listened to me—meek little Lisa just out of college. You remember my first job, that dreary bookkeeper thing?"

Wil nodded yes, recalling her letters describing it, the words trying to make light of how frustrated she was. Lisa went on as the rain beat harder on the roof.

"Paul talked me into going back to school during your last tour even though it meant no second income and more expenses. I wouldn't have done it otherwise." She bit her lower lip. "You remember when Daddy had his heart attack? What I didn't write was that he had no insurance—everything then went to the greenhouses. Paul gave me money to cover it. But he made me promise not to tell you. I'd have gone back to that lousy job, Wil. Do you see that?"

"What about the money?"

"I paid it back a little at a time—more as things improved. He and Raeann weren't rich, but they never asked me when."

Wil made tight wet circles with his mug on the Formica tabletop. "I took a swing at him once," he said. "In a lousy beer joint."

"He knew you didn't mean it."

Wil shook himself out of it. "Your loyalty to Paul isn't the point, Lisa. Killing is a way of life to these people, whoever they are. It's what they do, the way their problems get resolved. Understand?"

She said nothing.

"Let me clarify. I saw what they did to Paul—"

"Zavala did to Paul—"

"Same thing. They took him out like a pig in a slaughterhouse. In case I haven't said it, I'm running scared here. And you want me to send you after them? Use your head."

"*Damn you*, I just want to help. Is that so hard to grasp?"

He blinked against the pain, saw colors moving, and opened his eyes. "I don't even know what I'm up against, let alone how I'd use you."

"Try thinking about what you need but aren't able to get yourself. Like sober, to start with." The line of her jaw was set hard now and her grim, shadowed expression in the weak light of the kitchen fixture reminded him of kabuki theater. Wind drove the rain in bursts against the outside glass.

Running on empty, Julio replaced coffee cups in the mahogany sideboard and brooded over last night. It seemed to him the sheriff's men would never leave. They'd searched everywhere, found nothing, gone over everything twice. *Madre Sagrado!*

And the questions—out in the garage, Señor Guerra distracted by the big man inside the house. He'd been so tempted, deputies looking at him, expecting more. Why hadn't he told them?

He slumped in a chair. They were police, and he knew about police who came in the night. Paramilitaries, death squads. Killers who'd dragged his family into the front yard by the jacaranda tree, hung his father inches off the ground, his father kicking while his mother screamed and pleaded. The fat one hitting her in the face with his rifle and the blood on her nightdress and him trying to go to her, but the thin one holding him back.

The questions then, lowering the rope just long enough to ask—pulling on it when his father didn't answer. After a while they looked to Julio: Save your old man, give up the Farabundo Marti. We know you sleep with the FMNL, that you are traitors. Tell us and you will live.

Nothing he could say, nothing he knew. Finally they tied off the rope and watched his father's face go purple, the kicking stop, the tight, creaking ellipses. To his body they pinned a copy of his newspaper. Then they started on Julio's sister.

As it always did, the sweat came and the fast swallowing.

Two of them took her behind the hedges, her cries cactus spines in his heart. Silence then and the men returning, one wiping his knife, the other with a handful of auburn hair. Julio knew then he was going to die; he ran, but the fat one's rifle butt was quicker.

He'd opened his eyes to bright sun and black flies.

Drifting north then: hopping buses, begging food, sleeping in sewers, being invisible. Stealing to survive. Borders meant nothing: El Salvador, Guatemala, Mexico. Moving to an inner current: America, a vague notion fueled by television and his father's newspaper. In a year, he'd made it as far as Sonora. Then the woman from Los Amigos de Hermosillo and the slow road back from hepatitis and malnutrition and dysentery.

He should have died.

Selected for adoption, he'd gotten as far as Los Angeles when it fell through. Hearing his adoptive parents had burned to death under a gasoline truck on some freeway, that he'd be going back. And then the miracle: the gentleman who felt sorry for him, agreed to take him under his wing.

A vulture's wing.

At first Julio had been grateful; he was beyond love by then, but life at least looked promising. Being given a home by Señor Guerra meant enough to eat, enough to live, escape from the bad dreams. Señor was good to him, demanding but generous.

Then the massages, coming at night to his bedroom—touching, putting his mouth on Julio's; Señor whispering to him that he and Julio were alike, that people didn't understand, and if he told anyone, he would have to go back there.

Back to hell.

He was a whore now, a fourteen-year-old *puto*.

He wondered what his father would think. Back home, when something troubled him, he'd go to church, discuss

it with Father Jaime—maybe he could confide in Father
Martin the same way. Yet every time he came close to
Father Martin, after the others had left the altar boy class,
he was too ashamed to form the words.

That left the officers—why hadn't he spoken up? The
big one's face stood out again in his mind. From the moment he came into the house, the one named Freiman reminded Julio of the man who had hanged his father. From
then on they all looked the same. Men with guns.

Julio put his head down on the cold wood and waited
for the storm to pass.

Lenny Guerra poured, the aroma restoring him somewhat.
When he wasn't so tired, he enjoyed grinding the beans
himself, sweetening the black brew, adding the *leche eva-
porada*. He never stirred it, though, preferring to watch the
white cloud form and swirl—destiny in a cup.

He drank some, anticipating its boost. From the Niños
front desk Carmen routed a call. Jennette, he assumed;
probably needing more Valium.

"Did Leonardo forget our meeting?"

Goddammit to hell—all he needed right now. "Fuck the
meeting, Martin, I had visitors last night. Sheriff's people.
With a search warrant."

There was an intake of breath. "What were they looking
for?"

"Don't play innocent with me. What do you think they
were looking for?"

Hesitation, then: "I think what you are doing is absolute
madness."

"Be careful what you say, Martin."

"I can't permit it. I won't."

"Do you happen to have the Cardinal's office number
handy? Save me the trouble of looking it up. Two-five-one
something or other—"

Martin DeSantis's voice was barely audible now. "In God's name, don't do this."

"Tears, Martin? Really!"

"I'm begging you—"

"Good-bye, Martin."

TWENTY-THREE

They came up with the plan sometime after two that afternoon, Wil wasn't sure. All he knew was that he was against it, his head hurt like hell, and Lisa was on the phone talking about her skills and volunteer opportunities with Isabel Diaz, Father Martin's secretary. They concluded by setting up a late-afternoon appointment at St. Boniface.

"I'm as good as in," she said. "They need finance people. Something big's going on."

"Rebuilding their Mexican outreach mission," Wil said through the damp towel over his face.

"Los Amigos de Hermosillo. You know about it?"

"Some. DeSantis talked about it at the mass Paul and I went to." He pulled the towel off and sat up gingerly. "No tricks, Lisa. You use your maiden name, you get as close to Guerra and DeSantis as you can, and we play it by ear from there. The Polaroid is only if an opening presents itself. Ditto the tape recorder. No—I repeat no—heroics. That's the deal. Period."

"Why would someone of Father Martin's reputation get mixed up with someone like Guerra?"

"I don't know. Men like DeSantis—called charismatic types—are also ambitious. It's what drives them. What I suspect is that Guerra's tapping in, using DeSantis's ambition for his own agenda. How, I have no idea. But with guys like him it's generally for money."

"You think Guerra could be skimming off the Catholic Church?"

"Don't ask me to prove it."

"Surely the archdiocese must have auditors."

"Judging by the articles I read, Father Martin is extremely important to the church right now, and not just the archdiocese. He's doing incredible things. Millions are flowing in. The media love him. That would make him an awfully big fish to jerk around."

Her almond eyes looked thoughtful; one hand swept a wisp of black hair off her face. She said, "I can't believe he'd condone something like that."

"He's hiding something. I'm convinced he lied about Paul."

"I'd better get going, Wil. I need to shower before I go." She stood up, cinching the pink cord of her robe tight at the waist. The gesture was completely reflex, but it defined her figure: slim with small breasts, nipples standing out against the silk.

"I'll wash your back," he said, instantly regretting the crack. It was forced and inappropriate, and that's the way she took it.

She flushed, looking at him as though something dammed up for miles was about to spill out in a rush, but she said nothing. Just turned and walked away.

He felt her touch on his shoulder and realized he'd drifted off to sleep on the couch.

"I'm going now, there's a break in the rain. How do you feel?"

"Fine," he said. It was partly true anyway; the sharp pain in his head was gone, replaced by a queasy stomach and the sensation of his blood coursing. For some chemical reason, his system craved tequila with lime and salt. He sat up and checked his watch: four o'clock.

"Will you be here when I get back?" she asked.

"Depends." The question, the accountability inherent,

felt odd but welcome, and he amplified: "Guerra's due at his office at five; I called while you were in the shower. I'll tag after him, see where it leads."

"Won't he spot you on the Harley?"

Mentioning the motorcycle in front of Guerra came back, but he said, "I bought a helmet, one of those faceless things."

"Wish me luck," she said. She was wearing a navy sweater over a white button-down shirt and pleated green pants. Over her arm was a Ghurka bag and a bone-colored raincoat. Sunlight from a rift in the clouds sent shine off her straight black hair and a little zip of electricity through him.

"Luck," he said. "And remember our deal," the words sounding rote and vacuous to him. When she turned and closed the door behind her, she left a hint of jasmine and Wil fighting a sinking feeling of déjà vu.

It was getting dark when he edged onto 405 South and into the lit river of slowly moving cars heading up the grade toward West L.A. and Santa Monica. The city's glow reflected dully off the re-formed overcast; the promise of more rain hung in the air like a damp curtain. Spray from the roadway patterned the smoke visor of his helmet and his leather field jacket.

He made Stan's Café at five-fifteen, staked out a table that gave him a clear shot at Guerra's black Mercedes in the Niños lot across Olympic. A thin girl with heavy makeup told him Cindy was off duty and brought him a club sandwich, which he paid for. Then she left him alone to wonder how Lisa was doing at St. Boniface, how that whole thing had come together. It still seemed unreal, one more thing to worry about. Yet by her presence, she'd lifted something dark and oppressive off him. He realized he hadn't thought about a drink in nearly two hours.

Guerra strolled out just after seven, put his raincoat and briefcase in the backseat, nosed the SEL out of the driveway, and turned left. He slowed briefly at the jammed-up northbound 405, then kept going on Olympic. Wil maintained several cars between them as the neighborhoods upscaled, downscaled, commercialized, got dismal, and became respectable again. Lit signs hawked Kona coffee, then kimchi, then *pan dulce*.

L.A., he thought: Don't like what you see, you drive awhile.

Guerra picked up Alvarado Street, then drove northeast on freeways 2 and 134. Just before the freeway arched over Arroyo Seco and into Pasadena, Guerra swung off and followed the west side of the arroyo up a winding street overhung with camphor trees, then slowed at an open-gated property with about a dozen luxury cars parked along the curving drive. He swung the Mercedes in; a garage door opened automatically; the Mercedes slid inside. In a moment Guerra came out a side door and strode under the portico and into the house.

It was a dark-shingled Craftsman, modified and set back from the street. Multilevel decks circled the exterior; brick walks led off in different directions. Through brightly lit windows Wil could see a telescope pointing toward the mountains and people standing with drinks in their hands. Mist was beginning to float and swirl in the glow.

He put the Harley between a couple of photinia bushes; at the front door he was met by a white-coated houseman who eyed him up and down, took his card, then slipped back into the crowd of people. Wil stepped inside. The place was warm feeling and beautifully decorated, the people as well. Prosperous and late-thirties eager, they stood talking in small groups beside spotlit artwork, alcoves of antiquities, Plexiglas-framed ethnic weavings. Their champagne glasses caught sparkles of light from candles that flickered on a long table set with silver, wineglasses, and flowers. Classical music eased from tall speakers.

He recognized Jennette Contreras, then Diane Sumner across the room, and smiled at her as Leonardo Guerra approached with the houseman.

"Mr. Hardesty, I figured that must be you following me. I'm hosting a dinner party here. Is there something you want?" He was holding a cut-crystal tumbler, something clear over ice.

Wil brought his eyes up from the glass. "Yeah, to give credit where it's due. With your friends around." He looked beyond Guerra, saw people glancing his way. "I want them to know the real Lenny. The civic-minded one who put up a faulty hospital that fell down and killed people. In Hermosillo, of all places."

Guerra drank from the glass; through aviator lenses his gray eyes held dark glints. Conversation fell off as guests began looking openly now. Wil could see them eyeing his clothes.

Guerra nodded at the houseman. "Show Mr. Hardesty the door, Jesús," he said. "Now, please."

Wil raised his voice a notch. "The caring, compassionate Lenny who ordered my friend Paul Rodriguez killed." He felt the houseman's hand on his elbow and jerked away. He had the full attention of the group now and played to it; Diane Sumner's eyes were very large. "God-fearing Lenny had Paul's throat cut by a psychopath named Zavala who worked for him. Authorities say Zavala murdered seven children, then kidnapped his own daughter. He is now conveniently dead."

"Jesús!"

The houseman made another grab for Wil's arm. "No offense, Jesús," he said. "But I am not ready to leave yet. *Momentito más, por favor.*"

A well-built man with the logo of a catering company on his white shirt moved toward them. "Come on, man," he said. "Be nice."

"Sorry, I just don't feel nice." Wil's eyes encompassed the guests. "Maybe you folks weren't aware that last night the sheriff's department served a search warrant on our Lenny. Right here where you're standing. Seems they had evidence Lenny was hiding Zavala's little girl." He took the snapshot from Donna's out of his shirt pocket, flipped it on the dining table. "Her name is Jessie, Jessica Pacheco. Best to take a close look if any of you are thinking of adopting a child from Niños de Mexico. Wouldn't want any of you arrested as accessories."

Lenny Guerra's neck and face were red-blotched, and a vein in his forehead pulsed. He turned away from Wil. "My friends, please pardon this unforgivable intrusion. This man is a failed private investigator, a liar, and a drunk. Some years ago his recklessness was the cause of his own child's preventable death. Now he seems to exist for no other purpose than to cause trouble. Spoiling our evening is precisely what he wants."

"My, aren't we well-informed."

Diane Sumner said, "Please, Mr. Hardesty, this isn't right. Can't you see we're happy here?" She sounded confused and hurt.

Wil felt himself gripped on each arm, the picture shoved back in his pocket; this time he didn't resist. "That little girl's mother used to be happy, Mrs. Sumner. Tell it to her."

At the door, he shrugged off the escort and walked out into the rain. Midway down the drive, he looked back to see them all watching and, standing at a separate window, Lenny Guerra, one hand jammed in his coat pocket, the other holding a flip phone to his ear. Beside him, Jennette Contreras's face was as white and rigid as sculpted marble.

Wil wound the Harley down into Brookside Park, where he found a phone by a deserted Little League diamond. Raindrops cratered the wet dirt of the infield.

"Wil," she answered. "I just got home. Believe it or not, I've been out there all this time. Working."

"That's great, Lisa."

"You sound funny. Are you okay?"

"I didn't want you to worry—think I was boozing or something."

She was quiet a moment.

"It's a bitch, Leese, that's why I'm calling." He was still sweating from Guerra's, could smell himself under the field coat. His knuckles were pale peaks on the hand holding the receiver. "I want to," he said. "A lot."

"Come home, Wil," she said, then hesitated. "I have a surprise. The Polaroids you wanted of that statue? I got them."

"Unbelievable. How?"

"Father Martin held a press conference for his big fund-raiser event coming up. They all went but me; I volunteered to answer the phones. Are four shots enough?"

Wil found his voice. "Nobody saw you?"

"Nope."

"I'll be damned—nice going." He checked his watch. "Now we have to get them to Lindeman."

"Where is he?"

"UCLA, Anthro department, his card's in with my stuff. Take 405 South, then go east on Sunset, and you'll see it. It's about twenty minutes. If he's not in, slip them under his door."

"Done. What else?"

"I love you."

"Come home, Wil."

He was thinking of something clever to add when he saw the blur of motion, heard the whine. The car was bearing down on him, its headlights off, part of the dark and gaining speed. Wil jumped and felt it roar by him, heard the phone kiosk explode as though an artillery shell had hit, then he was rolling and scrambling in the mud toward the Harley.

He was trying to start it when the car completed a 180 and came barreling back. Three kicks, four, and then the bike caught and he was fighting for control as the car tried to cut him off. He spun away, roostertailing mud, then felt the surface change, the bike attempt to grip rain-slick asphalt and fail. He throttled down to stop the skid and stalled it.

The car, like a cape-maddened bull, completed its turn and gunned the engine as though sensing the kill. It was a black Dodge, an ex-CHP cruiser with tinted windows, the front doors still white, a faint outline where the shield had been. On the driver's side, a single windshield wiper swept back and forth like a twitching tail. The driver popped on his headlights, floored it, and the big engine threw the car forward, tire smoke streaming from the wells.

This time the Harley responded; after a brief jitter Wil was up and running, the Dodge gaining, then losing ground as Wil pushed the faster, lighter bike down a stretch and into a turn. Rain pelted his coat, burst on his helmet, stung his hands and neck. The Dodge's high beams were like twin searchlights in the rearview.

He torqued the bike past seventy, felt a surge of exhilaration. Almost to the freeway, he could see looming ahead the sweeping arches of the Colorado Street Bridge.

The pickup truck.

Pissed or disoriented by the three raised headlights coming at him, the driver hit his high beams. Momentarily blinded, Wil reflexed a feather squeeze on the brakes, knew his mistake instantly as the SuperGlide's rear end broke loose. He turned the bars toward the slew and almost righted it. But the drift was too deep and it went out from under him, and then he was down and sliding across wet pavement and gravel, his knee on fire, and he was trying not to let the front wheel dig in, and then he and the bike were airborne and that's all he remembered except for the feeling his head was being twisted off.

The young-looking doctor with the red buzz cut was finishing the stitches in his scalp when they let Lisa in to see him.

"How is he?" she asked.

Wil opened his eyes against intense light, closed them

again. "He's fine," he said, his words disjointed and far-away sounding.

"Lucky to be here," the doctor said. "You see his helmet?"

"Yes," Lisa said. "Doesn't that hurt him?"

"The area's deadened. And I gave him a pain shot for his knee. Nothing's broken, but I want to keep him overnight. I'll be around in the morning."

After the doctor left, Wil felt her touch his forehead, then take his hand. He was aware of dried blood tightening the skin on his neck.

"Guerra," he said. "As I left, I saw him on the phone. Setting it up. They must have been waiting outside."

"No more tonight, Wil."

"The pictures?"

"I put them under Lindeman's door."

"Not an accident, Leese."

"I know. Sleep now. We'll talk tomorrow."

"Not . . . *drunk*."

He woke up in a room looking out over a small park. The rain had let up recently; eucalyptus swayed gently in the wind, the wet foliage droopy and gray-green. Beyond them morning traffic hissed by on a four-lane surface street. He was stiff and bruised; where he'd been sewn up, he felt as though someone had left a fork in his scalp. Lisa stayed as long as she could, then left for St. Boniface, promising to call later. Wil remoted the TV on, flipped through silent channels, then turned it off. Vents exhaled processed air like a long sigh from deep inside the building.

Mo Epstein came by as Wil was picking at white-flecked scrambled eggs and pale toast.

"My, that looks appetizing," he said, regarding the plate. "And you look better than I was expecting."

"Put me back in, coach. I'm fine."

"Yeah, right." Mo regarded the stitches. "Nice even work there. I'm something of an expert, you know. How's the knee?"

"Got me to the bathroom and back this morning," Wil said. "What's up?"

Epstein sat down in a blue vinyl chair. "Casewise? Let's see: nothing on those file names you gave me. Every address had a different current resident."

"That tell you anything?"

"In the light of everything else that's checked out, no, it doesn't. As far as the infamous register receipt goes, that came from the SaverDrug on Alvarado."

"Guerra drove home that way the other night."

"How about giving the Guerra thing a rest, huh? Lots of people drive Alvarado. Some even shop at SaverDrug."

Wil downed the rest of his orange juice, shifted his weight off a sore spot. He threw a forced smile at Mo's look and waited for him to continue.

"The buyer paid cash. The checker was working late and doesn't recall the sale. I saw the accident report. You're kind of hard on the transportation, aren't you?"

"It's a weakness of mine."

"Among notable others." Epstein leaned forward on his elbows. "Guerra phoned the captain personally, said you were drunk and abusive to his dinner guests. There's a restraining order being cut." He paused. "You wouldn't be a little over the top here, would you, old buddy?"

Wil looked out the window. "You got something to say, Mo, say it."

"I saw my empty bottle of JD the other morning, and it wasn't me who emptied it. Maybe you get blitzed, go to Guerra's, spew all over him, then dump the bike seeing double. Doc said you must have been pretty damn loose to come out as good as you did."

"Or ridden one down before." He was suddenly flat-out weary of justification, raised eyebrows, swimming upstream. "I'm tired, Mo. Just drop it. There's money in my pants pocket for the Jack."

Epstein flushed to his ears. "Hey, fuck you—I didn't deserve that."

"No, I suppose not."

"You ain't the only one with problems, but here's another: Freiman's talking about running you in when you're well enough. I wouldn't want to tell you your business, but you might try lowering your profile for a change."

Wil sat up in bed, twisted his knee, and winced. "Am I under arrest, Mo?"

"No. At least not yet. But people who continue to futz around with the buzz saw usually wind up with the short end. *Pal*." He snatched up his nylon rain shell and walked out of the room.

Later, Wil dozed and woke up sweating from a dream about Devin and Jessica Pacheco playing at the edge of a cliff and his parents with blood all over them warning him not to die. He limped to the sink, splashed water on his face, and took another painkiller with some juice. He was in bed staring out the window when Lindeman called on the room phone.

"How'd you get this number?" Wil asked him.

"Your wife. She said you'd had an accident but would want me to call."

"Thanks. What about the Polaroids?"

"It's been an interesting day. Turns out your little idol is pre-Santería, all right, but not what I first thought."

"How's that?"

"It's sacrificial in nature—as in human. I'd stake my reputation on it."

"Then it's not Santería, right?"

"No. As I said before, Santería's doves, chickens, the occasional goat. Rum and flowers. Nothing like this."

"Then what is it?"

"Apparently some old African deity, at least an interpretation of it. Remember I mentioned there were myths? This is one—a spinoff sect that hit the beach in Cuba early on, then disappeared into the forests and never came out again. Through sources, we learned that all the governments down there have tried eradicating it. The last big push was in the forties, before Castro. Troops wiped out several whole villages—nothing they readily admit to.''

1945, Key West. Martin DeSantis. ''And the deity?''

''The name we got is Chawa Uve. It means lover of innocent blood. That's why the purges. Kids kept disappearing.''

''What was the purpose?''

''Of the sacrifices? Special favors, special blessings to accomplish certain things. Usually when a great deed was about to be undertaken.''

Wil was quiet.

''You there?'' Lindeman asked.

''Yeah, just thinking.''

''Kind of prickles your short hairs, doesn't it, what that little thing's seen. How did your collector respond to my suggestion?''

''Were you able to find out if it was stolen?''

''Uh-huh—August 17th, 1963, from the National Museum in Havana. Somebody ripped off the only three eyer found, replaced them with monkey heads to show their contempt. Well, if there's nothing else you need, I have to run. The ball's in your court.''

''Tell me about the fund-raiser,'' he asked Lisa in the car as they left the hospital. It was after seven and the rain had started again. She had a country station on for background, a Mary-Chapin Carpenter ballad about Carolina. The seats made soft leathery sounds as Wil shifted around to get comfortable.

''What do you want to know?'' she asked.

His fingers went briefly to the line of stitches, felt their wiry stiffness. ''Whatever you know.''

''All right. It's *the* event around St. Boniface. Cardinal Ennis is coming, and half of Hollywood. Media, of course.'' She had both hands on the wheel, race-driver style; oncoming headlights cruised across the lenses of her driving glasses. ''There's going to be a special mass and a reception afterward in a tent they're putting up. I've seen the renderings for Hermosillo and the initial projections. It's very ambitious. They need a ton of money.''

"When is it?''

"Sunday at three.''

"That soon?''

"Two nights and a day. Why?''

Mary-Chapin Carpenter segued into Bonnie Raitt. The Acura's wipers swept rain noiselessly off the windshield.

"Because I think we have until then to find Jessica,'' he said.

"And if we don't?''

"Then it's too late. She'll be in a grave somewhere.''

Suddenly she swung off the street and stopped at the curb in front of a group of stark apartments. She set the brake and turned toward him. "I thought you were afraid Guerra was going to put her up for adoption.''

"I don't think that anymore.'' He told her about Lindeman's findings—the violent nature of Chawa Uve, the wealth-gathering significance of the idols' cowrie shells—and watched her face darken under streaks of windshield rain. Christmas tree lights showed through drawn blinds in some of the apartments; a downpour rattled the car, then left as though running behind schedule.

"You're serious, aren't you?'' she said finally.

"Lindeman said great deeds. I think the Innocents were blood sacrifices for things like this fund-raiser. Seven kids, their throats cut—of course, the assumption these days is serial killings, sex murders. But each was buried with respect for the remains. You could even say reverence.''

She shook her head slowly.

"Hear me out, Leese. Zavala worked for Guerra; it would be logical bringing Jessica there while he stalked me. Meanwhile Lenny senses an opportunity. He not only sees what he needs in Jessica, but a chance to rid himself of the loose cannon Zavala has become. If Zavala kills me, great. If not, Zavala is still dead and the case is closed. Somehow he pulls it off. All except for the second bullet.''

She ran her fingers through her hair. ''What about Father Martin?'' she said.

''What do you think?''

Rain dripped steadily on the black coupe. As she turned away to face the windshield, he saw the shine in her eyes and felt something let go inside him, as if a spring had been stretched too far.

''I'm sorry,'' he said softly. ''I'll shut up.''

''No,'' she said bleakly. ''I just can't comprehend that we're sitting here talking about children being murdered, possibly by people I'm in with, working with. It's like this tight little box where I'd lock away the bad things is broken.''

Wil touched her hand.

''Lenny Guerra brought me a rose my first day,'' she said. ''He was charming, warm, welcoming. And yet I believe you when you say those things about him. But you can't convince me Father Martin is involved.''

''You've known him how long—two days?''

''I don't care. I just *know*. You ought to see him with kids.'' Fresh tears came. ''Wil, I keep thinking of Devin.''

''Me, too,'' he said.

''What's she like—Jessica?''

''You saw the picture—''

''*Tell me!*''

He let out a breath. ''A lively little thing, small like her father. She likes to play with Legos.''

''It's so goddamn real suddenly.''

''You can be home in an hour, and nobody'd blame you. One way or another, it'll be over soon.''

She drew a deep breath, wiped her eyes. ''Tell me,'' she said. ''Does Mo Epstein cry like this?''

Wil kissed her hair and stroked her cheek, held her to him. ''All the time,'' he said. Beyond the windshield, the bone-white underbelly of the moon peeked through clouds like the tail of a curtain tattered and whipped up by the passing front.

Donna Pacheco was elbow-deep in dishwater when it hit: the sound of a child crying, audible instantly over the lunchtime mutter and clink. A knife in her heart. In the kitchen, no one else noticed; so many families came to Papa Gomez, crying kids were as common as *refritos*. She remembered how easy it had been to tune out Jessie's little cries. Every mother did it.

It was tearing her apart. Again.

Kids with their mothers in the market, children playing in the street, pictures of little girls—that's all it took anymore, anticipating them was not enough. The tears were coming again. Plunking in the half-filled sink as the sobs swept across in waves.

TWENTY-FOUR

Saturday morning brought thundershowers, rain falling, and the sun shining, then the last of the clouds crowded out of the L.A. basin east toward Arizona. By nine the sky was clear and blue, odd contrast to the flash-flood warnings broadcast for some canyon and low-lying areas.

After dozing intermittently, Wil turned the clock radio from low to off, shook the cobwebs out, and took inventory. He was much sorer than yesterday. His knee was puffy and reluctant and tweaked him getting out of bed despite its Ace bandage. A centipede crawled in his scalp wound, evidence of healing. After slow stretching and the oatmeal Lisa'd left with her note about needing to get an early start at St. Boniface, he showered and eased into khakis and a navy sweatshirt, deciding he felt good enough to pass on his pain pills. As he sat with a coffee, he phoned to update Ignacio Reyes. Then he tried to make arrangements for the Harley to be flatbedded up to La Conchita. A recorded voice suggested he call Monday.

Mo Epstein he reached at home.

"You accept apologies during off hours?" he said.

"Apologies meant, or the chopped-liver kind supposed to grease somebody up for a favor?"

Wil felt the sting, knew he deserved it, and said nothing.

"Well, shit," Mo said disgustedly. "Our Lynwood hooker killer walked this morning on a technicality. Dead to rights we have this bird and now she's out on tainted evidence. You were saying?''

"I'm sorry I behaved like a jerk. No excuses. Sincere enough for you?''

"Why not. How you doin'?''

"Better.''

"You still on the sauce? I mean not that it doesn't do things for your personality, it's when it becomes your personality that friends say things, right? You do get that?''

"Right now I'm sober,'' he said.

"And you're smart enough to know there's help.''

"Yes. Look, I'm going to apologize again—sort of an advance.'' He heard the expulsion of breath at the other end. "You were right. I do need your help.''

"Goddammit. You have any idea the position you're putting me in?''

"I think so and I don't like it, but I'm asking anyway: You have any contacts at the sheriff's department, Monroe County, Florida?''

"Suddenly, from out of left field—''

"Humor me.''

"That's the Keys, right, Key West? No, I do not.''

"Okay.'' He left Mo an opening that went unfilled. "Thanks, anyway,'' he said.

"Why there? Not Guerra again.''

"Something I read. Probably nothing—my specialty these days.''

"Look, Hardesty. I'm going to eat my lox and eggs now and my Langer's onion roll and if I haven't called you by one, I ain't calling, right? And you can screw your instincts.'' He hung up.

Wil swallowed lukewarm coffee, checked the yellow pages for car rental companies, phoned a couple for rates, then a Valley listing for a cab. By twelve-twenty he was back at the house, a beige Ford Tempo running a day-rate tab in the drive. Lisa'd brought their answering machine from home and he checked it for messages, saw one flashing and punched it up:

All right. The best I could do down there is a Lieutenant Sawyer, my counterpart in Homicide.

Wil wrote down the number.

This is unofficial, he's agreed to talk to you as a favor to me. But push his buttons like you do mine and we're cashing in our chips, understood? Speaking of which, I think it would be a good idea for you not to call me for a while.

Wil erased the message, then dialed, waited, introduced himself, and explained what he wanted to a friendly-enough voice with a trace of South Florida.

"D-e-S-a-n-t-i-s, Martin," Sawyer repeated back. "Nineteen-forty-five through forty-nine. Hold a sec."

Wil heard the soft click of computer keys. A minute went by.

"Doesn't look as though he bothered our people any. You say he lived around here?"

"That was my understanding," Wil said. "You mind checking another name?"

"I guess not, long as this isn't some list."

"It's not. G-u-e-r-r-a, Leonardo, same time frame."

The clicks again, a chair squeaking. "Got a hit here," Sawyer came back. "Leonardo Guerra, age seventeen, resident of Stock Island. Arrested July 7th, 1949, suspect in a homicide. Held, questioned, cleared, released. Doesn't say when."

"Does it say what cleared him?"

"No idea, partner. Some of these old files got transferred over with just the basics."

"There any way of locating the hard copies?"

"Not on the Saturday before Christmas at four o'clock our time. You have yourself a good afternoon, hear?"

Wil replaced the receiver, poured himself a glass of milk, and drank it. He looked up the number of a nearby copy shop, called, and got their fax number. Then he dialed Key

West information and rang the library there. A Ms. Norris answered, to whom he explained he was investigating a murder and needed her help finding a story in a forty-one-year-old edition of the local paper. That it had a bearing on the case.

"Sir—did you say Lieutenant? We're closing soon. Can you call back on Monday when our archivist will be in?"

"I wish I could do that, Ms. Norris. You sound very nice, and I have no authority to insist that you help me. But the truth is a little girl named Jessica may die Sunday unless I get that information today."

The faint sound of long distance. "And if I find something?"

"I have a number where you can fax it after you call me collect."

Ms. Norris agreed to look; Wil gave her the information, then waited for her call, pegging the chances she would at maybe one in four—easier to just close up and go home. He cleaned up the kitchen, iced his knee, put on a wash, things to dissipate restless energy. Forty minutes passed, an hour; wind slid the hydrangea bushes against the windows. Lisa phoned, said she'd get back to him when he explained.

"Sorry to take so long," Ms. Norris said, calling after he'd written her off and was wondering what the hell to do next. "I had to wait until we closed and there were three articles, none very long. I hope they help."

After she hung up, he ordered flowers to be delivered to her Monday at the library. Then he drove the Tempo to the copy shop, where the three faxes had already arrived. He read in the order she'd marked:

LOCAL GIRL MISSING, FOUL PLAY FEARED

(July 3, 1949) Authorities, family and concerned neighbors of 8-year-old Anita Espinosa expanded search efforts to find the girl, missing from her Stock Island home since yesterday. Dolores Espinosa, 38,

told the Key West Citizen *that her daughter was not the kind to run off and described her as a loving, trusting child liked by all. Coordinating efforts to find Anita is Sheriff Forrest Biggio, who said he was "fearful of foul play." Anyone with information should contact him immediately at his Whitehead Street office.*

ESPINOSA GIRL FOUND DEAD, ARREST MADE

(July 7, 1949) The search for little Anita Espinosa ended tragically today with the discovery of her remains in a mangrove thicket two miles from her Stock Island home. Preliminary reports by Medical Examiner Hector Torres indicate the 8-year-old was murdered. "With a knife, we think, taking into consideration the advanced state of decomposition," he told the Citizen. *The lone bright spot in this tragedy is the arrest of a suspect, Leonardo Guerra, 17. Guerra, who lives with his aunt and guardian in the same rural neighborhood as the murdered girl, was described by Sheriff Forrest Biggio as a known troublemaker who carried a knife with which he often intimidated other boys into "doing things they weren't born to." Biggio revealed the boys broke silence to come forward about the incidents following Guerra's arrest. The* Citizen *joins all right-thinking residents in the hope that justice for young Guerra will be swift and sure.*

ESPINOSA SUSPECT RELEASED, CASE STILL UNSOLVED

(July 9, 1949) Sheriff Forrest Biggio has released Leonardo Guerra, 17, from custody, the Citizen *learned. The prime suspect in the heinous murder of Anita Espinosa, 8, was provided an alibi and cleared of wrongdoing in the case by Martin R. DeSantis, 18, a highly respected resident of Stock Island who left July 3 to enter Catholic seminary in Baltimore. When contacted there, DeSantis testified that Guerra had been helping*

*him prepare for the priesthood July 2, the day Medical
Examiner H. Torres speculated was the time of death.
Prior to his religious calling, DeSantis lived with
Guerra and Guerra's younger sister at their aunt's
residence following the trio's arrival here from Cuba
in 1945. Other unspecified charges against Guerra
also were dropped due to an apparent change of heart
by Guerra's youthful accusers. Biggio vowed to continue the search for Espinosa's killer but agreed that
valuable time had been lost.*

New pieces of the puzzle spun and floated:

Anita Espinosa, the first Innocent.

Martin DeSantis/Lenny Guerra, pals from Cuba going in
different directions.

Lenny owing his freedom, his life, to Martin's "alibi"—
backward sounding if Martin is Lenny's blackmail victim.

Other unspecified charges.

Wil had the faxes spliced together onto one sheet and
ran off a dozen copies. Then he headed for St. Boniface,
picturing as he drove a chain under great stress snapping
at its weakest link.

The Santa Ana was blowing hard as Wil pulled the Ford
Tempo into the church lot just after four. He found a spot
away from Lisa's Acura and Guerra's black Mercedes and
limped toward the administration building. Warm dry gusts
bent the deodar cedars on the lawn and sent dead leaves
whipping down the drive.

"Father Martin isn't in his office this afternoon," the
girl told him. "He's hearing confessions."

Wil glanced around for Lisa, thought he heard her voice
coming from behind a closed door, then backtracked to the
church. Dust blew in the side entrance with him and forced
it shut with a bang. Several people in the vicinity of the
confessionals looked up sharply, then returned to their
prayers. As Wil slipped into a pew near the door with the

light on and the Father DeSantis sign, a Hispanic girl left the confessional and began saying her rosary. Late-afternoon sun threw reds and blues off the stained-glass windows.

They'd faded by the time Wil entered the confessional.

He waited in the dim close space until the portal slid open and the familiar voice asked him how long since his last confession.

"Hello, Father," he said.

After a pause, the priest said, "Mr. Hardesty? Forgive me for sounding surprised."

"I was taught confession is good for the soul."

"You have something you wish to confess?"

Wil pushed a copy of the three articles through the portal. A light was snapped on, Father Martin backlit through the screen. He put on reading glasses. Minutes passed; the sound of wind finding cracks in the building, then of paper folding. Father Martin removed the glasses, pinched the bridge of his nose, then snapped off the light. Wil could hear him breathing.

"What is it you wish from me, Mr. Hardesty?" The voice was empty of resonance.

"The truth," Wil said. "That Lenny has her."

"Has who?"

Wil waited.

"Are you going to tell me who?"

"You're still covering for him, aren't you? Jessica—the little girl I was telling you about. Lenny's going to kill her to bless your fund-raiser."

"Do you realize what you are saying, and to whom? Excuse me, but I have much to do for tomorrow."

"Don't underestimate me, Father. You may not fear the Catholic Church, but the media will wallow in this. Throw in what I've learned about Chawa Uve, lover of innocent blood, and everything you've built here is burning big-time."

"You would threaten St. Boniface as well as me?"

"To save her? To end the killings? Try me."

"What we do here is far bigger than one man." The flatness was gone from his voice now.

"You know better than that," Wil said. "First the Hollywood crowd will disengage, all your image-conscious types. Then the money dries up. Then the dream. Pretty soon it's just you and the *rebozos* again—if they let you stick around."

"You are—beyond belief."

"And what are you, Father? Does the name Benito mean anything? He was a beautiful boy with dark eyes, six years old when Lenny cut him. And the others—Anita Espinosa. Why do you continue to protect him?"

"You have no idea what you're talking about."

"Blood sacrifices, children's lives traded for wealth. You an accessory to murder."

"That's what you think I desire—wealth?" He spat the word.

"Lenny I can see killing. But what happened to Martin DeSantis, the respected young man who wanted to be a Catholic priest?"

The wind moaned and slacked. Father Martin said, "You remind me of a child peering into a kaleidoscope, thinking he sees lions and tigers."

"Talk to me, goddammit. Where is Jessica Pacheco?"

"I don't know."

" 'Which of you can be happy knowing others are suffering, can live knowing others are dying?' Your words, the other Sunday. How long can you go on being two people?"

"I tell you I don't know where she is."

"But Lenny's blackmailing you, isn't he? Something to do with the Espinosa killing."

"Each of us has his cross, Mr. Hardesty. No one but the very young is completely innocent."

Wil took a deep breath. "Look, I don't care about that.

All I want is to stop him, to save the girl. Give Lenny up and I'll try to leave you out of it."

Father Martin leaned back in his chair, the copy crinkled in his hand. When he spoke he sounded like the scratchy soundtrack to an old travelogue: "Lenny and I met in school in Cuba. We were drawn to each other, we became like brothers. He was a loner, usually in trouble because his father had been kicked to death by *policía*, and his mother was too ill to handle him. I was forest people, the one pointed at and whispered about—the only one in my village permitted to attend outside school.

"One day Lenny was arrested for stealing. At the police station he heard talk of my village, of soldiers coming there that night. Lenny was thirteen—a year younger than me—but he knew I couldn't go back, which is what I wanted desperately. We fought. Afterward he pulled my face close to his and told me I was coming with him and Sissy to Key West. By then his mother was dying, and an aunt there had sent for the children. Next morning, Lenny hid me at his house when the soldiers came with guns. That afternoon the three of us were on a fishing boat, sick and retching, but alive." He cleared his throat of sudden emotion, then went on.

"Twice the boat nearly sank. But God had a plan for me, and it was St. Boniface, and whatever Lenny is he's been a part of that plan. Give him up? You should not underestimate me either, Mr. Hardesty."

Wil applied pressure to temples that had begun to throb and ventured in another direction. "Why were you the only one of your people to attend school?"

"I was—special. I'd passed tests. We were poor, and the others were needed for work."

"Your people sacrificed children."

The priest's sigh was resignation itself. "Chawan tradition was the way of the blood, Mr. Hardesty. Very primitive, very misguided. A very long time ago."

"And something that Lenny never abandoned after learning it from you."

"That is absurd."

"Lenny stole the Chawa idols from a Cuban museum in 1963. He was running guns to Castro then, easy to get them out of the country. Today they'd be worth plenty, yet he's never sold them. Isn't it obvious why?"

"Lenny is a collector as well as a seller of antiquities. He uses those pieces to generate business. I see many people in my office. In exchange for inquiries, our missions receive half the profits. To serve the greater good, I choose not to delve beyond that."

"And because he also makes you money selling babies he doesn't kill to rich parishioners you steer his way."

"For an intelligent man, Mr. Hardesty, you disappoint me. Even if I were to accept such crudeness, my parishioners are in no way coerced."

"And I say your splitting profits with Lenny Guerra might perk up some ears at the chancery. Last chance: Where is Jessica Pacheco?"

"I don't know."

Wil took a deep breath. The air in the closed space seemed fetid and used up now, and he hurt from being in one position so long. It all seemed upside down and out of sync, a dark twisting Möbius strip of truth and lies.

"Who confesses you, Father?" he said.

"DeSantis is lying, but it makes no sense. Lenny-saves-him-he-saves-Lenny seems like a wash. Yet the SOB is still into him for something." Wil winced as Lisa applied antiseptic creme to the scalp wound. They were in the guest bedroom, his shirt off to check progress on the bruising.

"You mentioned his ambition."

"It has to be more than that."

She touched the stitches gently. "You're pulling a little bit there, but it looks pretty good."

"I figured he'd crack."

"Maybe he really doesn't know," Lisa said. She screwed the cap on the tube, replaced it in his Dopp kit. "How's your knee?"

"Tender. They're too tied-in for him not to know."

"Can't Mo do something?"

"With what—more of my speculations?"

"I'm sorry," she said quietly. "It's not going well, is it?" She began to rub his shoulders, cautiously at first, then more intently.

"Feels good," he said, closing his eyes. "How did you do with Guerra?"

She kept rubbing.

"Ouch, lighter please. Well?"

"I don't know, nothing concrete yet—just a feeling that more money is coming in than going out. I keep trying to poke around in the files, but—"

He unblinked. "But what?"

"I look around to see where he is, what he's up to, what I might be able to do, and it's as if he's reading my mind. Following me with his eyes. When I ask questions I pretend I don't know the answers to, he's all smiles, but indirect and evasive. Wil, I need more time."

"I know."

"Are you sure about the fund-raiser?"

"Let's get a pizza or something, forget about it for one night."

"Don't be patronizing. I hate that." Her fingers hit a spot, causing him to wince. She bit her lip.

"Hey," he said. "It's all right."

"No, it's not. It's frustrating. I want to do more."

Wil drew her to him and held her around the waist. "We still have most of tomorrow; Lenny'll be tied up with the event. Whatever happens will be afterward."

"How can you be sure?"

"I'm not. But sometimes thinking that way is all you have to keep from going crazy." Her fingers smoothed the hair over his ears. "I'm glad you came, Leese."

She softened against him, and he pulled her down onto his good knee, lightly touched her cheek. "I was afraid I'd lost you."

Her eyes swept his face.

"And myself," he added.

"It's different now?"

"What's different is I'm not drinking even though I'm tempted. That's been you. Having something not to drink for."

"Wil—"

He kissed her tentatively, felt her kiss back, soft then harder. A chord struck and resonated in him, and he felt it surge against his khakis. After a bit she broke from him and traced his lips with her fingernail, smiled as he undid her blouse and took each breast in his mouth. They tasted perfumey of lotion and warm wind, the nipples firm under his tongue, and there was a tightness at his heart, as if she'd reached in and put her hand around it. She undressed first, her skin reminding him of the pale honey they'd trek to Ojai for in the fall. She helped him pull the khakis off over his erection, pushed him gently back on Raeann Rodriguez's bed, straddled him, and guided him inside. As they moved together in familiar symmetry, easy at first in deference to his knee, then more passionately, Wil felt himself floating away from everything, all the wrenching drama, lifted beyond it by the cresting sounds of two instruments lovingly played.

Patty McGann slumped in the red chair and exhaled smoke from her True cigarette; assistant news directors—even recently promoted ones—didn't cover fund-raisers, for Christ's sake. Before the Innocents she would have jumped at it, but now— Hell, women's groups had her booked six months in advance for speaking engagements. No looking back. Across from her the news director was saying, "Come on. Tell me you haven't heard the Nobel Prize talk."

"I'll put somebody good on it," Patty McGann said. "No problem."

"Look," the news director said, "I'm running it lead local with international overtones, the Mexican consul's primed. You can swing by there before you interview Father Martin. That's early news. At eleven we broadcast what you get at St. Boniface." He saw her expression. "It's hot, guaranteed. This guy's the next Mother Teresa."

Patty McGann rolled her eyes.

"Most of Hollywood's coming. Pick a name. . . ."

She sat forward. "All right, I'm weak. What do you have on it?"

Smiling, the news director briefed her.

Afterward, Patty McGann said, "I'll take Lombardi. He's luck."

TWENTY-FIVE

Lisa left for St. Boniface early Sunday morning, the event, including a three-o'clock mass and donor reception afterward, requiring every available volunteer. Wil showered, had breakfast he hardly tasted, then chafed and paced for an hour, anxious to move on what he had planned. At ten-thirty she called: Guerra had arrived, Julio in tow, to organize the financial part of the evening's presentation. She'd slipped away to get him some numbers and had to go now, bye.

Wil hung up, transferred his B&E tools from the torn-up field jacket to a windbreaker, put Lisa's beeper in his pocket, then locked up the house. As he drove east the sun's glare found the windshield streaks from Friday's storm. The Santa Ana had blown itself out, allowing an infusion of cool air into the basin, a new buildup of smog toward downtown and scattered clouds against the mountains. Forty-percent chance of thundershowers for later, the radio said. The air smelled of ozone and exhaust.

From the gate, Guerra's place looked empty; no cars in the drive, garage doors shut, curtains pulled across the windows. Wil cruised, found a cul-de-sac a block up, and parked. From here he had a bird's-eye view of the Arroyo and the Rose Bowl. Ahead, the big Craftsman's shake roof showed through close-bunched myosporum, bottlebrush, and eucalyptus.

Pretending to admire the view, he found a way through the greenery and slipped into it; minutes later, he was cursing an impenetrable rear door lock, feeling around a window for alarm wire, finding none. Interesting, Wil thought, scoring and removing a glass circle near the latch: Guerra preferring to take his chances with a burglar entering the house than with a security guard who'd report what he found.

He did a fast scan of the interior, found no evidence of Jessica, then came back to what had to be Guerra's bedroom: large, with French doors facing the mountains, gold-veined mirrors, recessed lighting, thick gray carpet, and a huge bed with a black-and-gold tapestry spread. Across from a walk-in closet was a two-person, multijetted spa surrounded by an apron of black marble. The room exuded the sweet-tart essence of citrus cologne.

Wil checked his watch: twelve-ten. He did a cursory check of the closet, then came back and tossed the bureau drawers. Nothing, personal effects. Next he returned to the wood-paneled den just off the living room and started through the desk and bookcases. Zip—until he saw the photo album. It was on a floor-level bookshelf, a corner of it sticking out from a crevice between two anthologies of Latin American poetry, their leather spines ornately embossed. The photo album, by contrast, was plain and water-spotted, deteriorating suede that cracked as he opened it.

She was there between them, a serious-looking young girl in glasses, peering out from deckle-edged snapshots blotched by time. In most, Martin was on the right, Lenny left. In some she was petting a boxer dog or dwarfed by a heavy woman in bunned hair and a print dress. He recognized the girl immediately, but the caption under one of her and a sunburnt man with pocked features and thinning hair was mute confirmation:

Wedding Day, October 16th, 1949. Sissy and Fredo Contreras.

Wil almost felt for her, she looked so unhappy: Lenny's

little sister on her day of days. Jennette Guerra Contreras.

Christ, Wil thought, she'd been right under his nose the whole time. Jennette Contreras: Not the stolid Niños employee, understandably and expectedly supportive of her boss. Not the dutiful worker taking papers home to complete the night he broke into Lenny's office—*after* Lenny transferred a suitcase large enough to hold a small child from his Mercedes to her white Camry. He pictured her looking out at him from Lenny's arched window, her face a hard mask through the rain.

The next spread was empty save for a small pasted-in newspaper clipping showing the sunburnt man in a dark suit. *Local man drowns in fishing accident 2/15/51*, the caption read. There was no story.

More blank spreads, then in back, a fissured snapshot shoved in without mounts; Wil took it out. It was Martin and Jennette, he eighteen perhaps, muscular in tight swimming trunks, she younger and obviously pre-Fredo Contreras. She was smiling at him, feeling the biceps he'd flexed for her. Wil flipped it over, read the girlish hand: *Mi corazón y mi vida. Por todo tiempo.*

In the drawers he found a phone book but no listing for Jennette Contreras; directory assistance was likewise unhelpful. Mo? Not likely and too little time: one o'clock already. He began going through the desk again, anything with an address for Jennette Contreras. Nothing. He checked the bedrooms, the closets, anything with drawers, and came up empty.

Like the trash containers in every room, even the kitchen.

He bolted outside in search of the garbage cans and found them racked beside the garage. Full, awaiting a Monday pickup—his first break. He dragged them inside, dumped them out on the kitchen floor, and started going through them. Ripe table scraps, vegetable peelings, spoiled fruit, damp tissue and paper towels, milk containers, junk mail, bits of voided checks showing Guerra's Pasadena address, wadded-up yellow tablet sheets with English and math homework attempted on them, old newspapers, cans and bottles. *Bingo*.

Wil lifted out the Southern Cal Edison bill as if it were buried treasure. Stained barely legible, it was for a Palos Verdes residence, 844 Pájaro Lane, yet was addressed for payment to Guerra. The name Contreras showed under tomato seeds Wil scraped off with his thumbnail.

He was headed out the door when Lisa's beeper sounded. Wil called her back at the number she'd given him. She was on in a half-ring, asking when he'd be coming. He told her what he'd found, about Jennette Contreras being Lenny's sister.

"What does it mean?" Her voice had a furtive edge to it.

"That's what I hope to find out," he said. "But I think she's had Jess the whole time. Guerra must own the property."

"So you're going." The disappointment was audible.

"Can you hang in until I get there? It's important."

"Guerra's acting strange, Wil."

"How?"

"Omnipresent or something. He barely lets me go to the bathroom without him. Father Martin's been with the media nonstop since I arrived. Wil, it's nearly two-thirty."

"I know. This could be it, Leese. Beep me when you can, and I'll let you know what I find. I'll try and make the reception, okay? I love you."

Sunday traffic was heavy in places but moving; thickened overcast made the day oppressive, as though a lid had come down on it. Pushing the rental, Wil made Palos Verdes in forty-three minutes. As the road curved up and along the cliffs above the ocean, he stopped at a gas station for directions.

Eight-forty-four Pájaro Lane was set back on the hillside in a looping circle of large established lots: horse corrals and tennis courts, pittosporum and eucalyptus windbreaks, ice plant and bougainvillea, Mexican tile and turf-roll-perfect lawns, rain-birds going despite the prospect of rain. Through tall oleander bushes, he could see no white Camry. He parked a block away from the house, tried to look like an insurance agent going up the drive to an entry overhung by the second story. He rang the bell, heard it echo, waited. No one came. He found a side door, looked around, then put his shoulder to it; the wood gave grudgingly, but it gave.

It was an odd house inside, predominantly white in theme and more spacious than it appeared from the street. Wil drew the .45 from his waistband, slid a round into the chamber, and did a room-by-room. The ground floor was heavy with the smell of air freshener but clean and tidy, nothing out of place, nothing to give away a baby presence. It was upstairs that the need for the freshener became clear. In a small closed bedroom down the hall from the one with all the candles.

The shuttered window was latched tight, the room empty save for a closet with an open sliding door and a rug cleaner awaiting use. The urine smell seemed to be coming from everywhere, not just the stained carpet with the playpen-sized imprints. He ran his finger over one, the fibers rising slowly.

He checked the rest of the upstairs, found two unopened bottles of Johnson's lotion under the bathroom sink, baby aspirin in the medicine cabinet, no-tears shampoo by the tub. For a minute he sat on the edge, imaging Jessica Pacheco here, feeling her, his gut twisting at how close he'd come. Then he went outside.

The trash cans beside the utility shed were empty and oddly free of the smell from upstairs. Puzzled, he searched the enclosed yard: unpruned rosebushes, patchy lawn, medium-size pines, a pile of recently raked needles in a shaded area, wire rake up against the fence. Wil moved the pine needles aside, then put weight down where they'd been; his chukka boot left a deep imprint. He broke the handle off he rake and began poking the sharp end into the soft spot. About eighteen inches down he felt it penetrate something, was widening the hole when the smell hit. He went back to the garage, found a shovel, and began digging.

The black plastic garden bag was full of old diapers, the stench like a slap in the face. Credit for thoroughness, he thought. With all the publicity about Jessica, she'd buried them to avoid any trace of suspicion by sharp-nosed garbagemen. He reburied the bag, was washing his hands off at the faucet when something caught his eye. Where the house seemed smaller than it was from outside, the garage seemed larger. It didn't take long to find the reason.

The space meant for cars was claustrophobic with old furniture, appliances, storage cartons, sacks of fertilizers, bottles of pesticide, paint cans on shelves, sprinkler hoses looped over hooks. But its depth lacked about three of the strides he'd measured off outside. Behind a workbench, the rear wall was festooned with tools; beside the bench a ladder leaned up against a padlocked door. Wil moved the ladder, found a crowbar, and went at the lock. It was a big Master, the kind bullets bounced off, and the wood around it gave before it did.

Unlike the raw garage, the inner room was carefully finished and painted white. It had a small roof vent through which sunlight angled and a marbled Formica surface anchored to white legs against the far wall. The smell of burned candles was like that from Jennette's bedroom, yet here were no candles. Roses hovered in the air where there were none.

The thing that drew him, however, locked his eyes onto it and set off a roaring in his ears, was the drain. It was in the center of the gently sloping concrete floor. Nothing unusual—just a couple of inches across with a gleaming steel grate. Yet it was everything, a vortex that dizzied and pulled him in, the portal to some dreadful dark place that sucked out hope and life and left behind a bloodless world.

•   •   •

It began with a blast of organ music; halfway through the mass Father Martin took the pulpit. He spoke of feeding and clothing, sheltering and healing; of bringing forth the means to lead a dispossessed generation back to grace. He had something he wanted them to see.

As Lisa watched from her seat on the aisle, a big-screen video projector was rolled out, the lights dimmed. Underscored by haunting flute music, the production's visuals hit with a wrenching directness. In the end the appeal of the actor-narrator was passed back to the priest like a baton.

For a moment Father Martin surveyed them, then his smile vanished. With the remote, he reversed the video to a child's face, freezing anguish made memorable by angelic features.

"This is Lourdes," he said. "One of our workers found her living in a dump, her home a rusted-out boiler. Anything she could find she ate—garbage, grass." He paused. "It wasn't enough. Lourdes—she hadn't even a name when we found her—died three days ago."

There was a murmur from the packed church.

"You see, we had no room for Lourdes. Because we hadn't room, because humanity hadn't room, she died. And because she died, we could wait no longer. Lourdes is why you are here tonight, my friends.

"How old would you say she was from the picture—seven, eight?" Seconds passed. "She was twelve."

"*Twelve!*" He banged the pulpit. "We feel the pain of hunger a few hours after eating—let a day go by and we're fainting. But try it for twelve years."

His face was cold stone.

"I want you to do something for me now. I want you to be silent for *two minutes* while you think what it was like to be"—he pointed to the image—"that child."

By the end of two minutes, much of the gathering was moved to tears. Lisa was not ready for what followed.

"Tears?" Father Martin raged suddenly. "For Lourdes? She could not eat your tears then, and she can't now. She could not be comforted by your tears then, and she won't be now. She could not draw warmth from your tears then, and she certainly cannot now.

"You are too late!" His voice thundered off the hard walls of St. Boniface.

"Yet even Lourdes, who was given nothing her whole life, found in the end something to give." His voice broke. "Before she died, she gave us her smile.

"If I had only known, you say. Only helped." He shook his head at them. "Lourdes had one thing, and she gave it gladly. How much will you give so that no more like Lourdes die?"

For a long moment he scanned their upturned faces. "For God's sake, help us," he said. *"Now."*

His silence was like a call to action. Baskets were passed. Every few rows, empties replaced full ones, the scene reminding Lisa of the loaves and fishes in reverse. Then the baskets were gone, and Father Martin retook the pulpit. The video unit was replaced by a carousel projector and screen.

"Are the slides ready?" he asked. The lights dimmed again in response. "My friends, these charts will help you understand the magnitude of this project. *Your* project. And why tonight's donation, generous as it is, can be only the beginning—"

Familiar with this part, Lisa's mind began to drift. Where was Wil, what came next? She swiveled and tried to locate Lenny in the projector light, but he'd evidently left his seat during the interlude. So strange he was—courteous and deferential one minute, sinister the next. And Martin DeSantis: Wil's logic to the contrary, there was no way the man she'd just heard could be involved in . . .

Lenny was beckoning to her from a shadow. She nodded, saw him slip out via the baptismal entrance. Lisa eased out of her seat, gave a last look at the audience. Every eye was on Father Martin and the figures she'd helped prepare. Powerful, well-dressed people held rapt.

Outside it was almost dark, the sky heavy with approach-

ing rain; thunder sounded faintly in the San Gabriels.
Across the lawn, though, all was festive readiness. Twinkling lights and the sounds of a string quartet warming up
came from the big reception tent. She checked her watch:
five o'clock, time to call Wil again.

"Over here," Lenny said. He was standing under a deodar near the parking lot, the red carnation a spot of color
on his black tuxedo jacket.

"Sorry to drag you out," he said as she approached.
"But we need to get some things for your presentation."

"What?" A chill went through her: the persistent fear
of speaking in public, something she hated about herself.
"What presentation?"

"Later at the reception," he said. "The tax ramifications
of donating. Father Martin thought of it earlier, giving that
part to you, and I forgot to mention it. It is your area, isn't
it?"

"Yes, but—"

"Come on, I'll brief you on what to say. I need to get
some things for my own talk."

"I thought that was all set," she said. He was steering
her toward his car. "Where are we going?" *Dammit, get
to a phone*.

"Only take a second to get what I need. We thought you
could open with a short review of that part of the tax code."

"Father Martin for sure wants this?"

"You've impressed him. Look, they'll be through any
minute, and we're up next. Are you coming?" Reflection
from the lot lights flared off his glasses, making it impossible to see his eyes.

She didn't like it, tried to weigh the consequences, wondered what Wil would do, cursed her inexperience. Her fear
decided it. Ever since eighth grade—the speech class when
she'd gone mute and fled the podium—she'd had night-
mares about being unprepared. As she got into the big Mercedes, Julio raised up in the rear seat from where he'd been
sleeping. He blinked and took her in with vacant eyes, then

settled back down on the leather cushions. Calmed by his presence, she snapped on the seat belt and began running through possible opening remarks as Lenny Guerra headed out of the lot, the first big drops of rain pelting the windshield.

Wil was aware of the rain only as a vague presence on Jennette Contreras's roof, its sound lost in the pounding of his pulse and the dumping of bureau drawers onto her overturned mattress. Her bedroom was a mess but a controlled one; with no trace of blood, old or new, in the shed, he needed another Saint Christopher medal, the knife. Something tangible.

One more bureau left. He pulled out a drawer, emptied it, found nothing to speak of.

Lisa's not beeping him since Guerra's was becoming worrisome. It was after six now and dark: probably she'd given up on him coming and was stuck at the reception. Still it wasn't the plan, and possible scenarios squirmed in his head like snakes let loose from a basket.

Middle drawer: more slips, bras, lace panties—blue this time. Bottom drawer: white satin robe, carefully folded. He shook it out, wadded it up, and threw it at the wall in frustration, heard something hit. Something more substantial than satin.

It was sewn into an inner pocket of the robe, the space inside the prongs just large enough to slip over his held-together fingers. The bracelet was tarnished almost beyond recognition as silver; he had to wet his finger and rub hard to bring out the name enscripted on the flat part.

Anita.

He was going to do it anyway, take his chances with Mo, knowing how Mo would react to the break-in and his meager evidence, when the phone rang. He wavered, decided, picked it up, listened. There was music and a faint sound like someone moaning, a voice robbed of its dignity and composure that sent icicles through him.

"Ah," Lenny Guerra said. "So glad we caught you in."

For seconds Wil said nothing, concentrating instead on the background voice, which had gathered itself into small familiar gasps. Then he said, "I've seen what's in the garage, Lenny. It's over. Tell me where your sister took the baby, and maybe we can deal."

"I have a message for you from a loved one, Mr. Hardesty."

Lisa screamed then: agonized, unremitting pain and terror, the sound of a baby bird in a cat's jaws. Wil shut his eyes, opened them. The room blurred momentarily, and he fought for air.

"Vise-grips are such useful tools," Guerra said. "Did you know a knuckle makes a sound just like a walnut cracking?"

"Pain for pain, Guerra. I swear it."

"The ring finger next, I think." Lisa's groan went soprano.

"WHAT DO YOU WANT?"

"*Already* you're giving up?" Disappointment in Guerra's tone. "I must tell you about another snitch we worked on once, uncooperative, not like your wife. She's told me a great deal. I appear to have underestimated you, Mr. Hardesty."

Wil wiped away sweat as the room steadied.

"You made a terrible mess in my kitchen," Guerra said.

"What do you want?" His voice was someone else's.

"From you? I want you to join us at my house. Make up for the party we had to miss. You'll come unescorted, of course, or she's dead. That is a promise."

"Let me talk to my wife."

"By all means."

There was a muffled bump, then, "Wil—? He found the Polaroid things in my desk. Stupid of me—" She sounded weak and sick and hurting.

"I'll be there, Leese. Can you make it?"

"Think so—"

"Good girl. He won't hurt you anymore."

"Wil? Did you tell Jennette Contreras I was Japanese? It's how they knew for sure, he said—"

The truth of it was like a jolt of high voltage, searing his ability to feel, leaving only his brain to recall his slip at the Niños office, playing it over and over in his mind like a shorted-out doll voice. *My wife is Japanese; wife is Japanese, wife is—*

Guerra broke the connection.

Wil replaced the receiver and put his hands over his ears, his self-righteous admonishment of Paul loud in them now as well. Then, strangely, he was conscious of the rain.

Jennette Contreras sat behind the tinted windows of her car in a shadowed section of the parking lot. Over the steady beat of the rain, she could hear thin snatches of music and people laughing—salt-in-the-wound sounds. Earlier she'd seen them exit the church in their fancy clothes, put up umbrellas, start across the lawn for the shelter of the reception tent.

Then *he'd* come out. Tall and straight in the black cassock he'd changed into, gray hair haloed by the glow from inside, sparks only she had the gift to see emanating from his fingertips into the darkness. Despite the rain, he paused a moment to look around, then raised his face to the sky. Then, as though reluctant to enter the realm of mere mortals, he descended the steps and strode powerfully toward the tent.

Like a thousand times before, after the initial pain subsided, she thought about what life with him would have been like.

Thunder and lightning. Fire in the sugarcane.

Babies they'd been then, but fast learners. Then her aunt: a sin, the meddling bitch called it when she'd found out. Conspiring with Monsignor Padilla to have Martin shipped off to the seminary in Baltimore and her married afterward to that imbecile Fredo. Were it not for her aunt, Martin

DeSantis would have renounced his precious calling.

Jennette lit a cigarillo, let the smoke curl past her eyes, and pondered what Martin had accomplished, the price of it, and who paid. Dark windows reflected the answer: She'd paid. With her life. Martin himself had said it: Where there is one injustice, there is no justice. He'd been stolen from her. Martin had been *hers*, and to hell with humanity.

The smoke from the cigarillo was making her eyes water. She cracked the window to let in air. The work was his sole passion now; all she would ever have was the memory of the mangroves, she knew that. Fed by deprivation and her one taste of him.

Jennette watched the first of the guests leave the tent and hurry toward their cars. Engines started, lights flashed on. At least she would see him tonight; at least there still was something she could do.

In the backseat of the Toyota, the baby stirred in drugged sleep.

TWENTY-SIX

Rain bent the camphor tree branches, swirled under the streetlights, danced and sheeted on the pavement. It ran off the shake roof of the big Craftsman as Wil pulled into the driveway and under the portico. Drawn curtains glowed upstairs; he could hear Guerra's big sound system playing. He got out of the car, thumbed the safety off the .45, and held it down at his thigh.

The front door was unlocked.

He slipped inside, scanned it from a crouch. The living and dining areas were dark except for minuscule greens and reds on the stereo panel. The furnishings were lumpy shapes. Light came from the stairwell. He was halfway there, remembering the old surf admonishment about never turning your back on the ocean, when Guerra's voice came from behind him.

"Drop the gun, please, Mr. Hardesty."

Wil froze, estimating Guerra's location and his chances to turn and fire.

"I am a very good shot. And you are a very large target."

The voice was from over his left shoulder and down low. Lousy odds.

"It would be a shame to come all this way and not see your wife."

Wil backed off the hammer, set the .45 down on the

carpet. He sensed a shape rising from behind a chair, heard footsteps, smelled citrus cologne, felt the touch of a silencer at his spine.

Guerra bent down and picked up the .45. "Up the stairs and to your left, please."

"The cops are waiting for my signal, Lenny. If they don't get it, you can blame yourself for what happens here."

"The very cops who are protecting me from you? Who'll sympathize with my having to shoot to defend myself and Julio from an armed intruder? I think not, Mr. Hardesty. Now move, please."

At the head of the stairs they turned left opposite the bedrooms, down the hall through paneled doors to a second living area with a fire going in the stone hearth. In the room was a wet bar, notched wooden beams, sconced lighting, gray leather couches, and around an inlaid game table, Windsor chairs.

It was to one of these that Lisa was bound with two-inch duct tape. A strip of it circled her head and covered her eyes; another had been put over her mouth. Her face was blotched and puffy as though having been struck. Drying blood patterned her blouse and the two swollen fingers on her right hand that bore ridged imprints.

On the table was a pair of vise-grips and a chain saw.

Wil felt a fluttering inside, as though something with wings and claws was trying to beat its way out of his rib cage. The air in the room was suddenly gone. He went to her, smoothed what hair he could off her face, kissed it, saw a tear roll from a gap in the tape. He tried removing the strip from her mouth, stopped when he saw how it hurt.

"I'm here, Leese," he said softly. "Can you breathe all right?"

She nodded.

"You son of a bitch," he said, turning to face Guerra.

"I'm glad we understand each other," Guerra said.

"She needs a doctor. At least let me free her broken hand."

"Later," Guerra said. He wore an embroidered silk jacket over black trousers, held a matte-finish automatic with a silencer as long as the slide. His gray eyes went to Wil's stitches. "You seem to have had an accident, Mr. Hardesty."

"Next time hire a better grade of scumbag."

"Gangbangers—losers who work without a stake in the outcome. Even at his worst Bolo was better."

"Is that the gun you killed him with?"

Guerra sighed deeply. "Poor Bolo. I could not risk his capture, and I certainly could not permit him to leave."

Keep him talking. Wil leaned against the table, put his hand on Lisa's wrist, and felt for a pulse. It was regular—at least she wasn't in shock. "So you waited at the tunnel and you took him out."

"I had a feeling his ambush would turn out the way it did. Would we even be here if his head weren't so hard?"

"It was you who saved him at the border, wasn't it?"

"Yes. Back then Bolo was worth saving." Guerra eased onto the arm of a couch. "He called me from a house he broke into after being shot. I was able to get him out, but he was never right after that. Morphine for the pain. Cocaine to function. Bolo made his own prison."

"Like Martin DeSantis? He's never been free of you either, has he?"

"Mr. Hardesty, I understand your wanting to extend this, but business calls. I want the name of the man who is paying you."

There it was. Juice, his bargaining chip. "Sorry," Wil said. "Client privilege. Besides, my client knows nothing beyond Zavala."

"That may be true, but I can hardly take the chance, can I?"

Lisa moved her fingers and groaned, the sound like a

scream in his ears. He went to the wet bar sink, dampened a towel, began bathing her face and neck.

"I'm curious," Guerra said, tracking him with the gun. "What kind of a husband puts his wife in a position to be killed by a man to whom it means nothing?"

Wil kept on with the towel but felt his chest tighten, a burning in his scalp.

"I suppose that shouldn't surprise me," Guerra went on. "Knowing how your son died."

Wil spun around, was steps from Guerra's throat when Guerra fired. The gun made a flat coughing noise, and the Windsor chair near Lisa's head disintegrated. The pistol then swung back to where Wil stood, his breath coming in gasps. Lisa was rigid, the tendons in her neck taut cables.

"Temper, Mr. Hardesty. The next one takes her head off. Now, who is paying you? Or would you rather I broke the rest of her fingers?"

Suddenly Lisa's head dropped to her chest and her body went slack; Wil ripped the tape off her mouth, determined she was breathing, then took off his jacket and cradled her head with it.

"She's fainted."

Guerra picked up the vise-grips. "These will bring her around."

"You think you can use that and still keep me off you?"

"You seem to have a death wish, Mr. Hardesty. And little concern for your wife."

"Touch her and I'll kill you. Shoot me, you get nothing. She can't reveal the name because she doesn't know it."

"Mr. Hardesty, where I put these next bullets, you will beg to tell me."

"Bolo supplied the kids, didn't he? But he didn't have the stomach to kill them. That's your specialty, along with blackmail. Using Jennette to get at Martin. Threatening to expose him because they're lovers. How'd you get your sister to go along—by blackmailing her, too? Or does she get a cut of what you suck out of St. Boniface?"

Seeing the color rise in Guerra's face, Wil kept pushing. "Why isn't she here, anyway? The sorcerer's apprentice have a mind of her own?"

Guerra stepped forward and lashed the silencer across Wil's face, the blow striking just below the cheekbone even though he turned with it. Pinpoints of light, bright fireworks; his face felt as though it was imploding into the cut. He touched blood, looked directly into the zinc eyes.

"How does it feel to kill a child, Lenny, let alone nine? Or haven't you done Jessica Pacheco yet?"

A glimpse of movement at the partly open door: red pajamas, black hair, wide eyes. Guerra saw, too. He backed up a step, keeping the gun on Wil's chest. Rain peppered the glass beyond the curtain.

"I told you to stay in your room, boy."

Julio said nothing. He was staring at Lisa.

Guerra raised his voice. "Didn't you take your pills?"

"I still can't sleep."

Wil realized he'd never heard him speak before; the words were heavily accented. "I heard things," Julio added, making no move to retreat. His eyes still were fixed on Lisa.

"Come here," Guerra said, and when the boy came within range, slapped him hard across the face.

Julio took the blow as if he felt nothing. No hand raised to the mark, no register of pain. His gaze shifted to Guerra. *"Es verdad?"* he said. *"Niños muertos?"*

"Go to your room. We'll discuss it later."

Julio seemed sculpted. Then he shook his head slowly.

Guerra was about to strike him again but stopped. "Very well," he said. "We will do this together, you can help. Down the hall, Mr. Hardesty. The second door on the right."

"Your guardian's a murderer, Julio. A killer of children."

Guerra put his left hand on the boy's neck. "These are bad people, they need to be taught a lesson. Now move,

Mr. Hardesty, or watch her die.'' The gun came level with Lisa's eyes.

Wil made a decision to play for time. Backing down the hall, he kept his eyes on Julio. ''You don't owe him this, you know. If you're a witness, he'll have to kill you, too.''

''Julio has every reason to obey. Don't you, boy?''

''He's going to shoot me to get me to tell him things. Then he'll start again on my wife. When we're dead, he'll have you cut us up with the chain saw.'' He couldn't tell if the boy had heard; his look was distant, and he was swallowing rapidly.

Guerra said, ''Julio, go to my room and turn on the water.''

''Don't do it. Run. Call nine one one.''

''Do as I say.''

Julio brushed past, and Wil heard the sound of water rushing. Then Wil was at the doorway and through it into Guerra's bedroom, standing on the black marble apron of the fast-filling spa.

''Cleaner this way,'' Guerra said, pulling the boy over beside him. ''You were quite right to insist on this, Julio, your education comes first. And you needn't look like that. Mr. Hardesty has caused us a great deal of trouble.''

Wil homed in on the boy's eyes, saw something there, with luck what he hoped: *Lenny, Key West, 1949. Boys intimidated. Unspecified charges.*

''It's all right not to care about me, but what about you? You like what he does to you, what he's doing now? You let this happen and there's no escape, no hope. Just more of it.''

Julio's shoulders sagged, and Wil knew he'd hit home. ''Think, Julio: How long before he kills you for a ten year old?''

Guerra smoothed his mustache. ''You will step down, Mr. Hardesty. Boy, pay attention to where I put the first round.''

It wasn't much: a bleat and a grab at the arm, but Julio's

move distracted Guerra long enough for Wil to complete his lunge. He grabbed, got a grip around the silencer, and hung on. Guerra ripped off three harmless shots, Wil feeling their heat before catching Guerra with an elbow to the throat. He twisted hard; the gun clattered on the marble, then they were in the tub, a single roiling, thrashing mass that bumped and skidded off the spa's contours. Wil freed an arm, drove punches into Guerra's middle, but without purchase they were feeble; he felt Guerra's jaws close to his face, fingernails clawing at his eyes. He managed to get a hand around one of the fingers then, wrench it back until it snapped. Guerra screamed, and in that instant Wil shoved his head under, knew Guerra had inhaled water from the changed nature of his struggles—fighting now for air. But the slick tub offered no leverage, and Wil banged Guerra's head on the bottom until the man went slack.

He got a knee then a foot under him and yanked Guerra's head up from the water. Gasping, he push-dragged the limp form up and over the marble lip, shut off the taps, and slumped back against the bed.

Gradually he was aware of Julio holding the gun. Pointing it at him.

Wil extended his hand. There was a moment when he wondered which way it was going to go, and then Julio put the automatic in it.

Wil nodded, still out of breath. *"Gracias,"* he said finally.

Julio said nothing, just fixed on the unconscious figure leaking reddish water on the marble, then sank to the edge of the bed, elbows on his knees, head down.

Wil stood slowly. "My wife—she thanks you, too."

No response.

"What you did was right, son. Sometimes that's not easy."

Wil left him there and went down the hall to the big room. With his pocketknife he carefully cut the rest of the tape off a still-out Lisa, then put her on the couch, raised her feet, wrapped bar ice in the towel, and touched it to her face. When she groaned, he laid her damaged hand on it.

Next he dialed Mo Epstein, caught him coming home late from an officer-involved shooting—deputies responding to a carjacking, one dead, one wounded. Mo said he'd send people, come himself, get an ambulance for Lisa.

She stirred on the couch. "Wil—?"

He went to her, told her what happened. "It's over, partner. You were incredible."

"I never faint—"

"You held out Reyes from Guerra. I'm not sure I could have."

She took a deep breath. "I told him things you'd found out. Tried to act scared. When I said I didn't know the name, he believed me—"

He hugged her, felt her wince from it. "I'm sorry, Leese. It's all my fault."

"Our fault."

He held her, eased her back on the cushions. Then he went to check on Guerra and Julio.

Both had moved. The boy was on the floor, fists clenched, knees pulled up under his chin. His pajamas were soaking wet in spots and he was trembling as he stared at Lenny Guerra, who now lay facing the ceiling from the bottom of the spa. Guerra's hair floated languidly out from his head and his eyes were partway open as though he were trying to awaken from a dream. One of his shoes lay on its side on the black marble.

Wil went to Julio's bedroom and got a robe, which he put around the boy's shoulders. Then he knelt down next to Julio. "Listen to me. He came to, tried to get up, slipped, and hit his head. You tried to save him but couldn't. The rest of it is our secret. Are we clear on that?"

"He—made me do things. In the tub and—"

"He can't hurt you anymore."

"They'll send me back."

"Julio, I need your help now. I need you to stay with my wife, take care of her while I do something. She's very important to me. Do you understand?"

Slowly Julio nodded.

"Friends are coming, a man named Epstein, who knows what happened except for how he fell back in the water. You tell him, okay? I'll be back as soon as I can."

Julio looked away and began to blink rapidly.

"It'll be fine," Wil said. "I promise."

TWENTY-SEVEN

St. Boniface loomed ahead in the rain—damned lucky with the way he'd driven. Gutter runoff thumped in the rental's wheelwells as he made the turn into the parking lot; raindrops looked like falling snow in the floods illuminating the church. It was almost one.

The white Camry was in a far corner of the lot. Wil braked beside it, saw no one inside, then tried the church doors and found them shut tight. On the lawn the big tent was flapped and dark and sounded hollow as the rain tattooed it. He checked each building, but no light shone in administration or the rectory. As he turned back toward the church, sodden grass squished underfoot.

Dammit, where were they?

The scream was so faint that at first he thought it must have been a night bird seeking shelter. Until it came again, more distinct this time, and he saw a sliver of light at a window above the sanctuary. He tried the side door: no luck.

He circled the church, found the door to the sacristy unlocked, entered a room with vestments, cabinets, drawers, the smell of incense, a single light burning. Closing the door behind him, he drew the .45, cocked it, eased toward the sounds of fighting that were coming from the open door to the sanctuary.

Where he stopped.

Poinsettias and mums from the special mass had been

knocked down and trampled; near the altar unlit candles lay scattered, the broken tapers so many pick-up-sticks. Carpet runners undulated like sea serpents.

Shadows became human. Martin DeSantis. Jennette Contreras raging:

"Why—won't—you—under—*stand!*"

It was as if they were dancing: Father Martin in his black cassock leading Jennette—teeth bared—in a violent waltz as the sanctuary flame flickered and the agonized Christ looked down.

"Let—me—*go!*"

Another candelabrum fell. The two figures caromed off the altar where Jessica Pacheco lay motionless. Jennette let loose another scream; in her hand was a long, curved knife, held there by Martin's grip on her wrist. She kicked, snapped at him, cursing now in some language Wil couldn't make out.

Martin DeSantis saw him coming. He managed a desperate-sounding "Hurry" just before Jennette broke his hold on her wrist and arced the knife downward. There was a sound of fabric tearing and DeSantis fell back, grabbing at his arm. Red showed brightly through the rip.

Jennette Contreras made a frenzied lunge toward the altar.

"*No!*" Father Martin's cry was hoarse with exertion. Wil leaped between Jennette and the child; Jennette raised the knife and leered at him. Her voice was shrill, compressed:

"Kneel, disbeliever, the child is His. *Menga para Chawa Uve.*" She charged, slashing. "*Hijo de Olosi! Muerte para los enemigos de Chawa!*"

The knife came close enough to feel its wind; Wil gave ground, then timed a jab and slammed the gun against her forehead. Jennette Contreras crumpled. He kicked the knife away, checked to see the baby was unharmed, then felt Jennette's neck for a pulse. He faced Martin DeSantis.

"She'll live. You?"

The priest nodded, gasping. Blood ran down his arm and

onto the carpet. Wil found a stole in the sacristy and
wrapped it tight around the wound. The stream became a
trickle, then stopped.

"I'd forgotten how strong she is," Father Martin said,
almost to himself.

"I was wrong," Wil said. "I had Lenny for the murders,
with Jennette helping him blackmail you."

Martin DeSantis held his arm. His face was the color of
ash.

Wil went on, "Until I got what he was blackmailing you
for." He reached into his pocket and handed over Anita
Espinosa's bracelet.

DeSantis took the bracelet and looked at the inscription,
then sagged heavily against the altar rail. "You seem—
reasonable, Mr. Hardesty," he said. "Someone who would
not knowingly instigate tragedy."

"Go to the law, you mean," Wil said.

"Destroy something that is of benefit to a great many."

Wil looked around St. Boniface, seeing Benito Reyes's
eyes, his drumsticks poised to play.

"An open mind is all I ask," Father Martin continued.
"You'll listen to what I have to say?"

"Don't expect any miracles of faith." Wil wiped rain-
water off his face; his wet hair was starting to feel cold.
Beyond the circle of light, empty pews became darkness.

"You understand the term *babalawo*?"

"No."

"I was ten when I became *babalawo* to my people. It
means high priest. You know what that meant to a wor-
shiper of Chawa?"

"I can imagine."

"The power of life and death. *Vida para vida*."

"Anita Espinosa," Wil said.

"Chawan tradition is the way of the blood and not
quickly washed away." He turned the bracelet in his
bloody fingers. "Anita Espinosa is my sin and my shame,
Mr. Hardesty. A sacrifice meant to obtain one last favor

from Him—to smile upon my upcoming endeavor with the Catholics. Since then, everything I've done has been to atone, though nothing ever will.''

Nuances: sanity and madness, saint and sinner, roads chosen versus those compelled; Wil corralled his thoughts. "Lenny must have gotten quite a kick out of putting a Chawa idol in your office.''

"Perhaps. But I made it remind me of what *I* chose.''

"What about Jennette?''

Martin DeSantis focused on the sanctuary lamp. "She helped me hold Anita while I used Lenny's knife—''

"Lenny wasn't even there?''

"No. We'd had a fight and Lenny was . . . with someone. His passions never included Chawa anyway—even in Cuba.''

It was like having the piece that defied you suddenly fit the puzzle, the last key twist in the lock. "Two outsiders against the world,'' Wil said. "Lenny was in love with you back then, wasn't he? It's how he could do all this to you now, use you. To him the money's been secondary; he was rich when he came here. But you threw him over for his sister, then you left them both for this. No wonder he hated you. Saving his life with that alibi was only what you owed him.''

"Love and hate are two sides of the same coin, Mr. Hardesty.''

"So are his revenge and your ambition.''

A twinge of pain crossed the priest's features, and he adjusted the tourniquet. "After I left Key West, Jennette was never the same, he told me. Slipping in and out of reality, worsening over the years, imagining herself my priestess. All this time Lenny's protected her.''

"While she killed the Innocents.''

Martin DeSantis sighed heavily. "They were for me, all of them. Sacrificed to Chawa so the charitable missions of St. Boniface would succeed. Seven missions, seven sacrifices.''

"With Jessica intended for Los Amigos."

"Yes."

Wil felt a wave of fatigue. "Seven dead children—damn near eight—to bless the work of a man of God."

"The irony is not lost on me, Mr. Hardesty."

On the altar, Jessica Pacheco stirred. Wil took off his jacket, covered her with it. "Why risk bringing Jessica here?" he said.

"Jennette is not well. She told me she thought it would give us what we once had—what her aunt robbed us of by sending me off to Baltimore. Tonight she waited until everyone had left. I'd been up praying for the little one."

Wil sat on the altar steps and massaged his hurting knee. "At what point did you learn about the others?"

"I'm not a monster, Mr. Hardesty."

"Maybe not. But Jennette did this because she still loved you—from the beginning she'd have wanted you to know. Explain to me how turning a blind eye to murder is doing penance for Anita Espinosa?"

Jennette Contreras snorted, then raised up and looked wildly around before curling into a tight, rocking ball from which whimpering sounds emitted. Martin DeSantis shook his head.

"She wrote me notes after each one," he said. "Rambling explanations, deeply disturbed. Lenny kept them from me until one day after we'd quarreled."

"Yet you said nothing."

"Try to imagine how I felt, Mr. Hardesty, what was at stake. What would it have accomplished except to tear apart everything I'd worked for, create more innocent victims of poverty and despair?"

"You're not God. Your silence almost got another child killed tonight."

"He promised me he'd keep her under control."

"Lenny knew all along what she was doing. And you trusted him to keep his word after he'd allowed seven children to die?"

The priest's eyes drifted to Jennette. "She was his sister. Despite her condition, he refused to have her institutionalized. Covering up was a small price to pay, is how he put it."

"And Julio?"

"No matter what you think, he's better off than when Lenny found him." Martin DeSantis looked at his arm, flexed the fingers. "Leonardo Guerra *made* St. Boniface, Mr. Hardesty, I told you that before. Somehow he found me here, me with big plans and no way to make them happen. Well, he figured out the way. Tonight we took in nearly three million dollars in pledges."

"Of which he gets what—twenty percent, a third? Easy when you control the finances."

"Whatever Lenny holds out is bread on the water. What he does for St. Boniface is all that matters."

"You knew he ordered Paul Rodriguez killed, the kind of a man he was. But why rock the boat—money pouring in from the donors, from Niños." Wil brushed away ooze from the cut on his face. "How does it feel to be a Guerra enterprise?"

The priest straightened. "Do you realize how many men, women, and children we help each year? The suffering we alleviate? The unloved and unwanted given new hope and life? Extraordinary achievements are worth extraordinary measures. Surely you can see that."

"The greater good again."

"Exactly. Paul Rodriguez said you'd been in Vietnam. You must have known innocent children were dying there, yet you participated, I assume for the greater good. Do you get my point?"

"Unfortunately, yes."

"I'm asking you only to be reasonable, Mr. Hardesty."

"To walk away."

"You know what we do here, how high the regard for it. The demand. Let Anita and the others live on in the

work. That's how I came to terms. For me it was either
that or go insane.''

"Your work here is the only reason I came alone, Father.
I kept hoping I was wrong, that you'd sort it out for me—
happy ending or something. That maybe you weren't in
league with the devil and the greater good is really what it
sounds like instead of what people like you twist it into.
How many more kids were you prepared to let die?''

"Don't you see? From now on there will be only children saved. As for Jennette, I know places where she'll be
cared for. Discreet places. After this, Lenny will go along.''

From the altar, Jessica Pacheco gasped and started to cry.

"I see,'' Wil said. He stood up stiffly and went to her,
picked her up and held her, was aware of her heart beating
against his chest, her warmth and the smell of baby shampoo. "Lenny Guerra's dead, Father. To hell with discreet.
And to hell with you.''

They were gone now: Jessica and Donna Pacheco, Jennette
Contreras, Martin DeSantis, the cops except for Mo Epstein
and August Freiman. Paramedics had taken Lisa to the hospital for observation and tests preparatory to having her
hand operated on in the morning. On the phone she'd
sounded dulled from painkillers, but okay.

As Freiman paced, Wil checked his watch: almost five.
The rain had stopped, although hollow plunks still came
from a gutter somewhere. Gray was beginning to show in
the windows, the stained glass figures in monochrome. In
the right front pew, Julio tightened his grip on the cassock
covering him, his breathing audible from the altar steps
where Wil and Mo Epstein sat.

"Congratulations, Mr. Hardesty,'' Freiman said. "You
managed to cross me and still come out smelling like a
rose.'' A candle snapped under his foot. "You know how
much I'd like to see you selling heating oil in North Da-
kota?''

"I have some idea, Captain.''

Freiman pulled on his trench coat, jammed his hands in the pockets. ''Your kind stink. You play it fast and loose with the rules, risk everything, and give it all a bad name. Maybe this time you grease through. But be forewarned. Whenever I can put an asterisk by your name or a red flag in a file or a black mark on a request, consider it done. And try bending a law sometime. You dig?'' His coattails flapped as he turned and left.

''Means you impressed him,'' Mo said finally.

''Pretty obvious.''

Mo nodded. ''What about the boy?''

''I'm working on it.''

''You have an idea?''

''Yeah, maybe.''

''Sad we couldn't bottle that look on Donna Pacheco's face, we'd make a fortune. She sure dumped off some pounds. Not a bad looker underneath it all.''

Wil replayed joyous shrieks that still echoed.

Mo looked around. ''Nice time to be in a church,'' he said. ''Quiet.''

Wil nodded.

Mo said, ''They turned up some things at Jennette's, stuff you missed. Dried blood, effects from the victims. Enough to prove they were killed there.''

''Anything to ID the kids?''

''Lab people thought no, but they're giving it a shot. Where's this put Bolo Zavala, you think?''

''Guerra had him in a vise for killing those federal agents at Calexico in 'seventy-one,'' Wil said. ''Not to mention saving Bolo's life. Over the years he'd have ordered Bolo to bury the bodies in the desert per Jennette's instructions. Guerra probably found it amusing that Bolo's kid was going to be number eight. My guess is he tried to sell Jessica first, then gave her to Jennette when she proved to be too hot.''

Mo pulled out a handkerchief, ran it over his face. ''Still not without risk. Why didn't Guerra just stop her if it meant nothing to him?''

"Each one she killed twisted the knife deeper in De-Santis, bound him to Guerra a little tighter. Worth it to him, I suppose."

"Anything so long as the money kept flowing. Speaking of which—"

"Earlier I talked to a guy named Warren Sumner—church counsel. The dust needs to lift a bit before he knows whether the work will survive intact. That and a few prayers." Wil bent forward, elbows on his knees. "What did you take DeSantis in for?"

"Questioning for now," Mo answered. "Conspiracy and/or adoption fraud later—depends on what the D.A. decides. You want a guess, they'll probably let the church handle it. Some nice parish in Siberia."

"And Anita Espinosa?"

"That old a murder—the lone witness a crazy? Be up to who's in office down there. Still, the bracelet may be enough for some hotshot to build a case around. As for the Innocents, we got Jennette, Guerra, and Zavala. Nobody here's gonna want to put Father Martin in jail. What'll bring him down is his association with them."

"With Guerra and Jennette anyway," Wil said. "I doubt he had much to do with Zavala."

Behind them in the sacristy there were noises; an altar boy poked his head out, saw them and the disarray, and retreated.

Mo stood up. "It's all right, son, we're outta here." He turned to Wil. "I tell you nice work? You really hung in. Now come on, Hardesty, they want to open for business."

Wil looked around. As he did the boy came out and was joined by another—two scrubbed-looking blond kids in black and white. They started cleaning up the mess.

Watching them made something resonate inside, a chord that brought to mind a time when the questions and answers were simple. "You go," he said. "I think we'll stick around for the six-o'clock."

TWENTY-EIGHT

Mass was over by six-forty; Lisa not due in surgery till eleven. Wil called Ignacio Reyes, apologized for the hour, and told him they needed to talk, explaining that he'd be bringing a friend along. On the way, he and Julio stopped for coffee and scrambled eggs, then headed out again, feeling somewhat revitalized. The morning was bright and sunny after the storm, no clouds showing and a north wind shaking the last of the rain from the trees. L.A. sparkled; the foothills were green with new growth. Already it was warm enough for Wil to crack his window as they drove.

Instead of talking, they listened to Christmas carols on the car radio. Julio fought it, but his head was against the rest when Wil finally parked the rental in front of the big white house. The boy stretched and yawned, then they were squishing wet leaves up the pebbled walk.

Ignacio Reyes answered the bell. Man and boy shared a handshake, then Reyes asked in Spanish if Julio would like to use the pool while he and Mr. Hardesty talked. Julio's eyes lit up, but he glanced at Wil before accepting. Marta found him a suit and Wil a fresh bandage for his cut, then Reyes closed the office doors.

It took an hour to explain.

"There is still the matter of Julio," Wil said after he'd finished. It hung there in the silence until Wil wasn't sure if Reyes had heard. Reyes finished his coffee and walked to the window; for a minute he watched the boy dive and climb out, shake off and dive again. Little waves threw sunlight around the patio and into the quiet room.

"What will happen to him?" Reyes said, his eyes fixed outside.

"Quién sabe," Wil said.

The old man sighed and turned from the glass. "What you are thinking is impossible."

"Like all this, not so long ago." Wil rubbed day-old beard. "You're right, I'm sure. But it occurred to me you had more restaurants than sons. And a pool that never splashed." His eyes felt grainy with fatigue. "We'll be leaving now," he said. "I'll send you an accounting."

Reyes turned back to the window. "What will you do with him?"

"Keep him with us, I suppose. Until his immigration hearings."

"I'll think about it," he said. "No promises. Now, what about your wife?"

Wil told him about the operation.

"Send me the bill," Reyes said; then, after a pause, "and leave the boy with me while you take care of her. Papa Gomez is respected at the INS. Standing up for him is the least I can do."

A smile started that Wil was too tired to finish. "You'll let me know when you want me there?"

"Of course."

Wil's hand was on the knob when Reyes stopped him. "One thing I have thought about, Mr. Hardesty. I want Benito."

"I see. So far, you're unknown to the police," Wil said. "You're aware of what it may mean to come forward?"

"I want my son."

"Then I'll find out about it and have a man call. Lieutenant Epstein."

Ignacio Reyes stood straight and nodded. "Thank you," he said.

"Another name, a good man." Wil found Montoya's card in his wallet and handed it to Reyes. "He'll show you the grave should you wish. Gilberto asked about it once."

Julio followed him out to the car, got in, eyed him solemnly from the passenger seat as Wil explained that he'd be staying with Reyes for a while.

"What will happen to me?" he asked, biting his lip.

"Good things," Wil said. "Already you've made three friends. You can take the train up to visit us. Go surfing, have fun. We have a room where you can sleep. A boy's room."

Julio's eyes dropped. "I see things. Señor's face in the water and the air coming out of him. Will they go away?"

"Yes. Maybe not right away, but in time. How soon depends on what you let in. Look at me, Julio. People are grateful for what you did. It seems to me that one of them should be you."

The boy thought a second, then nodded.

"Thank you for my life," Wil said.

Julio got out and shut the door; one hand rose in a shy wave as Wil made a U-turn and drove away. Through a gust of Chinese elm leaves, Wil could see him following the car with his eyes.

He caught the freeway to Pasadena, made good time in the thinned-out Monday commuter traffic. The hospital was the same one he'd received treatment in after going down on the Harley. He parked in the near-full lot, checked in at the nurses' station, walked past the Christmas cards standing at attention on the counter. He figured he had a half hour with Lisa before she was due in the operating room.

She was sitting up in bed reading a magazine. She had a shiner under one eye and her right hand was swathed in white; she was turning pages with her left. As he held it, he told her about St. Boniface, what Donna Pacheco had sounded like, about Father Martin, Jennette, Julio, and Ig-

nacio Reyes. Then the doctor came in. After a short briefing
on the anesthetic she'd be getting, an attendant wheeled her
down the hall.

Wil went downstairs to the gift shop, bought flowers for
her room, then stamps and an envelope into which he
slipped a check for a thousand dollars, addressing it to 542
Hibiscus Place. He then wrote a second check for the remaining bonus—his Zavala money from Reyes—wrapped
a thank-you note to Raeann Rodriguez around it, and put
both envelopes in the mail drop.

Four hours later, he was awakened by a touch on the
arm. As the waiting room came into focus, he saw the doctor, still in his greens, mask hanging down.

"First of all, Mr. Hardesty, your wife is fine," he said.
"Despite some splintering of the bone, I think we can expect only minor inhibition of the range of movement in
those fingers."

Something else. Or was it him, his groggy state—sinus
pressure he always got sleeping around air-conditioning?
"If she's okay, Doc, then why the look?"

The doctor regarded him, then cleared his throat. "Unfortunately, she miscarried in surgery. We stopped the
bleeding, but it's a good thing it happened here."

Wil had a sensation like the room tilting, of freon pumping in his veins. "Miscarried . . ."

"While we were closing up." Seeing Wil's expression,
the doctor added, "I'm very sorry. It's apparent you didn't
know about the pregnancy."

Late sun bounced off the stainless-steel cover on the untouched food they'd brought him, then faded from the wall,
the ceiling, and finally the window glass. Wil stared out at
the headlights coming on, traffic filling the lanes in waves
generated by signals up the street. The mountains behind
Altadena were deeply shadowed under a last splash of pink
light at the top. Sterile air hissed softly from the vents.

Approximately two months old, the fetus had been—a

boy, the doctor revealed when pressed. Telling him also that Lisa had been given two units of blood and would be weak for a while but projected to go home tomorrow if she passed inspection. Follow-up, medication, etc., could be discussed then. Get some sleep, he suggested; with the sedation she might be out awhile.

"Wil—" The sound of her voice broke into snap-click thoughts ranging from Devin in life and death, to his mother and father, to all the things he'd do differently if he could, the self-serving, self-pitying ass he'd been to any and everybody, especially Lisa. To almost losing her, then this. Sadness like a spasm in the soul; guilt that he hadn't been man enough for her to tell him the truth.

He went to her, kissed her, held the straw for her, watched her as though he'd never seen her drink before.

"Feel so weak . . ." she said, her eyes filling up. "So sorry. I was going to tell you . . ."

A peppery feeling spread out from back in his throat and threatened to engulf him. "It's okay, Leese. Just be okay. We'll talk tomorrow."

"My fault. I wanted another one so badly. Another us."

"You still want that, partner?"

"Takes two. . . . Not the way I did it."

She was drifting now; he squeezed her hand. "I know, Leese," he said. "That I do know."

She smiled at him and her eyes closed, and she mumbled something about tomorrow he didn't quite catch. Then she was asleep, her breathing steady, and suddenly his heart felt buoyed, as filled with light as the moon beginning to show through the swaying eucalyptus trees out beyond his reflection.